WING COMMANDER

Also available from HarperEntertainment

Wing Commander Confederation Handbook

WING COMMANDER

The novel by Peter Telep
From the screenplay by
Kevin Droney and Mike Finch

Based on the characters
created by Chris Roberts

HarperEntertainment
A Division of HarperCollins*Publishers*

HarperEntertainment
A Division of HarperCollins*Publishers*
10 East 53rd Street, New York, N.Y. 10022-5299

ISBN 0-06-105985-4

First printing: March 1999

Printed in the United States of America

Visit HarperEntertainment on the World Wide Web at http://www.harpercollins.com

❖ 10 9 8 7 6 5 4 3 2 1

FOR THE FANS . . .
"I GOT YOUR WING."

ACKNOWLEDGMENTS

Special thanks to my editors John Douglas and Caitlin Blasdell for thinking of me, and to my wife and daughter for smiles that eased the stress.

Robert Drake, my long-time friend and agent, did the usual, the unusual, and, as always, a professional job.

The folks at Digital Anvil were extraordinarily generous with their time and help. Chris Roberts, Maddie Fox, Ashley Galaway, and Katie Marye all answered my questions and sent material that helped to better this manuscript.

Chris McCubbin and David Ladyman at Incan Monkey God Studios gave their much-needed advice and criticism. Chris read the manuscript the same day I e-mailed it to him. He is a fine writer and a dedicated professional.

Mr. Ben Lesnick, Wing Commander fan par excellence, served as my research assistant and sent pages and pages of material, including an exhaustive list of the names of every capital ship in the Wing Commander universe. I thought relying on a fan for help would be a good idea. I had no idea Ben would be so friendly and determined. I met him through Mr. Dan Finkelstein, who runs a wonderful *Wing Commander: The Movie* website. Be sure to visit it at http://users.nac.net/splat/wc/.

My next-door neighbors Glen and Diane Martin provided me with information on the early Wing Commander games and were kind enough to give me the WCIII strategy guide. Yes, it's still possible to have great neighbors.

Finally, I need to thank all of the writers who have worked in the Wing Commander universe. Their contributions to this book and to the universe itself have made Wing Commander one hell of an exciting milieu in which to write.

PROLOGUE

VEGA SECTOR FLEET
HEADQUARTERS

TERRAN
CONFEDERATION
ASTEROID WORLD
PEGASUS

MARCH 15, 2654
0900 HOURS
ZULU TIME

ULYSSES CORRIDOR

700 LIGHT YEARS
FROM EARTH

WING COMMANDER

Seated at his console in Pegasus Station's NAV-COM control room, nineteen-year-old Radar Officer Thomas Sherryl stared through a wide viewport at the swirling blues and reds of the Charybdis Quasar. He looked past the whirlpool of gases, past the black hole lying at the quasar's core like an interminably deep maw, until his inner gaze rested on a gentle blue orb bathed in a soft glow.

Earth. Homeworld. So near. So far.

Thomas Sherryl dreamed of things green. Of the smell and taste of real air. Of foamy ocean waters rushing up and across his chest. Of beach barbecues. Of bikinis. He no longer sat in his chair, surrounded by billions of tons of durasteel and ice-slick rock; he no longer felt the rumble of the naval base's enormous ion engines propelling the converted asteroid deeper into the corridor; he no longer had to pull the graveyard shift and oversee instruments that did a fine job of sweeping the sector without human scrutiny. Thomas Sherryl had found his freedom. *Good-bye towers, gun emplacements, and antennae. Good-bye Confederation capital ships sitting in your spacedocks. I'm no longer stuck on this rock. I got a ticket out. And it's a ticket no one can take away.*

"Hey, Tom? Can you cover for me? I gotta take a leak."

Robbed of his bliss, Thomas Sherryl scowled at fellow Radar Officer Rick Adunda as the other man set down his half-full coffee mug and left before Thomas replied.

With a loud sigh that drew stares from the other personnel on duty, Thomas switched seats to Rick's console and resignedly studied the long-range sensor report: a blank screen. He eyed his own short-range display and found the same.

"I love my job," he moaned.

And, as though on cue, a mass of red blips suddenly rippled across the screen.

Thomas's gaze shot up. Had someone hacked into the system to play a joke? He studied the other officers. No smiles. No laughter. He felt a tremor rise from his feet and rattle into his spine.

He looked to Rick's coffee mug as it began to vibrate.

A shadow wiped over the viewport, followed by a second, then a third.

Muffled explosions resounded from outside the control room.

Jakoby, the stocky security officer on duty, rushed to the viewport. "Kilrathi fighters," he said stiffly.

Klaxons blared. Overhead lighting switched to the dim crimson of battle. Behind Thomas a panel of life-support monitors sizzled and shorted out, heaving a pungent scent that wafted through the control room. He glanced to a bank of screens that showed images from the station's external cameras:

Twelve comm dishes on the base's northwest side blew apart in succession under the unrelenting Particle cannon and Meson fire.

Dozens of Dralthi medium fighters swooped down and caught the great Confederation cruisers and destroyers still sitting helplessly in their berths. The fighters resembled glistening gray discs cut through their centers by sleek, single-pilot cockpits. Long, narrow laser cannons extended from the pits and blazed unceasingly. Though only twenty-eight meters long, the fighters' formidable, talon-like appearance made them seem much larger. And they packed more than just laser cannons. Heat-seeking missiles streaked away from the starfighters, locking onto the Confed ships' now-warming engines. The cruisers and destroyers retaliated with streams of tachyon fire, but scores of missiles navigated through the glistening gauntlet to impact on and weaken the Confed ships' shields. Another wave of those missiles would tear into hull armor, flesh, and bone.

A resonant drumming seized the NAVCOM control room as asteroid-based gun batteries finally came on line, belching out thick bolts of anti-aircraft fire as they swiveled to track targets.

Thomas kept a white-knuckled grip on his chair as he continued to watch with a horrid and inevitable fascination. Like an angry horde of plastisteel insects, the fighters dove at the station, dropped their poisonous barbs, and pulled up, leaving trails of floating debris in their wakes. For every Dralthi destroyed, another soared through the rubble of its predecessor.

One of the heavy cruisers, the *Iowa*, launched a half-dozen F44-A Rapier medium attack fighters. The Rapiers' silver, battle-scored fuselages and barrel-shaped rotating laser cannons that formed their brassy noses gave them a fearsome if not sleek appearance. Short, slightly upturned wings and huge twin thruster cones stated most clearly that the Rapier had been built for speed. And it usually did an excellent job of catapulting a single pilot across the laser-lit cosmos. But as the starfighters cleared the flight deck, Kilrathi fighters methodically picked them off with salvos of Meson and missile fire that fully obscured each ship before blasting it to gleaming fragments.

"We're gonna lose," an astounded navigator said behind Thomas.

Rick Adunda pounded over, his young face creased in terror. "Get out of my chair."

With a shudder, Thomas returned to his own station as Rick dialed up a commlink so they could listen to the skipchatter from outside.

"Goddammit! Cut our moorings! Get us out of here!" a capital ship commander cried, her voice already hoarse.

"Mooring release systems, uh, damaged," came a nervous ensign's reply. "Unable to . . . to initiate."

A fighter pilot cut into the channel. "Christ almighty! They're everywhere! Bug out, people. Bug out. Regroup at the southern pole. Go now!"

"Belay that order," shouted the capital ship commander. "We need air support, Lieutenant—not your announcement of retreat."

"Forget it, Commander. We . . . are . . . outgunned," the pilot said, spacing his words for effect. "There's a fine line between bravery and stupidity."

"See you at your court-martial."

"If we live that long."

"Mayday! Mayday! This is Senior Spacehand Eric Popkin in Watchtower Three. We can't hold 'em back anymore. Batteries are wasted. They're coming over the fence. Wait. What's that? Ohmygod. OHMYGOD! AHHHHHH!"

"Popkin? Report! Popkin, do you copy?"

"And it is you, Dear Lord, who will deliver us from this evil because we ask it in your name, and—"

"You wanna piece of me? I don't think so. Open wide . . ."

Something struck heavily on Thomas's shoulder. He turned to find Rick staring wide-eyed at him. "What are you doing?"

"I, uh, I don't know. I guess, well—"

"Make your report!"

Thomas swallowed and regarded his scope. "I count one-nine-zero bogies inbound. Vector three-seven-four, attack formation."

"Shields are not *responding*," Security Officer Jakoby announced.

The viewport filled with a harsh white light that peeled off the blackness of space. A tremendous thunderclap shook through the entire station as though a fusion bomb had detonated at its core.

"What the f—" Rick began, then shielded his face as his console sparked and smoked.

"I don't believe it," Ordnance Officer Scott Osborne said, squinting at the viewport as the glare subsided. "That was the *Iowa*." He turned toward Thomas, his face paling.

"Confirmed," Comm Officer Rene Gemma said. "The *Iowa* is gone. And the *Kobi.*"

Loud footfalls caught Thomas's attention. He cocked his head toward the lift doors as Admiral Bill Wilson double-timed into the control room with an armored Confederation Marine in tow. Twin rows of large buttons on Wilson's dark uniform flashed as they caught the overhead lights. He wiped the sweat from his balding pate, and his face seemed to grow more gaunt as he took in the scene with weary eyes.

Rick, who had moved to the console on Thomas's left, tipped his head in Wilson's direction and muttered, "It's about freakin' time."

Wilson turned toward them. "Status?"

Thomas jerked and studied his screen. "Four Kilrathi capital ships coming to bear, Admiral. They are powering weapons."

With a crooked grin, Wilson asked, "How did they get past our patrols?"

"We lost contact with our patrols for a few minutes," Comm Officer Gemma said. "But we reestablished. I thought it was quasar interference. The enemy must've taken them out and transmitted false signals."

Before Wilson could respond, a low-pitched alarm added its voice to the already rising din of the control room.

Security Officer Jakoby bolted to his terminal. He touched the screen several times, then winced. "We have a station breach. Levels seven, eleven, and thirteen. Kilrathi Marines."

Wilson hurried to a bank of security monitors beside Jakoby. Thomas stood to peer over the admiral's shoulder.

Towering forms in copper-colored armor skulked through the dim corridors, throwing markedly inhuman shadows on the walls. Rebreather tubes partially concealed their faces and snaked down from elongated heads to bulging chests. Exhaust fumes lingered behind them as they forged efficiently and inexorably forward.

A pair of Confed security officers fired upon them suddenly, but two of the Kilrathi withstood the point-blank hits and thundered on to seize the officers. Thomas turned away as he listened to the women shriek, gurgle, and fall silent.

"They're headed for Command and Control," Jakoby reported.

Thomas may have only been a radar officer, but he knew very well what the aliens wanted. He flicked his gaze to the opposite end of the control room, to the massive computer system shielded by a synthoglass wall, a mainframe that represented the very heart and brain of Pegasus Station. At the system's center lay that small, most precious black box with the letters NAVCOM stenciled across its side.

Clenching his teeth, Wilson charged toward the computer system. "Destroy the NAVCOM AI. Now!" he ordered Benjamin Ferrago, the chief navigator.

Ferrago typed frantically on his touchpad, then, balling his hand into a fist, he smashed a glass panel to gain access to a red handle. Grimacing, he threw the handle forward and looked to the black box.

Nothing.

He tried the handle a second time, his eyes now glassy.

No response.

"What's wrong, son?" Wilson demanded.

Ferrago shook his head. "Command codes have been overwritten."

Wilson whirled and seized the Confed Marine's conventional rifle, dropped the slide back, then aimed at the NAVCOM. Thomas flinched as uranium-depleted rounds ricocheted off the synthoglass. Wilson emptied the entire clip before turning the rifle around. With a howl, he charged toward the NAVCOM and drove the rifle's butt into the glass. The stock shattered.

"Back off," Jakoby said, pushing the button on a concussion grenade the size of a ballpoint pen. He tossed it at the synthoglass.

The others retreated as Thomas crouched behind his console and held his ears. The grenade went off with a terrific boom. He lay there, listening to his own breath for a moment.

"Did it work?" someone asked.

Someone else cursed.

Peering furtively above his instrument panel, Thomas glimpsed the bad news.

Another concussion echoed from outside. The lift's massive, reinforced doors began distorting, bending in, as the Kilrathi Marines outside unloosed a flurry of rifle fire.

"Here," Rick said, slapping a sidearm in Thomas's hand. He winked. "Special *arakh* rounds. Kilrathi catnip. We Terrans stick together."

"Where'd you get this? We're gonna get in—"

"Big trouble? You kidding me?" Rick clicked off the safety of his own pistol. "Let's go."

Remaining hunched over, Thomas followed Rick past the radar and navigation stations to a partition opposite the lift doors, where they huddled and watched the doors grow hotter and weaker.

Admiral Wilson regarded Comm Officer Gemma with a grave look. "Prepare a drone. Get me a coded channel."

Gemma seemed lost for a moment, then she touched the correct keys and nodded to the admiral.

Wilson faced the camera at Gemma's station as it pivoted toward him. "This is Admiral Bill Wilson, Pegasus Station commanding officer. Four Kilrathi capital ships are closing. Station has been breached. They want the NAVCOM. Repeat. They want—"

The lift doors blew off their glide tracks and *thwacked* the deck with twin thuds. A cloud of toxic smoke swelled into the control room. Within that smoke, Thomas made out the unnerving outline of a Kilrathi Marine as it hunkered down and ignited its weapon.

Rick pumped rounds into the smoke, as did some of the others. Thomas saw a half-dozen more outlines appear behind the first, and the sight sent him ducking behind the partition.

"Drone away!" Gemma shouted.

Thomas looked back at the viewport. The tiny drone streaked away from the dying station, bound for the nearest Confederation carrier, the *Concordia*, some twelve hours away. It passed in front of the Kilrathi battle group that included a dreadnought, two destroyers, and the largest vessel, a Snakeir-class cruiser. Transports and smaller escort ships flew abreast of the capital ships, exploiting their cover.

An explosion stung Thomas's ears, and he saw Rick fall against the partition, his uniform melting into a black cavity in his chest.

Thomas wanted to act, but he could only tremble. He detected heavy footsteps. Close. Loud breathing, mechanized. *Oh, God. What's that smell?* He looked over his shoulder at the Kilrathi Marine standing over him, its polished armor reflecting explosions from outside, its pale yellow eyes wide, menacing, drinking him in with sinister delectation as it breathed through its tube.

Shoot him! he screamed at himself.

He lifted the pistol.

The Kilrathi plucked it effortlessly from him, grunted, and kicked him onto his back. The soldier pressed its boot on his chest, cutting off his air. A rib popped.

In those last seconds, Thomas took himself away from Pegasus, through the jump point at Charybdis, and back home, where palm trees bowed to the coastal wind, where waves lapped endlessly at the shore, where he lay under a canopy of fronds and drank from the lips of a dark-eyed woman until night fell.

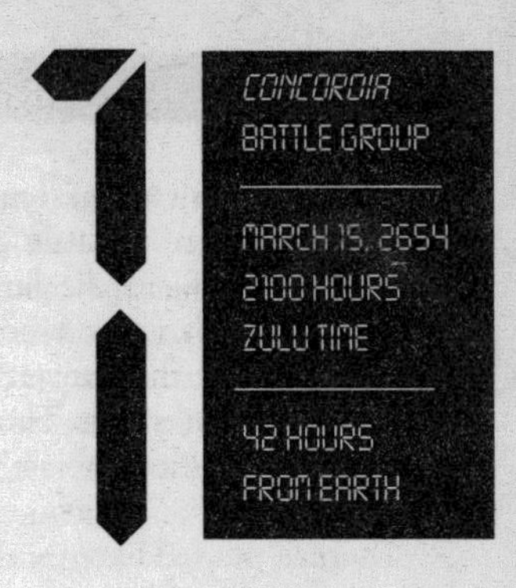

In classic battle group formation, the Confederation-class carrier *Concordia*, flagship of the 14th Fleet, glided majestically amid five cruisers, five destroyers—including the formidable TCS *Beowulf*—and ten support ships. The pride of the Confederation Navy, the *Concordia* stretched into space nearly 984 meters and weighed in at an imposing 73,000 tonnes. She doubled as a dreadnought so she could stand up to Kilrathi cruisers and destroyers in a one-on-one fight. Three heavy flak cannons discouraged light fighters from becoming intimate, and eight anti-matter guns warded off attacking Kilrathi corvettes, heavy fighters, and bombers. Fore and aft phase shields guarded her from an assortment of Kilrathi weapons, as did her 500-centimeter-thick armor. She carried 120 fighters piloted by the most respected and experienced officers in the fleet.

Admiral Geoffrey Tolwyn suspected that every time the *Concordia* appeared before the Kilrathi, she turned their alien blood cold.

As she should.

Twelve fighters presently on security patrol veered off to allow a changing of the guard. Tolwyn shifted away from the external monitor and scratched at a graying sideburn, then at his neck. He loved the smell of his new cologne, a thank-you gift from his nephew Kevin, but the damned stuff had the strange effect of making him itch only when he wore his uniform, as though chemicals in the cologne reacted with the fabric. This effect had, of course, not been mentioned on the cologne's label, nor had Tolwyn remembered the last time he had served as a human catalyst for an unlikely chemical reaction. He tugged at his collar, swore, then stepped across the carrier's wide, pristine bridge to lock gazes with Commodore Richard Bellegarde, who had just exited the lift. Stocky, with neatly trimmed dark hair, Bellegarde had thus far been an excellent officer but a poor liar. He assumed that no one knew of his alcoholism nor his frequent extramarital affairs, both born of a midlife crisis that threatened to ruin him. Tolwyn hated to see a man slowly destroying his life, but he would keep on his side of the line. At least for now.

"Did we get it, Commodore?" Tolwyn asked.

Bellegarde nodded vigorously. "It's just been decoded." He hurried toward a video monitor at the commander's station. Tolwyn fell in behind him.

The screen lighted with a shaky image of Admiral Bill Wilson, whose eyes pleaded as he spoke. "The NAVCOM command codes were somehow overwritten. We can't shut it down, can't destroy it. Station self-destruct programs have been locked, passwords changed. Jesus, I'm sorry, Geoff. I'm so damned sorry." Laser fire pierced the air around Wilson. Small explosions lit the shadowy Command and Control room behind him. Then static whisked away his face.

Tolwyn repressed the urge to pound his fist on the commander's chair, having learned long ago to govern his emotions, use them as a tool, and never let them overwhelm him. He stood there, focusing on his breathing, clearing his thoughts, then guiding them toward an appropriate response.

Contrarily, Bellegarde paced the bridge, muttering to himself, rubbing his jaw. Were his thoughts visible, they would be wildly orbiting his head. He whipped around and faced Tolwyn with a madman's glare, releasing a short, bitter laugh. "I've been considering ways Wilson could've protected it from them. But he . . . think about it . . . the Pegasus NAVCOM. My God, if they have it—"

"Calm down, Richard. Let's assume they have it," Tolwyn said, his voice a placid lake. "Now, what shall we do about that? Speak to me, Commodore."

Bellegarde snorted. "Go after them."

"Exactly. And I'm sure the Kilrathi counted on that." Tolwyn turned toward the open expanse of bridge between the commander's station and the lift. "Tactical. Give me the Vega and Sol sectors."

A swirling holographic projection took shape as overhead lights dimmed. Dozens of star systems appeared in each of the selected sectors, their tiny planets rotating in real time about their suns. Glowing blue orbs indicated the positions of Confederation capital ships. Red orbs representing Kilrathi cruisers, dreadnoughts, and destroyers dotted the display like blood. The Pegasus Station's last known location stood as a small blue dot at the core of the celestial maelstrom. Behind it, thin white lines formed a tube depicting the Ulysses Corridor. The tube funneled toward a small but comprehensive model of the Charybdis Quasar. Hundreds of yellow lines emanated from the quasar's back, each representing an avenue through space-time. One yellow line, much thicker than the others, led directly to the Sol system, to Earth.

Tolwyn walked into the projection, intent on the images surrounding him. As he neared the Sol system, the holograph zoomed in on Earth, illustrating the precious planet in sharp detail. A hurricane swirled off Florida's east coast. Clouds blanketed California. Lightning backlit the thunderheads. Tolwyn glanced sidelong at Bellegarde. "What is the fleet's position?"

The commodore stepped closer to the holograph and gestured toward the blue dots. "We're spread all over the sector." He rushed to the commander's station and tapped in coordinates on a touchpad. Then he looked up and shook his head. "The earliest our advance elements could reach Sol is forty-two hours. And that's piecemeal and taking risks with the jumps, sir. If we do make it within that time frame, we'll be breaking every Confederation jump record."

"And with the NAVCOM, the Kilrathi can reach Earth in forty hours through the Charybdis Quasar." The irony tasted so bitter in Tolwyn's mouth that it made him cringe. "A mere two hours could decide the outcome of this war."

"That's not true, sir."

Tolwyn furrowed his brow. "What?"

"Even if Earth falls, we still have the fleet and support from the rest of the Confederation."

Stepping to the edge of the projection, Tolwyn locked gazes with the commodore. "What is it you fight for, Richard, if not Earth?"

"Permission to—"

"Granted."

"I'm sorry, sir, but Earth's not my homeworld. I'm aware of its strategic importance, but I don't place as much emphasis on it as those like you with family connections in government and industry."

"But it's the world of your forefathers. Think of Scotland, of Glasgow. That accent still lingers in your speech. You cannot deny your heritage."

"Sometimes I wish I could."

Tolwyn looked away, glaring into nothingness. Then he abruptly faced Bellegarde with renewed steel, his tone a direct challenge. "Signal all ships to mark our course and make full speed for Earth."

"All ships to mark course and make full speed for Earth. Aye-aye, sir," the commodore said tersely. He spun on his heel toward the situational display on his monitor.

"Richard. I suggest we lay our political differences aside for now. I suspect we'll return to this conversation later."

Bellegarde kept his back to Tolwyn. "Yes, sir."

Tolwyn stared at the holograph once more, his gaze directed

to the Vega sector and traveling past McAuliffe to Trimble to Baird's Star. "Now. I need to know what the Kilrathi are up to. I need eyes and ears, and I need intelligence. Do we have any ships left in Vega?"

"Checking." The commodore's fingers worked quickly on his touchpad.

As Tolwyn waited, he realized that with the luck they had been having, the answer would surely be no. In that event, he needed to devise an alternate plan, one that would somehow get Warning and Control mission fighters in close enough to run intelligence on that Kilrathi fleet—but fighters deployed from where?

"We have seven capital ships in that sector, sir," Bellegarde finally answered. "The closest one to the Pegasus Station's last known coordinates is the *Tiger Claw*. But she's in the Enyo system and out of communication range. A drone will take two standard days to reach her."

Tolwyn moved toward a blue orb that quickly materialized into an image of the Bengal-class carrier *Tiger Claw*, 700 hundred meters of Confederation fury. Dammit. If they could only alert her. He winced once more over the taste in his mouth.

Then he accidentally spotted a tiny dot on the projection. Granted, whatever ship it represented lay in the Sol sector, but judging distances and factoring in a jump point, it might be within communication range and might be able to reach the *Tiger Claw* in time. He pointed at the dot. "Who's this?"

Bellegarde studied the holograph, then typed on his pad. "It's a requisitioned merchantman, sir. The *Diligent*."

"The *Diligent*?" Narrowing his gaze, Tolwyn watched as the dot grew into the rather bulky, purely functional form of the transport vessel. What she lost in appearance she gained in strategic position.

"She's captained by James Taggart," Bellegarde added.

With that, bad luck and operative words like "might" got burned away by Tolwyn's recognition. He had been meaning to check on Taggart's whereabouts. Now fate had stepped on the bridge to whisper the coordinates in his ear. "Can you pull up her log?"

"Already have. She's en route to the *Tiger Claw* with two replacement pilots: First Lieutenants Todd Marshall and Christopher Blair."

Blair. Another name from long ago. In their quest to end humanity's future, the Kilrathi had inadvertently summoned up two distinct figures from Admiral Geoffrey Tolwyn's past. If nothing else, the immediate future would prove bittersweet. He stared through the merchantman's ghostly hull and said, "Open a secure channel to the *Diligent* immediately. I need to speak to her captain—"

"Right away, sir."

"—and this First Lieutenant Blair."

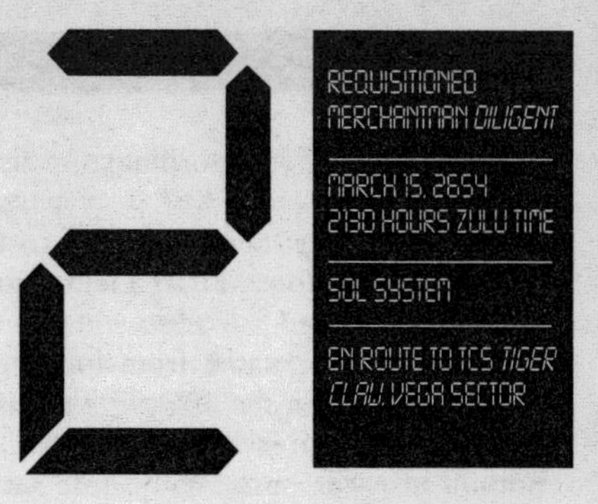

After graduating from the Terran Confederation Space Naval Academy on Hilthros just a month earlier, First Lieutenant Christopher Blair had entertained a number of fantasies concerning his first non-training assignment. He, like many of the other fledgling pilots, had put himself on great carriers like the *Concordia* or cruisers like the *Waterloo*. Some of Blair's classmates had actually been awarded those prestigious assignments, much to his jealousy and chagrin, because for a month he had been shuffled around, leading him to believe that his superiors could not find him a home. He had served a brief, thirty-hour stint on the destroyer *Gilgamesh* before being ferried back to the academy. The commandant had asked him to give several testimonial speeches to the new classes. But Blair felt that his wisdom had fallen on the deaf ears of bright-eyed baby birds too excited to listen, their hearts pounding at the thought of strapping on starfighters and hauling their particular asses across the cosmos. But Blair couldn't blame them. He had behaved the same way when graduates had come to speak to his freshman class.

Christopher Blair needed a home. And at last they had given him one: the TCS *Tiger Claw*, the largest carrier in her class, with a crew of over 750. Less than two minutes after receiving word of the assignment, Blair had voice-activated his Portable Personal Computer, a fingernail-sized device embedded in his wrist, to learn more about the carrier's service record.

In 2642 the Confederation military command had authorized the design of the Bengal-class carrier line, and by 2644 the *Tiger Claw* launched for her shakedown cruise with a minimal space crew and inexperienced command. She ran headlong into a Kilrathi invasion force. With clever tactics her crew managed to suppress the superior force. Shortly thereafter, Vega sector became the carrier's permanent assignment.

During 2649, the *Claw* performed a delaying action to allow Confed transports to retreat out of Kilrathi-occupied space. The engagement, subsequently known as Custer's Carnival, concluded with the ship badly damaged but able to return home. She lay in spacedock undergoing repairs and refitting until early 2050. Veteran crewers swore the old girl never fully recovered from that mission, that battle damage still haunted the deepest regions of her hull.

Besides hearing about the *Tiger Claw*'s history, Blair had wanted to review the personnel roster, but that access had been denied, since his computer account had not yet existed. No matter. He would meet his fellow officers soon enough.

Now he lay sprawled out and bare-chested on his rickety bunk in one of the *Diligent*'s tiny cabins. Exposed conduits spanned the ceiling like rubber and durasteel cobwebs. Even the standard cot-and-locker arrangements aboard carriers afforded more living space. And their crews actually kept the floors clean and addressed problems such as foul-smelling mattresses, two items clearly overlooked on the *Diligent*.

Trying to ignore the uncomfortable surroundings, Blair fixed his gaze on a hard copy of *Claw Marks*, the onboard magazine of the TCS *Tiger Claw*, a gift from one of his flight instructors. As he read the latest news from the Terran Confederation Armed Forces CommNet, he absently touched the four-inch-long silver cross hanging around his neck. He let his fingers play over the strange symbol carved into its center. Resembling the old Earth scales of justice, the symbol stood on a circular gold background with three points of silver radiating from it to support a semicircle also trimmed in gold. That semicircle ran the width of the cross and served as its glimmering top. From a distance, the object appeared like a cruciform set against a rising sun.

Out of the corner of his eye, Blair saw a magnesium-bright flash appear on the shelf above his head. Merlin had decided to show himself. A half-meter tall and generated by Blair's PPC, the holographic old man/interface tossed his waist-length ponytail over his shoulder, then smoothed out his black tunic and breeches, as though he had been somewhere to wrinkle them.

"I know there's a war going on—but a requisitioned merchantman? What are we on, a garbage run? Delivering groceries?" Merlin's clean-shaven face tightened like a piece of stretched leather.

Blair ignored him, having learned since age five that Merlin's ranting would soon evaporate were he denied an audience.

"The *Diligent*?" Merlin continued. "Please—the *Dilapidated* is more like it. The *Deluded*. The *Dilatory*."

Frowning, Blair glanced at the disgusted little man. "*Dilatory*?"

Merlin snorted. "Of course. Inclined to delay, tardy, slow. From the Latin *dìlâtor*." He smirked. "I'm not keeping you up, am I?"

For a moment, Blair felt taken aback. Had he heard right? True, the program knew quite well how to complain over every situation, but cutting remarks of this kind should not have been at its disposal. "Where did you pick up that sarcasm? My father didn't put that in your program. And I know I didn't."

"Well, I don't just sit around waiting for you to power me up. I have my own life, too, you know. I have aspirations. I dream that one day you'll finally come to your senses and adjust my program so that I am the proper size."

Blair rolled his eyes. "I'm not changing my mind."

"What's the point of my being scaled down?"

"My father wanted you this way. Besides, you're less obtrusive."

"Obtrusive? I am *not*—"

"Run a diagnostic. You are. And while you're at it, tell me where you picked up that sarcasm."

"I downloaded it from the mainframe at the academy while you were in—" Merlin looked up.

"What is it?"

"Lieutenant Marshall is approaching the hatch."

Slapping the magazine over his chest to conceal his cross, Blair flinched a little as the hatch opened and Todd Marshall stepped into the cabin, his regulation blue uniform hanging loosely from his lanky frame, his closely cropped blond hair grazing a sweaty pipe. He raked fingers through his hair, scowled a moment at the conduit, and muttered, "What a bucket." Then that slightly crazed gleam returned to his eyes, and his oversized Adam's apple worked overtime. "I was going to come down here and get you." He smiled devilishly, raising his brow. "I found some holos in the rec that I know you'll wanna see."

Blair drew in a deep breath and nodded his understanding. "Don't you get tired of that stuff? I don't think those women exist."

"Of course they don't. It's all part of the fantasy. But like I said, I was going to come down here and get you so we could watch them. But the captain stopped me on the way. Up and at 'em. He wants you on the bridge. Top priority."

"Really? For what?"

Marshall shrugged, moving around the bunk to stare at Merlin. "He didn't sound thrilled."

Merlin, now in standby mode and immobile for the most part, continued to stare around the room, as though his face had become a mask for another entity behind it. Blair had seen the effect many times, and it didn't bother or fascinate him anymore.

But Marshall still found it spooky, intriguing. "What are you looking at?" he asked Merlin, then regarded Blair. "What a waste of artificial intelligence."

"Funny, Lieutenant. I was thinking the same about you." The holograph glowered at Marshall.

"Merlin, off," Blair ordered.

"Of course I have no difficulty obeying your command, but if I may—"

"Merlin, off!"

With a huff, the little man vanished.

"Sorry about that," Blair said. "He's been hacking where he shouldn't."

"I'll hack him," Marshall said, shaking his head. "There weren't enough know-it-alls in the universe . . . your father had to program another one."

Blair chuckled. "What? You don't want any more competition?"

"Now I know where the little man gets it," Marshall said, nodding. "Did I tell you about the time I reprogrammed Marty Pinshaw's PPC so that it would automatically read aloud his diary every time he said the word *waxed*? Remember that guy back at the academy? That's all he ever said. I *waxed* his ass. I *waxed* her ass. You get tired of listening to a guy talk about how great he is, you know?"

"I totally agree."

"Hey, now. Come on. We'd better get upstairs." Marshall started for the door.

"I'll meet you," Blair said, reluctant to rise and reveal his cross.

Marshall began to mouth something, then simply shrugged and left.

Lowering the magazine, Blair sat up and took in a long breath. A chill needled up his spine as he whispered the words, "Top priority." He reached for his shirt beside him and bolted from the bunk.

On a day when you're feeling generous, Blair thought, you could call the *Diligent*'s bridge a bridge. But were you to be accurate, you might call it a machine room like the ones used a half-dozen centuries ago to house the huge, noisy compressors of large refrigeration units. Low-hanging conduits, exposed circuit panels, torn crew seats, and poor lighting completed the unglamorous effect. Blair got the feeling that he now stepped into the bowels of a cyborg with a strong inclination for spicy food. He ducked as he shifted by a small hatchway and moved farther onto the bridge, careful to duck once more to avoid a major contusion from a low-hanging hydraulic line. He found Marshall seated to starboard in the co-pilot's chair, studying a navigation screen mounted on a swivel arm. Glancing to port, he saw the captain stepping out from the adjoining galley, blowing on a steaming mug of coffee.

Captain James Taggart hadn't said much during the voyage. His reticence, Blair figured, stemmed from the embarrassment of commanding a tape-and-coat-hanger transport like the *Diligent*. Funny, though. Taggart didn't look the part of a gypsy cabby contracted by the military. Dark, neatly groomed hair. A face that barely betrayed his middle years. And there seemed something rugged, something handsome, something pirate-like about the guy that made you just know he had seen a lot more in the universe than would ever escape his lips. Marshall could take a few lessons from the man.

Blair found the captain's gaze. "Sir?"

But the man's stare lowered to Blair's chest, and a strange look washed over his face.

A quick glance down revealed that Blair's cross had slipped out from behind his V-neck shirt. He quickly tucked it behind the fabric and stiffened nervously to attention, waiting for a severe interrogation.

"I don't know who you know, Lieutenant, but you just received a Confed One Secure Communication." Taggart gestured with his coffee mug toward the bridge's center console.

Releasing a long mental sigh over the captain's decision to ignore the cross, Blair hurried to the console, slid over to the comm screen, and keyed an activation code on the touchpad.

"Identify," a computer voice said.

"Blair, Christopher. Lieutenant."

"Voice print recognized. Communication establishing . . ."

The screen filled with the god-like face of a man for whom the phrase "living legend" remained as inadequate as it was trite. "Admiral Tolwyn."

"At ease, Lieutenant."

"Yes, sir."

"I need a favor," Tolwyn said matter-of-factly, his gray eyes flashing.

Blair swallowed. "Anything, sir."

"You're currently outbound for Vega sector and the *Tiger Claw*. I need you to hand-deliver an encrypted communications disc to Captain Sansky. Message is incoming."

As he waited for the download to complete, Blair grew more confused. The comm recorder beeped. He removed the minidisc and held it up. "Begging the admiral's pardon, sir, but why not send it via drone to Pegasus? It would be quicker . . ."

Slowly, Tolwyn shook his head, driving Blair into sudden silence. "The Pegasus is gone, destroyed by a Kilrathi battle group twelve and a half hours ago."

Blair's mouth fell open. Two of his classmates, Trish Melize and Sandra Sotovsky, had been assigned to the Pegasus. He thought suddenly of their parents, mothers and fathers he had met at the graduation ball, at the barbecue, at the ceremony.

The war had snapped its fingers.

And two daughters were no more.

"See that Captain Sansky gets that disc," Tolwyn added.

"With all due respect, sir. Why me?"

Tolwyn's lips curled in a remote smile. "Right now you're all I've got." His gaze averted a moment as he seemed to consider something. "I fought with your father in the Pilgrim Wars. He was a good man—you look like him."

Without trying to offend the admiral, Blair pointed out a fact that had shadowed him all of his life. "People say I have my mother's looks, sir."

At the mention of Blair's mother, the admiral's eyes narrowed, as though he remembered something. "Yes, it must've been hard. They were both good people. Godspeed. Tolwyn out."

Blair stared at the empty screen a moment before Marshall's voice ruined the silence. "Can you believe he fought with your father? Man . . . you got an in now. I'm you, I don't even worry about promotions."

Turning to Marshall, Blair closed his eyes. "Just shuddup."

On the *Concordia*'s bridge, Admiral Geoffrey Tolwyn read the obvious look of displeasure on Commodore Bellegarde's boyish face. The commodore rarely wore that look, and Tolwyn found it impossible not to address. He cocked a brow. "You don't approve, Richard?"

"Of using Blair's kid? No, sir. I do not."

"Why?"

Bellegarde stepped forward. "I think we both know why."

The *Diligent*'s navigation screens woke from their powerless slumber to create 3-D grids as Captain James Taggart began tapping in coordinates. Blair stood behind him, watching. "This milk run just got a little more interesting," the captain said. "Set a course for Beacon One-forty-seven, one-quarter impulse."

Marshall nodded and worked his touchpad. "Course for One-forty-seven. One-quarter impulse." He frowned at a flashing red warning that appeared at the top of his screen. "One-forty-seven is off-limits, sir. There's a one-hundred-thousand-kilometer no-fly zone around it."

Taggart puffed air. "I said *Beacon* One-forty-seven. It's a short cut. Lose the sir."

With an exaggerated shrug, Marshall regarded his screen, banged in the course, then booted the engage pedal.

As Taggart fell back into his chair and yawned, Blair noticed a small, dark tattoo emerge from beneath his collar. Blair recognized the writing: a set of four vertical lines that comprised the Kilrathi language. Taggart caught him staring, and Blair flinched toward the forward screen.

The *Diligent* streaked by the mottled red orb of Pluto, its tenuous atmosphere escaping in tendrils toward its gray moon, Charon.

Taggart got abruptly to his feet. "I'll be in my quarters. Call me when we come within a hundred klicks of the beacon."

"You got it," Marshall said. He waited for the captain to leave, then stage-whispered, "I don't trust this guy. What does he mean by a 'short cut'?"

"Got me," Blair said. "Did you see his neck?"

"What about it?"

"He's got a tattoo. Kilrathi writing. Wish I got a better look at it. Maybe I can get something on it from Merlin."

"Tell you what I think. I think he's intentionally delaying us. One-quarter impulse? Why don't we get out and push? And now you're telling me he's got a Kilrathi tattoo? Hello. I can't find anything right with this picture."

"Stay cool. Let me talk to him. We just don't know what he's about." Blair stood and turned toward the hatchway.

"Hey," Marshall called out.

Blair faced the pilot, who now waved a small sidearm he had withdrawn from a hidden calf holster. "I know what I'm about."

KILRATHI BATTLE GROUP

SNAKEIR-CLASS CRUISER KIS *GRIST'AR'ROC*

MARCH 15, 2654
2140 HOURS ZULU TIME

ULYSSES CORRIDOR, VEGA SECTOR

39 HOURS 20 MINUTES FROM CHARYBDIS QUASAR JUMP POINT

For the fourth time in the past five standard minutes, Captain Thiraka nar Kiranka shuffled through the dense nutrient atmosphere that filled the *Grist'Ar'roc*'s bridge to check the radar screen as the immense cruiser traveled at maximum drive toward the quasar. The attack on Pegasus Station had gone exactly as planned. The absence of difficulties had Thiraka wondering when those difficulties would arrive. His experience fighting Terrans told him they always did.

Born of the most powerful clan on Kilrah, Thiraka had a reputation to uphold, a fact that weighed upon him too heavily and preoccupied too much of his time. His father did not believe him worthy of the clan. His father did not believe he could present even a single Terran death as a gift to Sivar, war god of the Kilrathi people. And his father's beliefs had become public knowledge by way of servants' loose tongues. Thiraka suspected that most of his crew doubted his capabilities. The presence of Kalralahr Bokoth, the Kilrathi fleet's most revered admiral, underscored those doubts. Thiraka considered how his own intimidation had become heightened by the fact that he and Bokoth belonged to the same clan and that Bokoth would undoubtedly report Thiraka's every move back to his father. The emperor had not entrusted Thiraka with the mission and had turned his cruiser into the kalralahr's flagship, thus relieving him of battle group command. *I am a lowborn peasant at the kalralahr's beck and call,* he thought. Thus, Thiraka's intimidation remained fused with contempt.

Commander Ke'Soick rested a heavy paw on Thiraka's shoulder. "Kal Shintahr, our officers complain that you're oversupervising them. I've watched you check this screen four times now. Should the third fang here find a discrepancy, he'll report it directly to you."

Thiraka lowered his massive brow. "To me and not the kalralahr?"

"We've only served a short time together, but I already know your pain. You can rely on my loyalty, Kal Shintahr. I'm oathsworn to you and you alone."

Pursing his lips, Thiraka nodded. "A debt is owed. A debt shall be repaid."

"Have you forgotten how your family strengthened my clan by killing the weakest of us? Now we rise in power and serve aboard the empire's deadliest cruisers and dreadnoughts. But my clan also believes that those who bargain with the Terrans are the lowest of born, cowards despised and condemned by Sivar."

Thiraka moved closer to his Ke'Soick, and with eyes capable of seeing the infrared spectrum, he gazed through the green effluvium to see if others watched. "Those opinions are better kept silent. But, dear Ke'Soick, I agree."

Behind them, the lift doors parted to reveal Kalralahr Bokoth. Without a word, the admiral paraded across the bridge, his armor flexing, the colorful clan and battle plumes affixed to his shoulders fluttering behind him. He paused at the forward viewport to gaze at the quasar.

"And thoughts become flesh," Ke'Soick said, eyeing the kalralahr with unflappable contempt.

Second Fang Norsh'kal, tactical officer, approached them with a computer slate. "Kal Shintahr. Sector report of

Confederation ship movements." He proffered the slate.

But Thiraka had grown weary of staring at holos and computer screens. "Read them to me."

The Second Fang purred his acknowledgment. "One vessel remains in the sector, the TCS *Tiger Claw*. Intelligence reports that she is still out of communication range with her fleet and holding position."

"Very well," Thiraka said. "Your report tells me nothing new."

"But Kal Shintahr. One of our surveillance stations on the border of Sol sector intercepted and decoded part of a long-range communication from the *Concordia* to a merchantman bound for the *Tiger Claw*. An officer on board that merchantman is delivering an encoded message to the carrier's captain."

"ETA of merchantman to *Tiger Claw*?"

"We're not sure, Kal Shintahr. The merchantman is headed toward Beacon One-forty-seven, just outside the Sol system."

"They're not headed toward Vega?"

"No. And we don't know why."

Drawing in a long breath that made his throat grumble, Thiraka stepped away from his officers and crossed the bridge, heading toward the kalralahr.

As he neared the old one, Thiraka bowed his head and spoke in a low hiss of respect. "The Ulysses Corridor is clear. As you predicted, the door to Earth is open. But new difficulties have arisen."

Kalralahr Bokoth turned his long, pale head toward Thiraka. Bokoth's face bore the ravages of the battle at McAuliffe. He had lost an eye in that ambush, and deep scars radiated from the gloomy socket like an improbable form of black anti-lightning. "Difficulties, Thiraka?"

"Yes. One of our surveillance stations—"

"I know." Bokoth stroked the long, fine hairs on his chin and bared his yellowed canines in a smile, as though over Thiraka's surprise. "I'm having all intelligence routed directly to my cabin."

"Kalralahr, this is my ship. I've paid you tribute enough in turning over command of the battle group. All intelligence will be routed to the bridge."

Bokoth's good eye widened. "I wondered how long I could push you before you would behave honorably and defend yourself. There's hope for you after all."

Thiraka frowned as he detected the musty stench emanating from Bokoth, from the kalralahr's ornamental plumes, which he apparently only donned on special days or missions. Repressing the desire to gag, Thiraka considered several responses to Bokoth's chide, but thought better of them. The wrong word might spark the killing-rage in both Kilrathi. That all-controlling feeling dwelled just beneath the skin of every warrior, and once ignited, the feeling would blaze until one or both Kilrathi lay dead in its embers.

"What is it, Thiraka?" Bokoth asked, his tone a notch less condescending.

"Nothing, Kalralahr. Nothing."

"Then let me address your supposed difficulties. Yes, it's unfortunate that the Terrans have learned so soon of our attack on Pegasus. But it's of no consequence. By the time that merchantman reaches the *Tiger Claw*, our lead will be too great for them to intercept. If by some small miracle they do reach us, we will finish them as efficiently as we destroyed Pegasus. That complication has already been addressed. And even without our contingency plans, one carrier is no match for this battle group. Even the lowest of born can recognize that."

"But answer this: why is the merchantman not headed to Vega sector? Doesn't that puzzle you?"

"It does. Which is why I've asked it to the bridge." Bokoth turned his head toward the lift doors as they closed behind a human wearing an atmospheric suit.

"Where's the celebration?" the hairless ape asked, its voice sounding tinny through the translator attached to its suit. "The door to Earth is open. And you have your prize."

As the human drew closer, Thiraka noticed a silver cross hanging around the man's neck. He recognized that cross from history holos he had been forced to watch during his training. It represented a clan of humans known as Pilgrims.

"The NAVCOM AI has been reconfigured to your jump drives," the ape continued.

"Excellent. Now answer me two questions," Bokoth said in his most demanding tone. "Why was the *Concordia* alerted of our attack so soon?"

"That, I'm afraid, was unavoidable. Next question?"

Bokoth growled. "Explain *unavoidable*."

"I think the word translates clearly."

Raising a paw and extending long, jagged nails, Bokoth said, "If I discover—"

"You're not in a position to threaten me—after what I've given you."

Slowly, Bokoth lowered his paw. "A merchantman has been ordered to alert the *Tiger Claw*. Why isn't it headed to Vega sector?"

"I don't know. I'd worry about that."

"If you're lying—"

"There you go again. Haven't I already expressed what I want?"

"Yes. Most clearly. You have betrayed your race on a scale unimaginable, Pilgrim."

The ape sniggered. "I've lived up to my part of our agreement. Live up to yours. Destroy Earth."

Bokoth stared long and hard at the traitor. At last, he nodded.

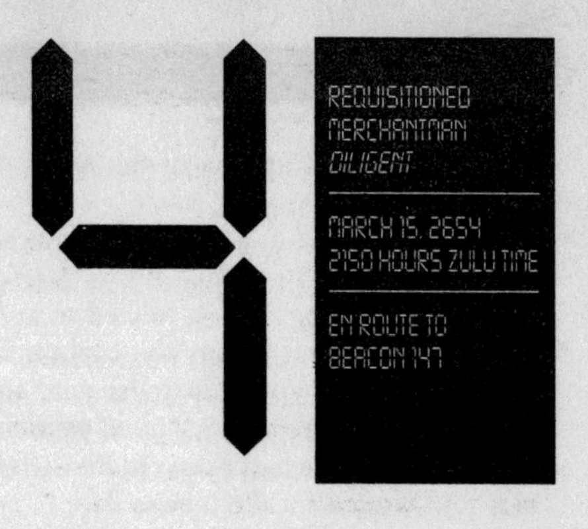

Taggart's hatch stood ajar, and Blair peeked through the crack. *If a man's quarters say a lot about the man, then this place isn't talking.* Taggart kept only the bare essentials: cot, nightstand, and wide, battered desk. Even the old gray walls were bare, sans the pinups or family photos that hung in the majority of pilot berths.

Taggart sat at the desk, poring over a collection of ancient star charts printed on real paper. A half-dozen of them lay rolled up and bound by rubber bands at his elbow. Still more of the scrolls sat in a pile on the floor. Amid the charts lay an unwrapped and half-eaten sandwich and Taggart's coffee mug.

Lifting a knuckle, Blair prepared to knock.

"Come in," Taggart said.

Grinning slightly over the man's keen senses, Blair entered and suddenly felt awkward at standing in this most personal of places. He blurted out, "We're holding steady on the beacon. Marshall has the helm." He neared the desk and ran his finger over one of the charts. "These must be antiques."

"Yeah," Taggart said. "They were made by the first explorers in the sector. Pilgrims."

"How did you get them?"

Taggart rolled up one of the maps. "Now that's a story too long to hear."

"I, uh, before . . . I couldn't help noticing the tattoo on your neck."

Smiling wanly, Taggart looked to an empty wall. Blair could only imagine what ghosts the captain saw there. "What about the Pilgrim cross you hide under your shirt?"

Retreating a step, Blair's hand went instinctively for the cross. Then, realizing he had betrayed himself, he thrust the hand to his side and waited for the inevitable.

"Don't worry. We all have pasts. And secrets."

Blair gave a slight sigh. "It was my mother's."

"May I see it?"

After hesitating, Blair lifted the chain over his head and withdrew the cross. He handed it to Taggart, who ran his fingers slowly, reverently over the semicircle. The glimmer in his eyes grew brighter, and his face tightened into the countenance of a priest staring at a recovered relic. He pressed the center symbol. A seven-inch blade telescoped from the cross's bottom.

As he traced the blade with his index finger, he smiled wanly again and said, "There was a time long ago when people looked up to the Pilgrims. They were at the forefront of space exploration. When I was a boy, I knew there was some kind of connection between God and the stars. I think the Pilgrims found that connection." He touched the plate again, retracting the blade, then returned it to Blair.

"You know," Taggart continued, "since the Pilgrims were defeated, not a single new quasar has been charted."

"It's so strange hearing someone talk like this. The word Pilgrim has always been . . . I don't know . . . a curse."

Without warning, a sudden surge of acceleration sent Blair reaching for the desk. He caught the edge and balanced himself as Taggart's coffee mug fell and broke.

"That idiot!" Taggart screamed. He shot to his feet and stormed out of the cabin.

Blair followed close behind, only then realizing what Marshall had done.

As Taggart entered the bridge, he shouted, "Get up!"

Marshall's face grew thin and pale as he quickly vacated the captain's chair and moved to the co-pilot's seat. "That caffeine's killing your attitude, man."

"Shut up. Did you change course?"

"You told me to shut up."

"Answer the question!"

"No. Just boosted the power. Why dog it when we can be at the beacon in an hour? Unless, of course, you want us to be delayed."

Blair watched Marshall's hand drift toward the sidearm concealed at his calf.

"That beacon is marking a gravity well," Taggart said through clenched teeth.

Marshall gave Blair a nervous look and mouthed, "Holy shit."

Swinging the navigation computer in front of him, Taggart's fingers danced over the touchpad until a Heads Up Display lit before them. A green, flat grid rotated and glowed as data bars on each side filled with coordinates. The grid began folding inward, creating a strange, swirling, elliptical spike in the concave surface.

Blair stood transfixed, knowing all too well what a gravity well could do to a Confed capital ship, let alone a rusty old transport.

Something sparkled near the floor, and Blair turned as Merlin self-activated and began pacing. "I told you this ship wasn't up to the job. My sensors indicate that there are a number of structural flaws—"

"What the hell is that?" Taggart asked with a lopsided grin.

"That's Merlin," Blair answered. "He's the interface for my PPC."

Taggart resumed his gaze on the HUD. "Well, get into his face and tell him to shut up."

Blair cocked his head to give the order, but Merlin had already switched to standby mode.

Shoving the navigation computer back on its swingarm, Taggart slid another display forward, one that offered multiple views of space via the *Diligent*'s external cameras. He chose the image from the centerline unit and adjusted the telescopic lens to bring a dim object, the gravity well, into focus. Blair spotted asteroids and space debris being sucked into the well, as though into a whirlpool, and disappearing. The *Diligent* screamed toward the same future.

Taggart beat his knuckle upon a thruster control button, throwing Blair and Marshall forward as retros violently kicked in. "One cubic inch of that well exerts more gravitational force than Earth's sun," he barked at Marshall.

"I screwed up. I get that. Stow the physics lesson," Marshall answered, his eyes not leaving the external camera display.

Taggart pushed that display aside and slid back the navigation computer. He frowned at the coordinates and tapped in new ones. "Come on, come on," he said, driving himself harder. "If I don't realign our entry vector, we won't make the jump."

"And if we don't make the jump . . ." Marshall began.

"We die," Taggart finished.

"Have we reached the entry vector's point of no return yet?" Blair asked. Once they hit the PNR, course adjustment would be a fond memory.

"Not yet," Taggart said, throwing a toggle to automatically stabilize the now-groaning transport. "She's reaching out for us. Hear that?"

The *Diligent*'s hull protested much louder now, and through the viewport, the gravity well appeared in all of its gluttonous furor. The ship's thrusters whined as they fought to obey Taggart's course corrections. Still, the well grew larger, more ominous, and the space distortions now seemed more like gelatinous hands reaching incessantly into the cosmos. Blair repressed a shiver.

Taggart took one look at the viewport and raised a hand. "Well, ladies, meet Scylla, bane to sailors and monster of myth."

Marshall frowned at Blair, then regarded Taggart, his frown deepening. "What's a Scylla?"

But Blair answered for Taggart. "Ulysses sailed between the whirlpool Charybdis and the island monster Scylla. She snatched six of his men and ate them."

"I didn't need to know that," Marshall moaned.

Shaking a finger at Scylla, Taggart said, "This beauty's got an even bigger appetite. Hold on."

Blair got to the navigator's seat behind Taggart and Marshall. The captain threw a pair of toggles, and a bank of afterburners kicked the *Diligent* onto her side. Blair clung to the arms of his seat as the ship continued to yaw and tremble like a piece of Los Angeles real estate. Every seam and conduit in the old transport begged for relief. Within a few seconds the tremors became so violent that Blair fell from his chair and crashed to the wall that now served as the deck. He rolled over and spotted Merlin, whose image shook so hard that it blurred. Marshall lost his grip as well, and thumped to the floor beside Blair.

Still glued to his seat, Taggart continued adjusting the *Diligent*'s course. The transport slowly rolled upright, sending Blair and Marshall sliding toward the true deck. As the ship finally balanced and artificial gravity readjusted, Blair looked over Taggart's shoulder at the Heads Up Display, which now showed a digital glide path that took them along Scylla's perimeter, the course steady and true.

"Broken your grip, old girl," Taggart said, regarding an external camera display that tracked the gravity well. "Better luck next time."

Blair stood and watched Taggart steer the ship along the glide path. The *Diligent* now skipped closer to Scylla, avoiding her maw, but nonetheless doing some serious flirting. Space wavered along the starboard quarter.

Clearly, Marshall had a rough time comprehending the gravity well. He stared at the external camera image, at the space distortion through the viewport, at the glide path. And he began shaking his head. "This isn't a normal gravity well. What the hell is this thing?"

"This *thing* is a distortion in space-time," Taggart explained. "Pilgrims were the first to chart it."

"So why is it off-limits?" Marshall asked.

"Because it's unstable."

"And we're going to jump it?" Marshall mouthed to Blair, having a hard time keeping his jaw closed.

A warning light flashed on the navigation computer, accompanied by a rapid beeping. The HUD winked out. The *Diligent* suddenly listed to starboard.

"Nav computer's off-line," Blair observed.

"It's the magnetic fields," Taggart said. "Blair. Take the helm."

Normal functions like breathing suddenly escaped Blair. "I've never made a jump before."

Taggart cocked a brow. "Now would be a good time to learn." He rushed toward the hatchway.

"Guess we both know what he's about," Marshall said softly. "He's about getting us killed."

Blair ignored that, focusing instead on the vortex as it now shifted to the center viewport. Without the nav computer's assistance, the *Diligent* would return to the previous course, and Blair, Marshall, and Taggart would learn the mysteries of the afterlife, free of charge.

Near the hatchway, Taggart had pulled off a maintenance panel and now considered the exposed intricacy of wires. He pulled out a pair of protein processing chips, studied them a moment, then tossed them over his shoulder. He opened another panel and withdrew fresh chips.

The gravity well now dominated all viewports, a malevolent queen at her banquet table. A pair of discarded O_2 canisters collided and exploded on their way into her stomach. Asteroids spun and broke apart, leaving trails of themselves across the whirlpool. Even a comet had strayed too close to Scylla's amorous arms and now painted an even streak across the watery blur of her physique.

A proximity alarm blared, and a digital countdown at Marshall's station read 9, 8, 7—

"Uh, Captain?" Marshall called out.

"What?"

"Five seconds to jump."

"So?"

"So if you don't get the nav computer back on line, this unstable gravity well is going to pull us in—one molecule at a time."

REQUISITIONED
MERCHANTMAN
DILIGENT

MARCH 15, 2654
2200 HOURS ZULU TIME

JUMP POINT: SCYLLA
GRAVITY WELL

"This antiquated vessel is riddled with structural flaws," Merlin said, appearing atop the copilot's console. "In my opinion, it cannot survive the jump."

Marshall shouted the final countdown: "Three . . ."

Taggart shoved a protein chip into place—

". . . two . . ."

—then jiggled a wire.

". . . one!"

The navigation system snapped on, panels warming to their normal glow, coordinates spilling across four screens in front of Blair. *Snap*. Everything went dark.

Snap. Everything came back.

"Come on!" Marshall shouted.

After a tiny spark and loud hum, the HUD returned with a suggested trajectory marked by a thick green line through Scylla. Blair read the coordinates and studied the course, but something deep inside him said the computer was wrong. He couldn't explain the feeling, but he had felt it before, at the academy, during blind navigation simulator runs. The feeling tugged on his mind, his heart, and something even greater.

"Plot your course, Mr. Blair," Taggart said.

Mother? Father? Be with me now. Blair pulled out his cross and squeezed it. Then he obeyed the feeling as it told him to close his eyes. His fingers glided over the touchpad as though it were a musical instrument hardwired to the quantum level. Then he opened his eyes and stared at the upper left screen: COURSE PLOTTED.

Drawing in a long breath and holding it, Blair steered the *Diligent* into the gravity well. The viewport grew darker as Scylla robbed more and more starlight. Shuddering again, the ship pressed harder against the barrier of space-time that lay at the singularity's core.

Marshall released a long howl over the cacophony of rattling consoles and conduits.

"As I was saying before I was so rudely cut off," Merlin cried, "I would calculate our chances of survival at twenty-seven point two percent. I implore you . . ."

Blair glared at the hologram as the screens shook so violently that he held them, fearing they would snap off their swingarms.

Three, two, one and the *Diligent* pierced the barrier

Though his eyes remained open, Blair could only see a dark void speckled occasionally by flakes of yellow light. He turned his head. The void surrounded him. He cried out to Marshall. The pilot did not answer. Then Blair realized that he hadn't heard himself call out, that all of his senses had been shut down, replaced by . . .

The feeling.

Never had he felt it so strongly, a connection to the universe that made no sense, that made perfect sense. The subatomic particles of his body had never belonged to him in the first place. They had always belonged to the universe. He understood at least that much of the feeling now.

Scylla's gravitational forces caused matter to have infinite density and infinitesimal volume, while also causing space and time to become infinitely distorted.

But Blair's coordinates somehow broke those rules.

The *Diligent*'s bridge reappeared as quickly as it had vanished. But life still hung between seconds, between particles, frozen. Taggart stood immobile on his way toward the bridge. Marshall leaned back in his chair, in midscream. Merlin pointed at the gravity well and bit his lower lip. And Blair somehow observed this while feeling as though he could move his body, but seeing that he could not.

His moment of inexplicable peace, silence, unity, continued for one minute, for a thousand years, for infinity, the distinctions became irrelevant.

Yet at some point, a point Blair could not single out, a nova-bright light engulfed the *Diligent* as she shed Scylla's arms and plunged back into normal space.

With his senses recovered, Blair recoiled from the still-rattling ship and Marshall's screaming, from the stench of frayed wires, and from the pain in his hands at keeping such a tight grip on his displays. The return left him feeling empty, as though he had forgotten part of himself and needed to head back. The others would not appreciate that desire.

"Stop this madness," Merlin demanded. "That man is quite probably insane. He'll kill us all." Merlin looked over his shoulder at Taggart's approach. "Oh."

But the captain shifted past the hologram to level his gaze at the nav computer's display. He opened his mouth, looked at Blair, started to say something, then just stared.

Unnerved by Taggart's odd look, Blair asked, "What happened?"

Taggart held back a laugh. "You just plotted a jump through a gravity well in under five seconds. A NAVCOM can't do that." His gaze averted to Blair's chest.

Seeing this, Blair gripped his cross for a moment before slipping it under his shirt. "I don't know what to say. I guess I just felt something back there."

"You didn't use the nav computer's trajectory. Why didn't you trust it?"

"I don't know."

Marshall, his face still flushed, turned to Blair and nodded. "Who cares how he did it? That was one hell of a rocket ride. Not bad for the second-best pilot at the academy."

"Shut up," Taggart barked, turning to Marshall. "The next time you fail to follow my orders, I'll dump you with the rest of the garbage. You read me, Lieutenant Marshall?"

Tensing, Marshall kept his gaze forward and replied, "Yes, sir. I read you clearly, sir."

Satisfied that Marshall had been duly reprimanded, Taggart redirected his attention. "Plot a course for the *Tiger Claw*, Mr. Blair."

"Yes, sir."

Taggart rubbed his eyes, sighed loudly, then walked off the bridge.

The flush that had filled Marshall's face during the jump lingered, fueled now by the young man's anger. He looked after Taggart until the man moved out of earshot. "That guy has some serious issues."

"He's all right," Blair said quietly.

"What?"

"You heard me."

Marshall snickered. "Yeah, I guess he likes you 'cause you kinda saved his ass."

"Kinda saved yours, too."

"Coincidence."

This time Blair snickered. "Fortunate for you."

"So, did you find out anything about his tattoo?"

"Not yet."

"You find out anything about him?"

"He knows a lot about history."

"Whose history? Ours . . . or the enemy's?"

"Let's not talk," Blair said, piloting the *Diligent* toward the distant carrier, ETA: fourteen minutes.

"Well, thank God we're almost rid of the man. Imagine having him for a wing commander? He wouldn't last a day."

"Or you wouldn't."

Marshall raised his lip in disgust. "Like you said, let's not talk."

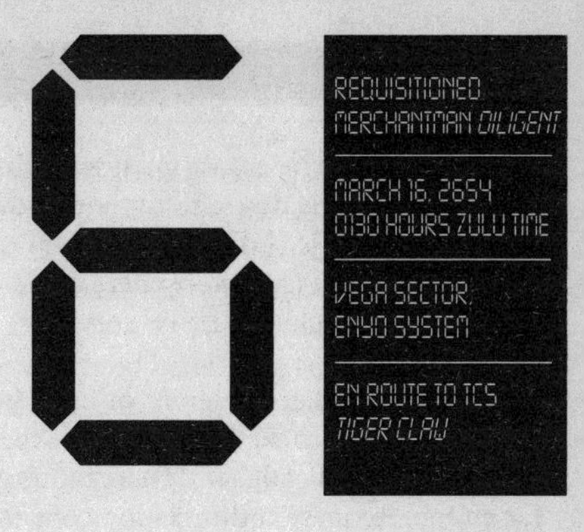

"Where are you going, Daddy?"

"I'm sorry, Christopher. Daddy has to go to work now. There's a war he has to fight."

"What's a war?"

"It's . . . I don't know. It's just bad."

"Then why do you go?"

"It's my job."

"Stay with me, Daddy. Don't go."

"Bye, Christopher. Give me a hug."

"Don't go, Daddy. Please don't go."

"Hey, what the hell's the matter with you, Blair? Hello, Blair. Come back to us."

After blinking hard, Blair looked at Marshall's angular face, then at his nav display. ETA to TCS *Tiger Claw*: three minutes.

Marshall shoved his shoulder. "You all right, bro?"

"Yeah. Just . . . thinking."

He gestured to the viewport. "Well, start thinking about those birds."

Two Confederation Rapiers flew straight toward the *Diligent*, their rotating nose cannons and short forward wings lending to them a deadly visage that would awe even the most casual spectator. Bright running lights flashed on both craft, switched on only during routine escort missions. Observing the fighters made Blair itch with the desire to fly one of them instead of the clunky merchantman. He slid over the comm control. "They've queried us. Better get the captain up here."

Marshall mocked a fit of vomiting. "Oh, that would be my pleasure."

Blair punched in the senior officer's frequency. First Lieutenant Tanaka Mariko clicked into view on the left screen, her face hidden behind her headgear. "Merchantman *Diligent*. This is Black Lion One. Request authorization code for approach to TCS *Tiger Claw*, roger. Broadcasting sign now."

"Affirmative, Black Lion One," Blair said. "Stand by."

"Send the countersign," Taggart said, coming up behind Blair. "And thank you for waiting. I see you've read and understand the regs manual."

Blair craned his head, even as Taggart stared unflinchingly at Marshall. The two held their gazes until Marshall broke the duel.

After dialing up the signal, Blair threw a toggle. A coded burst of static crackled over the intercom, followed by another burst. Blair read the display. "Identification acknowledged. They'll escort us in."

The Rapiers broke off and wheeled around to bracket the ship. A distant, shining fleck stood dead ahead.

Marshall moved to the viewport to glance at the fighters. "I never get tired of looking at 'em."

"You should get used to this view," Taggart said.

Spinning on his heel, Marshall pursed his lips tightly and poured poison into his eyes. "Sir. May I speak freely?"

"I suppose that's a threat. Go ahead."

"What's your problem?"

Blair shot to his feet and directed an index finger at Marshall. "Don't go there."

"Mr. Blair. Fly my ship. I'll handle this." Taggart marched up to Marshall and circled him like a rabid drill sergeant. "My problem is that I care too much, Lieutenant. I care too much about idiots like you who sneer at protocol and fly like you own the war.

You guys stand in line, waiting to get blown out of the sky. Yeah, I got your number, Lieutenant Marshall. I see you coming from a light-year away—and so will the Kilrathi."

Although Marshall did not move, Blair guessed that he wanted very badly to smirk and roll his eyes.

Taggart paused to get squarely in Marshall's face. "From here on out I suggest you get your priorities straight, understand the mission, your place in it, and stow that pathetic ego. No one ever flies alone. No one." After letting that sink in, Taggart plopped into his captain's chair.

Slowly, Marshall shifted back toward the viewport, mumbling something.

Blair sighed and regarded Taggart, filling his gaze with understanding, but the man would not look at him. Taggart studied the growing form of the *Tiger Claw* as her enormous flight deck doors rolled open.

Burying the awkwardness of the moment in his job, Blair slipped the *Diligent* into her final approach vector, then engaged the autopilot. The Heads Up showed a green outline of the carrier and the vector's "red carpet" runway grid. Blair looked beyond the HUD to marvel at the carrier as they drew closer to her bow. She resembled a 700-meter-long gray cylinder tapered at the ends and split into port and starboard halves. A narrow rectangular structure joined the halves and served as a runway to stern and a colossal hangar bay amidships. Massive doors permitted access to the bay from the upper deck or the stern (the latter approach most used by starfighter pilots who would plunge into the *Claw*'s innards to land). Far above the runway, past some of the hundreds of lights that dotted her hull, rose the carrier's bridge, a circular superstructure on the starboard side that stood in tribute to the ancient sea carriers that had clearly inspired the Trojan Four Spaceyards engineers who had designed her. Despite the tradition of her silhouette, she boasted state-of-the-art firepower. Eight dual laser turrets had been mounted equidistantly apart on her hull and covered the full sphere of vacuum. A main battery jutted out from each half of her bow, and triangular sleeves of battle-scarred armor shielded personnel operating the big cannons. The sealed hatches of missile tubes subtly reminded her enemies that even more death lay within her bowels.

Indeed, the *Tiger Claw*, though patched up here and there, remained powerful. In fact, if you took her in with a quick glance, you would swear that she reached out in challenge to any cap ship that dared defy her perimeter. She had attitude in spades; few would deny that.

As the escort fighters swerved away to continue their patrol, a broad tractor beam lanced out from a turret below the *Claw*'s flight deck and seized the *Diligent*. Blair's autopilot automatically disengaged, and retros fired, helping the beam to ease the merchantman down and through the clear energy field that separated atmosphere from vacuum. The beam's force grew weaker, and Blair took over. The ship settled onto a dull, ocher-colored deck heavily stained by hydraulic fluid, its landing pads outlined in bright yellow. The huge doors closed slowly over them.

"Switching systems to accept moorings," Blair announced, punching in the command.

"Good work," Taggart said. "Auto power down in progress. Message from flight control. The XO will meet you on the deck. Go fetch your gear."

"Thank God," Marshall muttered.

Five minutes later, two Confed Marines in burnt sienna deck uniforms approached the *Diligent*'s loading ramp. Blair and Marshall trudged down toward them, their shoulders already sore under the weight of their duffels.

"IDs?" the male jarhead said curtly.

Blair produced his identity badge, and the Marine waved a scanner over it. "Do you have your orders card, Lieutenant Blair? I'll need to see a hard copy as well."

"Duh," Marshall said, shouldering his way toward the Marine. "You think we're here to gamble and eat too much?"

"Don't mind him," Blair told the Marine. "He's having a little trouble with his bodily functions. I'll get him to sickbay right away."

The Marine gave Marshall a stupid grin, then his eyes snapped wide open. "Officer or not, you will shut your hole and wait your turn."

Marshall swore under his breath as Blair handed the Marine his orders card.

Once they finished the interminably long check-in, Blair suggested that they wait for Taggart to at least say good-bye.

"Now that," Marshall said, "is humorous."

Blair dropped his duffel. "I'm waiting."

With a hand on his brow, Marshall paced for a moment, then slipped off his own duffel. "You're right. We should wait. I'm not finished with him."

Having quickly developed a numbness to Marshall's belligerent remarks, Blair moved off to survey the immense rectangular flight deck. A half-dozen or more columns on either side of the deck rose thirty meters, joined overhead by a latticework of durasteel. Behind the columns stood rows of Hornets, Rapiers, Scimitars, Broadswords, and Raptors, many being serviced by orange-suited flight crews who hung from open cockpits, scorched wings, and pockmarked fuselages. One tech attached multicolored fuel and hydraulic lines to a Raptor whose nose had been removed to repair her electrical system. A miasma of heated metal, jet fuel, hydraulic fluid, and burning rubber hung heavily in the air, despite the best efforts of the ship's recyclers. While civilians would crinkle their noses at the smell, Blair smiled. *I'm home.* As he touched a bulkhead adjacent to the lift doors and came upon a patch welded there, he noticed the carrier's age, evident in that patch and the hundreds of others that freckled her walls. "You've seen a lot of action," he whispered. "Guess you'll see a lot more."

"Hey, what are you doing?" someone familiar asked.

Blair turned in Taggart's direction. "Waiting for you. Just wanted to say thanks for the lift."

The captain paused before them. "Well, gentlemen, don't think I haven't enjoyed your company."

Marshall bore his teeth. "We won't. *Sir.*"

Not wasting a second on Marshall, the captain focused on Blair.

"I'm headed for the lift over there," he said, tipping his head toward the doors fifty meters away. "See you. And good luck."

Lifting his duffel, Blair said, "I'll walk with you."

"I won't," Marshall said.

Blair hurried after the captain. "Marshall? I'll meet you back here." He didn't wait for the expected reply and finally caught up with Taggart. "Before you go, tell me about your tattoo."

"You know what it is?" Taggart asked, lifting his voice over the collective whine of power tools.

"I think I got it figured out. It's a Kilrathi marker. You were a prisoner of war."

"I was on the *Iason* when they took her."

That caught Blair off guard. "The *Iason*? She was the first ship to have contact with the Kilrathi. You served under Commander Andropolos?"

Taggart nodded. "We encountered a spacecraft of unknown origin, transmitted a wideband, nonverbal greeting, and waited. Four hours later she fired upon us with all batteries. But you know the story."

"Yeah. And I know there weren't supposed to be any survivors from the *Iason*."

"I guess not."

They reached the lift doors, which slid apart. Taggart stepped inside and turned around.

"Why don't you have it removed?" Blair asked, staring at the captain's neck, the tattoo partially exposed.

"Let's just say it helps me remember."

"Remember what?"

"Why I fight."

The doors began to close.

Blair stepped forward. "Wait. I've seen photos and holos, but what do the Kilrathi look like? I mean, in the flesh?"

"They're ugly. Good luck."

The doors sealed.

"Right," Blair muttered, then hurried back to the other lift, where he found Marshall ogling a blonde tech whose smooth skin and lithe figure seemed incongruous with her greasy coveralls. She stood beneath a Broadsword bomber, dismantling one of its mass driver cannons with a power wrench.

"I don't see the XO," Marshall said, his gaze still riveted to the tech.

"I can see why."

"Maybe she can help." He strutted toward the woman, his boots barely touching the deck.

Blair ambled toward a row of Rapiers, still searching the room for their welcoming party. He came to the first fighter, number thirty-five. Her heavily patched armor and carbon scoring bespoke numerous round trips to Hell. He felt like a kid as he pictured himself in the cockpit, diving onto a Dralthi's tail, locking target, and—

He repressed a chill and lifted a computer slate from a rolling tool cart. The slate showed the fighter's mission status. She had come in less than eight hours earlier from a sortie on the fringe of the Enyo system. Her next pilot had yet to be assigned. Not bothering to read more, Blair replaced the slate and hurried up the cockpit ladder. He peered furtively around the deck for a second and, seeing that no one watched, climbed into the pit.

Although the instrument panels remained dark, he could easily imagine the left Visual Display Unit reporting battle damage, the right VDU showing options for the vidcom system and the targeting screen. The circular radar display, just left of center, depicted a wave of red blips above him. "Break and attack," he told his ghostly wingman.

"Two Dralthis on your tail—one above, one below."

Blair felt a jolt in his gut, then looked down toward his inquisitor. In her late twenties, she stood nearly as tall as him, her shoulder-length hair a deep brown laced with gold curls. The shadows beneath her eyes and streak of lubricant on her cheek did little to mar her beauty. However, the oil-stained disposable plasticine coveralls she wore weren't exactly flattering on anyone. With a socket wrench in one hand, an x-ray scanner in the other, she raised a thin brow and continued: "You've got five, maybe ten seconds—the clock is ticking. What do you do?"

"Simple. I go vertical and inverted, do a one-eighty at full throttle, apply the brakes, and drop in behind them."

"Bang. You're dead. Not fast enough. Dralthis are too quick—particularly in a climb. You've just taken a missile up your tailpipe."

No lower-ranked tech had ever spoken to Blair this way. What did she hope to prove? Was she bitter over not being a pilot? Why the callous shield?

"Okay. Reverse the situation," she said. "You're locked on a Dralthi. It goes evasive, enters an asteroid belt. Clock is ticking."

With a loud snort, Blair pointed ahead. "I'm locked on. There's no such thing as evasive because—"

"Bang. Dead again. It's an ambush. Five or six fighters hide behind rocks the size of your swollen head and pounce—a Kilrathi gang-bang."

An intense heat washed into Blair's face, and he balled his hands into fists.

She set down her tools and began untying her coveralls. "What's the matter? Did I bruise your ego?"

"No. I'm just not used to getting combat tips from a grease monkey."

As the words left Blair's mouth, he saw her step out of the coveralls to reveal her blood-red flight suit. The insignia on that suit indicated the extent of Blair's foolishness.

"I'm Lieutenant Commander Jeanette Deveraux—your wing commander. You have a name, *nugget*?"

Blair straightened and saluted her, not that his after-the-fact respect would mean anything. "Lieutenant Christopher Blair, ma'am."

"Well, Lieutenant. If you want to play at being a fighter pilot, I suggest you find a virtual fun zone. Meanwhile, step down from the Rapier."

Feeling as though his face would burst into flames, Blair rose and set foot on the cockpit ladder. As he descended, he noticed the pilot's name in bright yellow letters along the pit's edge: Lt. Commander Vince "Bossman" Chen. Twenty-six Kilrathi paws representing kills had been set in neat rows beside the name, a scorch mark slashing through them. "Ma'am, the mission slate said this fighter was unassigned. I apologize. I didn't realize it was Bossman's."

"Who?"

"Lieutenant Commander Chen. Bossman." Blair gazed back at the Rapier. Had he read the name correctly? Yes, he had.

Deveraux's face creased even more.

Puzzled, Blair crossed to the tool cart and lifted the computer slate. "If this fighter's not his, then who got these twenty-six kills?"

She wrenched the slate from his hand. "What are you doing on the flight deck, anyway?"

"Looking for the XO," Marshall said, arriving at Blair's side.

Shifting her gaze to the far end of the flight deck, Deveraux nodded to a tall officer. "You found him." She turned on her heels and strode off.

"I'm proud of you, Blair," Marshall said, patting his back. "Even from back there I could tell you were defying authority. Some day these hardasses will appreciate our creativity."

"That hardass is our new wing commander. And I've made a wonderful first impression."

"She'll get over it. They always do. Or she'll get whacked and you won't have to worry about it. Either way, you're in the clear, buddy. Now, c'mon. Smiley over there is waving us over."

Blair looked to the XO, a man with a deeply grooved face who had once smiled back in 2649, though no hard evidence existed to prove that rumor.

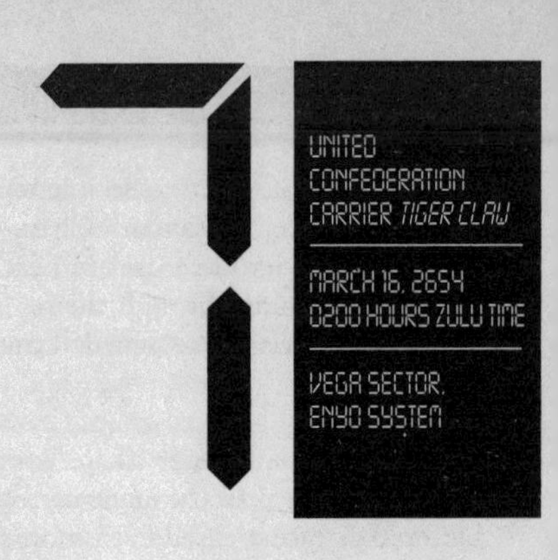

During Blair's senior year at the academy, he had flown training missions off the TCS *Formidable*, an Exeter-class destroyer assigned to the Vega sector. He had been on the *Formidable*'s bridge only a few times but had seen enough to fill his heart with awe.

Now, as he stepped onto the bridge of the *Tiger Claw*, a carrier nearly twice as large as the destroyer, he could barely contain his excitement. Viewports wrapped around the bridge, the synthoglass so clear it seemed that nothing stood between people and the vacuum. Dozens of officers and noncoms sat murmuring at dozens of consoles. Instrument panels at the radar, navigation, communications, tactical, and flight deck stations radiated a calming glow. Six holographic projectors shaped like inverted domes hung from the overhead, and one of them at the tactical radar board to Blair's left displayed a real-time, grid-enhanced image of six Hornets launching for patrol to replace the Rapiers now returning.

Captain Jay Sansky stood below the hologram, conferring with a radar officer and pointing to coordinates marking the fighter patrol's flight. The stress of command had robbed Sansky of his hair and the rest of his youth. Pride obviously stood between him and the partial recovery of that loss through surgery. Appearances aside, the way he talked with the radar officer suggested an avuncular quality, a benevolence that the XO, Commander Gerald, sorely lacked.

With few words, Gerald had escorted Blair and Marshall to the bridge. Yes, the commander had identified himself, but Blair didn't even know Gerald's first name, and the man obviously preferred it that way. He had looked annoyed over having to meet them on the flight deck. XOs typically didn't greet new pilots or give them the welcome-aboard orientation tour. That was the wing commander's job. But according to Gerald, Captain Taggart had called ahead, unbeknownst to Blair and Marshall, to make sure that the XO served as escort. In an attempt to quell Gerald's temper, Blair had explained the importance of the minidisc he now carried. Gerald had seemed unimpressed. And he had even forced Marshall to wait in the corridor, since Marshall had "no business on the bridge."

Not waiting for the commander to do an uninspired job of introducing him, Blair crossed to Captain Sansky, stood at attention, and gave a crisp salute that the captain returned. "First Lieutenant Christopher Blair reporting for duty, sir."

"At ease, Lieutenant." Sansky scrutinized Blair for a moment, then said, "I understand you have something for me."

"Yes, sir." He withdrew the minidisc from an inner breast pocket and handed it to Sansky. "An encrypted communiqué—from Admiral Tolwyn."

Sansky scratched his forehead and stared nonplused at the disc. "Why didn't the admiral send a drone from Pegasus?"

Blair's tone grew somber. "Sir. Pegasus was destroyed by a Kilrathi battle group seventeen hours ago. I'm sorry, sir."

The captain looked gravely at Gerald, then crossed toward a wall of consoles, holding up the disc and shouting, "Communications. I want this decrypted ASAP."

"Aye-aye, sir," a young comm officer said, pivoting in his chair to accept the disc.

"If there's nothing else, sir?" Blair asked as Sansky returned.

"We don't kill the messenger anymore, Lieutenant. Instead, I'll just say welcome aboard. And dismissed."

Drawing up his shoulders, Blair saluted and turned to go.

"Hey, Lieutenant," Gerald called. "You wouldn't be related to Arnold Blair, would you?"

Steeling himself, Blair looked back and answered, "He was my father, sir."

Gerald nodded, his lips rising in a self-satisfied grin that suddenly evaporated. "He married a Pilgrim woman, didn't he?"

"You don't have to answer that," Captain Sansky said.

After a moment's hesitation, Blair finally confirmed, "Yes, sir. My father married a Pilgrim, sir."

"Mixed marriages seldom work out." The commander shifted in front of Blair, his face a cold, dark knot. "Pilgrims don't think like us."

Blair returned the icy look. "You won't have to worry, sir. They're both dead."

Sansky placed a hand on the commander's shoulder. "I'm sure the lieutenant's heredity will have no bearing on his performance, Mr. Gerald."

"No, sir. I'm sure it won't."

"That's all, Lieutenant," Sansky said, obviously growing weary of his refereeing. "I suggest you stow your gear and take the virtual tour. Your onboard accounts have already been set up. You'll find hard copies of everything in the personnel department."

Blair nodded. "Thank you, sir."

Captain Sansky watched his new pilot exit, growing more and more troubled over Gerald's reaction to the boy. "You don't trust him?"

Instead of answering, Gerald turned to the tactical computer console. "Computer. What are the odds that a Kilrathi battle group could infiltrate Confederation space undetected and destroy Pegasus Station?"

"Calculating," the computer responded. "One chance in one-point-twenty-one million. To the tenth power."

Gerald's eyes grew wide as he lifted his gaze from the terminal. "Trust him, Captain? No, sir. I do not."

In the corridor outside, Blair stormed silently past Marshall, damning to hell both the recent and distant past. He suddenly felt trapped in who he was, cheated out of a fair life. All of the hard work, the training, the studying, the suffering—all of it—for nothing. *I'm a Pilgrim half-breed. That's all I am. None of you can see past that, you bastards.*

"Hey, hey, hey," Marshall said. He ran up behind Blair and yanked him around. "What? Are you having a moment?"

Blair mouthed a curse, stared teary-eyed at the deck, then said, "It never changes."

"Look. I overheard a little of that. So Gerald's another hardass XO, so what. Let it go. Because right now, we're about to meet our fellow pilots. The men and women we're going to fight with, perhaps even die with, and perhaps"

"Don't worry, Marshall. I won't let the fact that I'm pissed keep you from getting laid."

"Me? I'm worried about it keeping *you* from getting laid. You watch the old Marshall man in action. I'll teach you how to make friends." Marshall threw his arm over Blair's shoulder and led him down the corridor.

By the time they reached the pilots' mess, Blair's rage had cooled to a simmer. Marshall pushed open the hatch, and Blair followed him inside.

Considering the large number of pilots stationed aboard the *Tiger Claw*, Blair had assumed that the mess would be spacious, well-equipped, and at least somewhat orderly. But Captain Sansky obviously kept a long leash on his fighter jocks, perhaps in compensation for the dingy, cramped, and stale-smelling mess assigned to them. Uncomfortable-looking gray metal chairs lay scattered around chipped tables whose legs bore the tape of numerous makeshift repair jobs. Fading pinups of men and woman hung from every wall, flapping in the breeze of the air recyclers. A Confederation Navy recruiting poster had been affixed to the rear hatch and depicted a cruiser with a jump point exit beaming behind it. Beneath the ship stood a challenge in bold letters: THE NAVY WAY. IS THERE ANY OTHER? Someone had taken the challenge and had written a number of answers in indelible black marker that included combinations of epithets even Blair had never seen nor heard.

Two pilots played chess on a scratched-up old board. One of them, a tall, sturdy man with a high-and-tight crew cut and Roman nose, smiled to make the long scar on his face twist a little. He took the other pilot's pawn and laughed. "You're going down, Forbes."

"Mr. Polanski. It's good to know you still dream." Forbes, a beautiful, dark-skinned woman who had cut her hair short and dyed it blonde, stared determinedly at the board for a moment, then quickly made a move, took Polanski's bishop, and grinned. Something about her smile bothered Blair, as though the gloss on her lips were a poison only he could recognize.

The chess players noticed their entrance, as did the half-dozen other pilots seated at tables, eating and sipping drinks. Blair gave a quick nod hello.

But Marshall marched into the room with the joviality of a grand marshal at a Confederation victory parade. "Hey! How's everybody doing? Lieutenant Todd Marshall."

Silence. Dead silence. Blair swore he could hear molecules bumping against each other. He scanned the blank faces of the pilots and felt his breath shorten. A few returned to their conversations.

Undaunted by his audience's initial reaction, Marshall continued, "I'd like you all to meet a close personal friend, Lieutenant Christopher Blair—who just happens to be the second-best pilot on this hunk of junk."

Several of the pilots now looked up. One with reddish-brown hair and long sideburns that defied regulations removed the cigar stub from his mouth and spoke in an Australian accent. "Who you calling the best, nugget?"

Blair leaned toward Marshall. "So this is the secret to your overwhelming popularity?"

Still not fazed, Marshall took a step toward the cigar-wielding pilot, who quickly stood. "There's two ways to figure out who's the best," he said as he read the pilot's nametag. "One way, Captain St. John, involves you trying to kick the shit out of me—"

St. John frowned, having no idea what to make of Marshall. Blair knew the feeling all too well.

"What's the other way?" St. John asked.

Marshall smiled—a very dangerous look now. "The other way? Why, that involves my other close personal friend. Mr. Johnnie Walker Black." After quickly unzipping a pouch on his duffel, Marshall produced a bottle of Scotch, very good Scotch, the rare, real stuff. Now Marshall commanded the room.

Turning toward Forbes, St. John spoke her name as a question, as though she were the group's unofficial leader.

Keeping her gaze trained on the bottle, Forbes said, "We're on stand-down. One won't hurt."

Marshall moved quickly to a shelf, fetched a plastic glass, and poured one for Forbes. "This might even help."

The other pilots flocked around Marshall, who looked at Blair with an I-told-you-so expression plastered on his face.

Forbes tanked down her drink, exhaled loudly as the burn set in, then faced Marshall. "You got balls."

"You should see them."

"Mine are bigger," she said.

"I've been told that size doesn't matter."

"She lied." The other pilots chuckled loudly. Forbes eyed St. John and addressed him by his call sign. "Personally, Hunter, I'd have taken the third option: kick his ass first, then drink his Scotch."

That drew more laughter. For the moment, Blair felt accepted.

Standing in the chart room with the hatch sealed, Captain Sansky and Commander Gerald waited as the computer booted up and prepared to play the decoded message delivered by Lieutenant Blair. Sansky had already guessed what Admiral Tolwyn would ask of him, and he knew that he could not disobey orders at this juncture. He had, on more than one occasion, disagreed with the admiral, but too much was at stake now. Responsibility would rest upon the admiral's shoulders, and it felt liberating to be someone else's instrument.

Finally, the monitor showed Admiral Tolwyn standing on the *Concordia*'s bridge. "Jay, I'll be brief. The Kilrathi took Pegasus. They have her NAVCOM AI. By the time this communication reaches you, they will be approximately thirty-five hours from the Charybdis jump point and Earth. Confed capital ships are headed home now. The *Concordia* battle group will be there in approximately thirty-seven hours. I'm ordering the *Tiger Claw* to the Charybdis Quasar. You are to use any means necessary to gather information as to the Kilrathi whereabouts, capacity, and plan of attack. I need intelligence, old friend. Use Taggart. He knows Vega sector better than any man alive. He can get you to Charybdis quickly. Good luck. Tolwyn out."

Sansky looked to his second-in-command. Gerald had begun shaking his head halfway through the message. He caught Sansky's gaze and said, "I don't like it."

"No one asked for your opinion, Paul."

"Sir. The disc came to us on the *Diligent*, entrusted to a Pilgrim half-breed."

"I'm aware of how easy it is to fake communiqués, Commander. But if it's real and we ignore it, then we seal Earth's fate. Is that how you'd like to be remembered?"

"No, sir. But you're putting trust where it doesn't belong."

"Your reservations have been duly noted. Now then. Send for Taggart."

Gerald bit back a response and quickly exited.

Turning to the monitor, Sansky thumbed on the replay, switched off the volume, and stared at Geoffrey Tolwyn's face. "Oh God, Geoff. You've always known the right thing to do. I've always trusted you, and you me. It's been a long haul. A very long haul. I wish all of this could be easier. But it never is, is it? Good luck to you, old friend."

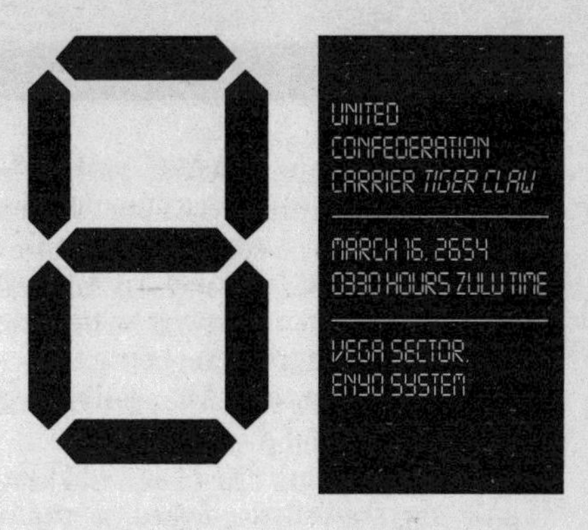

Riding a warm wave of Scotch toward an imaginary shoreline, Blair settled down into a chair and watched Forbes and Polanski play another chess game. Marshall, the bottle still clutched in his hand, wandered over to observe the competition.

The youngest of four sons, Marshall had grown up in a competitive household where his older siblings had constantly challenged him to meet their unrealistic standards—not that Marshall had ever volunteered this information. Blair had deduced this after meeting and spending time with Marshall's brothers. Never had he encountered a more demanding, ill-tempered, hard-core bunch of military brats. Two of them still flew for their father, Boomer Marshall, a retired Marine pilot who owned a charter service on Leto. Thanks to his father, Marshall had entered the academy with more logged flight hours than any other cadet, and he had made sure that no one ever forgot that fact.

Despite his constant boasting, Marshall's experience had actually come to great use during a training exercise in which he and Blair had discovered a Kilrathi destroyer hidden in the Hilthros system's nebula. With Marshall's fearless flying to counterbalance Blair's by-the-book combat tactics, the two managed to destroy the ship, which had already penetrated Confederation counterintelligence measures and had nearly gained access to highly classified data regarding fleet positions and strength.

But to look at Marshall now, you'd never think he was capable of such a feat. He could barely stand as he drew closer to the chess game. "Take his pony with your castle," he told Forbes, then took a swig from the bottle.

Polanski belched in Marshall's direction, then said, "We call them a *knight* and a *rook*."

"You're kidding me. That's what you call them?"

As she studied the board, a grin seized Forbes's face. She regarded Marshall, her eyes saying thanks.

Marshall winked.

She moved her "castle" and captured Polanski's "pony." Then she folded her arms over her chest. "Check."

Drawing back his head, Polanski stared incredulously at the board. "Where?"

"Mate," Marshall said.

"Damn," Polanski said in realization. "That's cheatin'."

Forbes gave Marshall a penetrating stare. "So there's a brain behind that mouth?"

Marshall flashed one of his trademark smiles, the kind that sometimes made women swoon and always made men, especially pilots, ball their hands into fists. He poured her another drink, and she stood. For a second, her gaze met Blair's, and he turned away, unconsciously jamming his hands in his pockets.

"Your friend always this talkative?" she asked Marshall.

"He just made the fatal error of mistaking Commander Deveraux for your average grease monkey."

She circled to face Blair and bent down to his level. Then her hand shot out, and she grabbed his crotch. He went to push her away, but found his hands trapped in his pockets.

"Feels like they're still here," she said.

St. John, who had been sitting quietly beside Blair, chuckled with the other pilots.

Forbes squeezed a little harder. Blair squirmed and finally wrestled her off.

"If Commander Deveraux was really pissed," Forbes said with a knowing grin, "well, you'd be testicularly challenged, Lieutenant."

Bringing his legs together and silently swearing over the pain, Blair forced himself deeper into the seat as he realized that every gaze in the room had found him. "All I did was sit in Lieutenant Commander Chen's fighter."

Smiles faded. Polanski shifted away.

Captain St. John looked up from his Scotch. "Who?"

"Lieutenant Commander Chen. Bossman."

The cigar came out. "Bossman? Anybody here know a Bossman?"

"No," someone said.

"Never heard of him," someone else added.

Shooting to his feet so quickly that he knocked over his chair, Blair said, "What's with you people?" The indifference in their faces infuriated him. Was this how they regarded their fallen comrades?

A burly black man with a widow's peak and a nametag that read Khumalo moved to Blair, his expression calm, his voice nearly a whisper. "Leave it alone, Blair."

"Leave what alone?"

St. John sniggered. "You're asking after a man who never existed, nugget."

"I'm pretty sure he did."

It all happened in a moment as blurry as Scylla. One nanosecond St. John sat before his drink, the next he stood and pushed Blair hard in the chest. "He never existed," St. John corrected. "Now, I suggest you change the subject. Or I'll change it for you."

Marshall threaded his way through the other pilots and came up behind St. John. "You have a problem with my friend, Hunter?"

"That's right. I do."

"Then you have a problem with me."

St. John whirled around. "Oh, yeah? You're going to love this—"

Expecting St. John to rush Marshall, Blair tensed, preparing to leap on the man's back.

But the pilot whirled back to him, grabbed his shirt, and drove him into the bulkhead.

Marshall employed Blair's original strategy and leapt on St. John's back, slinging an arm under the man's chin.

Likewise, Polanski slipped his arm around Marshall's neck and began prying Marshall away.

As St. John's hands got yanked back, Blair's shirt tore open to expose his cross.

"He's a Pilgrim!" St. John cried, then released Blair, who had suddenly become a live wire.

Everyone in the mess stared at the cross. Marshall cursed and pounded the bulkhead. The pilots closest to the hatch shifted back, blocking the exit.

Forbes elbowed her way through the others to get a closer look at the pariah named Christopher Blair. "Excuse me?"

"If you ladies don't stand down, you're going to have a problem with me." Blair knew who had said that, but he couldn't see her past the others. Good. She also couldn't see him. Exploiting his temporary cover, he slid his cross beneath his shirt as the pilots snapped to attention.

"I want an explanation. Hunter?"

But before the man could answer, Blair hurried forward to address Lieutenant Commander Deveraux. "Hunter and the others were just making Lieutenant Marshall and me feel at home, ma'am."

She stared dubiously at him, then at St. John. "Lieutenant?"

The captain gave Blair a slight glance and said, "Uh, that's right, Lieutenant, ma'am."

Blair couldn't hide his contempt for her, for all of them. "There, you see, ma'am? I guess this conversation *never existed.*" He bolted through the open hatch.

Out in the corridor, Blair charged toward a pair of green-suited munitions techs, who immediately shifted to the bulkhead, allowing him to pass.

I hate this place.

"Lieutenant?" Deveraux called sternly.

He stopped but wouldn't turn around, listening to her approach.

"I need to know that you have your priorities straight. Who the hell do you think you are?"

"I'm a fighter pilot on a capital ship in a war zone, ma'am. Which part confuses you?"

"Oh, I'm clear on you now, Lieutenant. You're a pawn in somebody else's game. We get ten, twelve replacements a month—as fast as the academy can spit out spare parts."

"Well, that really instills confidence, Commander."

She crossed in front of him, her runaway temper darkening her cheeks. "Let me give you a reality check. In all likelihood you're going to die out there—we all are. We don't need that reminder. So. You die, you never existed. Understood?"

Resigned to her illogic, Blair dropped his gaze. "Yes, ma'am. Understood."

"Good. 'Cause that's the only sensitivity training speech I can remember. Now. Carry on." She strode away.

Merlin abruptly activated to walk on air near Blair's shoulder. "She's kind of attractive when she's mad."

Blair made a face.

"Hey, I'm a hologram. I'm not blind."

In the dimly lit and silent chart room, Captain Sansky looked up to consider the group of red dots on the ghostly tactical schematic that Lieutenant Commander Obutu had pulled up for him. Those holographic dots moved toward the broad limbs of the Charybdis Quasar. Behind the quasar, a single yellow line unfurled toward a floating Earth.

Sansky knew his orders, knew very well the role he would play, but a deep-rooted feeling of hesitancy returned. Commander Gerald doubted the authenticity of the message. And now he had little faith in Sansky's decision to feel out Taggart before committing to the mission. Gerald's second-guessing could become unmanageable if the crew got word of it.

Though Gerald kept a tight rein on his people, they deeply respected his authority, evident in the many official and unofficial service awards they had given him. Sansky would simply have to wait and see. But the game turned his stomach sour.

The hatch opened, and Gerald stepped inside. Captain James Taggart followed, lifting a hand to cover a yawn. "Captain Sansky. From one captain to another—never wake up a tired sailor unless we're talking life-or-death situation."

"Then let's talk, Mr. Taggart."

Moving beneath the holograph, Taggart stared at the Kilrathi battle group arrowing toward the quasar. "They're in a hurry," he muttered.

"I know *of* you, Taggart, but I'm afraid I don't know you. You're a civilian captain flying a requisitioned transport, yet you come to me with classified orders from Admiral Tolwyn."

Taggart smirked. "And you don't trust me, Blair, or the disc."

"Would you?"

"No."

Sansky nodded to the holograph. "This tactical schematic outlines a nightmare, Mr. Taggart. It tells me that the Kilrathi have a NAVCOM, and with it, the capacity to jump into Earth space. Based on that nightmare, I must take radical action that, if it and you are a lie, could compromise this ship, her crew, and Earth—all of which are unacceptable. Before I put my command in harm's way, I must be certain that you and the orders you bear are legitimate." Sansky reached into his breast pocket and produced the decoded disc. "So, I ask you, Mr. Taggart, what proof do you have that this is authentic?"

Taggart reached into his inner vest pocket and withdrew a small, shiny object. He tossed it to Sansky, who caught and quickly examined it. Between his fingers rested a gold class ring, its surfaces worn, its emerald dull. Sansky held it to the holograph's light and read the inscription: ANNAPOLIS NAVAL ACADEMY, 1941. He closed his now-trembling hand over the ring and stared incredulously at Taggart. "How did you get this?"

"Tolwyn gave it to me eight months ago. He thought it might

be useful in situations like getting a captain to follow his orders."

Gerald crossed to Sansky and gestured to see the ring. Sansky handed it to him, then turned to the intercom. "Con. Plot a course for the Charybdis Quasar, full speed."

Lieutenant Commander Obutu shifted from the tactical schematic console to read the navigator's coordinates on another screen. Obutu, an earnest black man, tough as titanium, with a thick brow and a face that seemed regularly haunted by a past of which he would not speak, remained a comfort and a mystery to Sansky. As the lieutenant commander further surveyed the screen, a query creased his face. "Sir, the nearest jump point to Charybdis is four days hard travel from our present position. How are we supposed to get there in time?"

"There's a Class Two pulsar eleven hours from here," Taggart said. "We can jump there."

Obutu began a rapid-fire sequence of key commands, then looked to Sansky. "Not on the charts, sir. NAVCOM does not have those coordinates."

"I have them," Taggart said, stepping between Sansky and Obutu.

"No one's jumped a pulsar for forty years," Gerald pointed out, eyeing Taggart with disdain. "And even then, they were Pilgrims."

"I don't believe we have a great deal of choice, Mr. Gerald," Sansky fired back. "If the battle is to be decided at Charybdis, then we have to be there." He regarded Taggart. "Plot your course."

With a nod, Taggart headed for a navigation subterminal.

Swearing under his breath, Gerald watched Taggart plug numbers into the computer for a moment, then moved close to Sansky, out of Taggart's earshot. "Sir. This ring means nothing." He returned the antique to Sansky. "You shouldn't—"

"This ring has been in Tolwyn's family for sixteen generations. Any man who carries it has the admiral's full confidence."

"If it's real—which it may not be—then I can't believe Tolwyn gave it to a civilian."

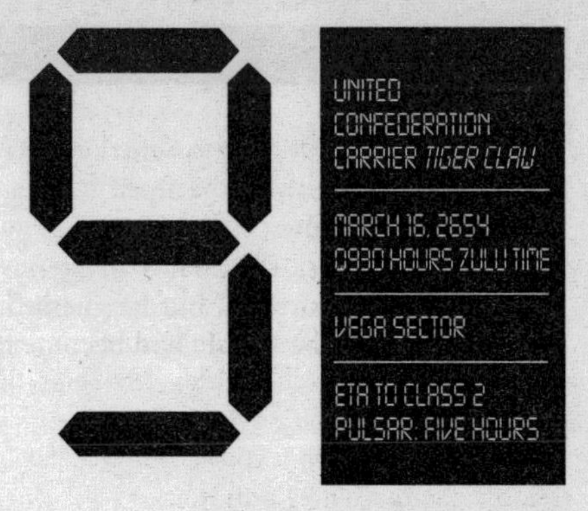

With the lights off and his eyes closed, Blair lay on his cot in the quarters he now shared with Marshall. He needed to sleep. Needed to dream. Dream about anyplace but the carrier. He thought of dreams he would like to have, dreams of home, of Nephele, of his aunt and uncle who had worked so hard to raise him after his parents had died. He thought of old girlfriends, of old summer jobs, of a particular July 17 birthday party that had marked the end of his teenage years. He considered his time at the academy on Hilthros, days that felt like several millennia ago. His life had become a streak of indistinct memories. Nothing stood out anymore. All of it seemed blighted by his depression. The only thing tangible was the Pilgrim cross around his neck. A blessing. A curse.

How did I get here? I was just a kid who liked to wrestle and was raised on a farm. I joined up to get flying experience, not to become another Confederation statistic. I remember my uncle telling me never to join the service. What has it done for me? What has it really done for me?

The lights snapped on. Covering his eyes, Blair sat up. He heard a shuffling of boots, a zipper being pulled up, and the rattle of metal on metal. He squinted and saw Marshall standing in a crimson flight suit, his battered helmet tucked in the crook of his arm.

"We going out?" Blair asked.

"No. Just me. I pulled security with Lieutenant Forbes."

"So why did you wake me up?"

Marshall shook his index finger at Blair's cross and opened his mouth.

But Blair beat him to the punch. "So I changed my mind. But I can't change who I am."

"No, you can't. But you made a promise back at the academy that you wouldn't wear that anymore. I'm not saying to throw it away. I think you know what I'm saying."

"It brings me luck, Todd."

"It's going to get you killed—*Chris*."

Blair took the cross in hand, as though to protect it. "I was wearing this when I made the jump. You heard Taggart. A NAV-COM can't do what I did."

"That had nothing to do with luck. It was about training and desire." Marshall reached toward Blair. "Take it off."

Drawing back, Blair held the cross tightly against his chest. "It's who I am. Or who I should be."

Marshall snorted loudly. "You don't even know what it means. They lost the war. Winners write the history books and make the rules. You want to play on a team that doesn't exist anymore? Think about it."

He recognized the truth in Marshall's words. But he still felt powerfully intrigued by his heritage, by the feeling, and by what the cross truly represented. He couldn't abandon the past just to make things right with the other pilots.

"This is the big show," Marshall went on. "It's either kill or be killed."

"Man, that's profound. Did it come to you in a vision?"

"Shuddup. You know what I mean. And you really messed up this time."

"I didn't do anything."

"Yeah, you did. And now you need someone watching your back. Let me tell you something, buddy. I can't always be there."

"I don't expect that from anyone—especially you."

"Oh man," Marshall said, turning away. "You're going to get whacked. If not by the Kilrathi, then—"

"This is getting old."

Marshall collapsed on his cot, smoothed back his hair, then kneaded his bloodshot eyes. "I'm trying to have a sensitive moment. I don't know why I bother." He sprang from the cot. "Wish me luck."

"Luck? What about desire?"

With a wink, Marshall said, "You've seen Lieutenant Forbes. You know I got the desire." He headed for the hatch.

"Hey, Marshall—luck."

The trademark grin came and went, along with its owner.

Blair fell back on his cot, pillowing his head in his hands. He gazed up at the lovely overhead, bedecked by flexible tubes and ductwork. He shouldn't complain. Having to share a cabin with just one other pilot might be the last luxury available to first lieutenants aboard the *Tiger Claw*. During training on the TCS *Formidable*, he had been assigned to a berth with seventeen other pilots and had slept on a lower bunk above a two-hundred-and-ten-pound Neanderthal with a hearty appetite for fried onions, cabbage, and broccoli.

What was it that Marshall had said that now troubled him so much? Something about the cross. That he didn't even know what it meant. That he didn't really know who he was and where he had come from. Without that knowledge, how could he forge a clear path for himself? How could he could keep the memory of his parents vivid? How could he stop wondering?

"Merlin. Activate."

The little man walked along the edge of a storage locker on the opposite side of the room. "My God. What time is it?"

"The Pilgrims. What can you tell me about them?" Blair sat up and crawled to the edge of the cot.

"Pilgrims. Yes. Earth history. They were English Separatists who founded the colony of Plymouth in New England, circa 1620."

"Wrong ones."

The hologram shrugged, his tone soft and sympathetic. "I'm afraid I have very little on the Pilgrims of this millennium. Your father wiped my flash memory."

"Why?"

"I don't know."

"Don't you have anything? A temp file you forgot to erase?"

"I'm sorry, Christopher."

"That's all right."

Brightening, Merlin added, "I do know that since the Pilgrims were defeated, not a single new quasar has been charted."

"You heard that from Taggart."

"Did I? Oh yes. I must've been monitoring. Sorry again."

Blair stood and crossed to the latrine. He leaned over the sink for a few minutes, splashing warm water on his face. He eventually looked to the mirror, but his dark hair and dusky skin remained blurred by condensation. After drying off, he opened his locker door and withdrew a clean uniform.

"Where are you going?" Merlin asked.

"To talk to someone who may know more about the Pilgrims."

Once dressed, Blair accessed the Shipboard Information Datanet and found Taggart's cabin assignment. He printed out a map that would take him there. With over twenty corridors and thirteen levels between him and the man, a map remained more than a good idea if he planned on talking to Taggart during this decade.

As he walked through the ship, taking a lift here, a stairwell there, his gaze buried in the map, he felt like a cadet on the first day of his academy training. No less than three times, crew members accosted him to see if they could help. Though grateful, Blair declined their offers. He would have to learn the ship's layout one way or another, and he welcomed the practice.

After twenty minutes of travel, he found the hatch and touched the bell key.

"Come," Taggart said through the intercom.

The door automatically opened, and Blair entered to admire the captain's spacious accommodations and bunk with thick mattress and comforter.

He found Taggart staring through a great bay window. The vacuum appeared especially dark, and for some reason the captain felt compelled to note that. "Except for a few specs of light, it's all emptiness. If it were up to me, I'd let the Kilrathi have it all—just leave Earth alone."

Blair hemmed. "We need to talk."

"I've been in a thousand different solar systems, and I've never seen anything in the void as beautiful as our own sun breaking through the clouds after a rainstorm. I'm a native of Ares, Lieutenant. But my parents were terraforming engineers from Scotland. They taught me that my home wasn't a space station in orbit around Venus. They told me the truth. Did yours?" He craned his head.

"You mean my real home is Earth?"

He nodded.

"The only home I've ever known is Nephele. I was on Peron when I was little, but I don't remember anything. You know if I went to Earth now, they'd call me an alien."

"If you went to Earth now, you'd really know why we fight. The Kilrathi see us as decadent and weak. They won't stop until we're all dead. If they let us exist, that would be admitting that another race deserves the stars. In truth, none of us does. But I suspect you haven't come here for a philosophy lesson."

"No, sir. Talk to me."

"About what?"

Blair crossed to a well-padded chair and took a seat. "All my life I've taken shit about being part-Pilgrim. And I barely know why. Most people don't want to talk about it or don't really know why humans and Pilgrims hated each other so much."

"That's right. Most people don't like to talk about it."

"C'mon. You know about them. Tell me the long story about how you got the star charts. Have you ever met a real Pilgrim—

not a half-breed like me? What are they like? What about the war? What do you know?"

"I knew a boy about your age who asked the same questions. Do you know what happened to him?"

"I don't care."

"You should."

Seeing the conversational dead end rushing toward him, Blair stood and started for the hatch. "I'm sorry to have bothered you."

"You are who you choose to be, Lieutenant."

The hatch opened.

"You're one of the last descendants of a dying race," Taggart added quickly.

Blair turned back, and the hatch sealed after him.

"Pilgrims were the first human space explorers and settlers. For five centuries they defied the odds. They embraced space and were rewarded with a gift: a flawless sense of direction. No computers, Blair. No compasses. No charts. They just knew. Then, in a small number, about one in a million, a change started to occur."

"What kind of change?"

A hidden importance now resided in Taggart's expression, something Blair could sense but not fully describe. "They learned to feel the magnetic fields created by black holes and quasars—to negotiate singularities. They learned to navigate not just the stars but space-time itself."

Blair shook as a powerful chill fanned across his shoulders.

To *feel* the magnetic fields created by black holes and quasars.

To navigate space-time itself.

It seemed impossible. And possible. And in his blood.

"So the Pilgrims could perform like a NAVCOM AI," Blair said.

"You've got it backwards. The billions of calculations necessary to lead us through a black hole or quasar are the NAVCOM's recreation of the mind of a single Pilgrim."

He nodded in wonder. How could one mind be so powerful? He most definitely lacked that kind of power. "How did the war start?"

Taggart moved back to the window, and as he did so, Blair saw his lips come together and his eyes well up. "You spend so much time out here alone, you end up losing your humanity. The Pilgrims began to lose touch with their heritage. They saw themselves as superior to humans. And in their arrogance, they chose to abandon all things human in order to follow their destiny. Some say they believed they were gods, others that they were angels."

"You believe they were gods?"

"No. But I do believe they were touched by God." He looked back, his eyes still glassy. "And like it or not, you've got some of that inside you."

Blair's people had done great things. And terrible things. Had they been gods? Demons? Where was the line? And now that he knew his heritage, where did he go from here? For every question answered, it seemed that Taggart had raised three more. Blair simply wanted to ask, "So how do I live like this? What kind of life should I expect?" But the captain did not have the answers. No one did. Except Blair.

Taggart sighed and said, "I have to get to the bridge. We'll be jumping in a few hours. I'd like you to be there."

"I will." He ambled toward the window. "You mind if I stay here a while?"

"No. Just don't drink my coffee."

Blair grinned, then listened to him leave.

Something flashed at the corner of his eye. Two patrolling Rapiers in tight formation pierced the night. Behind them, far in the distance, lay an enormous, flashing gulf that Blair recognized as a pulsar, a spinning, superdense mass of neutrons. Only high-energy photons, neutrinos, and Confed ships carrying Pilgrims or a NAVCOM could escape the pulsar's gravitational pull. Blair wondered how many of his forefathers had jumped here.

And he wondered how many other Pilgrims were still out there, contemplating their future among the stars.

"See, when I'm not flying I'm like a pit bull pulling on his leash. You know he's going to break the leash any second, but you don't dare reach down to set him free—unless you're in the mood to sacrifice a few fingers. And you go ahead and do your homework on pit bulls. They were originally bred for *dogfighting*. Pun intended here, baby. Pun most definitely intended." First Lieutenant Todd Marshall grinned so hard that it hurt. Then he accelerated ahead of Lieutenant Forbes's Rapier, leaving her in the maelstrom of his wash.

Dialing up the rear turret view, Marshall watched as Forbes expertly recovered, kicked in her afterburners, and burst toward him like a rabid hawk. "This is a security patrol, nugget," she said sternly. "Unauthorized maneuvers will not be tolerated. You'd better get with—or out of—the program." Her Rapier settled in beside his, and he looked over, but too many dazzles of reflected light from the carrier obscured her canopy.

"Unauthorized maneuvers?" Marshall cried. "What the hell does that mean?"

"I don't know," she said, then rocketed ahead of him.

As her thruster wash enveloped his fighter, the stick whipped out of his hand, triggering a beeping alarm and automated message: "Pilot control lost. Do you want to engage autopilot? If you do not respond in five seconds, autopilot will automatically engage. Five, four—"

Seizing the stick and cutting off the countdown, Marshall cursed, throttled up, and went hunting. He streaked after Forbes for thirty seconds, then got creative. He yanked the stick toward his chest, going ballistic for a handful of seconds before leveling off. Forbes now lay ahead, at his twelve o'clock low and in his cone of fire. He swooped down toward her, one eye shielded by the Heads Up Display viewer attached to his helmet. The smart targeting reticle superimposed on the HUD floated just ahead of her Rapier, a tiny green circle that said, "Shoot here, dummy."

"What the hell's the matter with you?" Forbes screamed. "You got missile lock on me?"

"I got you locked up so tight, Lieutenant, it's a miracle you can still breathe."

"Break off!"

"Can't help you there, Ace." He leaned a little more on the throttle and considered her next move.

She could perform a burnout, hitting afterburners and leaping so far ahead of him that she could pull a tight one-eighty to open up on him.

Or she could go for a fishhook: Make a ninety-degree right turn, then follow up immediately with a one-eighty that would put her on a starboard intercept course.

If she felt uninspired, she'd go for the old hard brake, in an attempt to make him overshoot her. But Marshall had responded to that textbook trick too many times. Once he overshot her, he would stall the thrusters and use retros to make the tightest one-eighty she would ever witness. While inverted, he'd lock on her nose. *Ciao,* baby.

She probably wouldn't attempt a kickstop or a turn 'n' spin, knowing all too well that making a simple ninety-degree turn would not cause him to fly by her, whether she killed her engines or not. Likewise for the shake, rattle, and roll. No combination of slaloming would lose him now.

"What are you going to do, Forbes? Tick. Tick. Tick. Doncha hear the ticking?"

Her answer came with a burst of afterburners. She tipped her nose up until inverted, then flew straight at him as his proximity alarm wailed.

Marshall had all of two seconds to comprehend the game of chicken. Even as he shifted the stick to dive, their canopies came within a few centimeters. A howl rose from his throat as her tail wings grazed his fuselage with a horrible screech, then—

The fighters cleared each other. He held course, panting into his O_2 mask, wondering what the hell had just happened.

"Are we ready to hit the first nav point?" Forbes asked. "Or do you still want to play?"

"You're the female version of me," Marshall said, dumbfounded.

"Correction, stud. You're the male version of me. With a lot of practice, you may one day fly in my shadow."

Marshall's left VDU switched to Commander Gerald's grim mug. "Lieutenant Marshall. We've been unable to contact Lieutenant Forbes. What's going on out there?"

"Stand by, sir." Marshall dialed up Forbes on a secure channel. "Hey, Lieutenant. Gerald's flipping out."

"I know. Flight control's been hailing me, but I've blocked their signal. They probably handed the problem to Gerald. I'll take care of this."

"Roger." He toggled back to Gerald's channel. "She's replying now, sir."

Then Marshall listened in as Forbes lied about communication and maneuvering problems and that both had now been solved. "En route to first nav point, sir."

Five thousand kilometers ahead sat an indistinct pocket of space designated as nav point one, the first of three stops on their grand security tour of nothingness. Marshall activated navigation mode and glanced at the white cross-hairs on his radar scope and HUD. He adjusted course until the cross-hairs each floated in their centers. The rest of the radar display had been divided by quadrants and would flash in the appropriate quadrant when he took a missile or laser hit, not that he had seen that flash very often.

Sometimes he wished the Rapier's controls were more sophisticated, more challenging. The Rapier was, after all, a very real fighter, not some funzone simulator used to zap computer-generated targets. Yet her controls were just as simple to operate. Then again, that simplicity gave him a hell of a lot more time to concentrate on whacking Kilrathi.

"Delta Two? I'm lined up," Forbes reported.

"Roger. Good light over here," he said, glancing at the autopilot display, the AUTO button now illuminated.

"Engage autopilot on my mark. Mark."

Marshall tapped the key and felt the familiar and humbling force of the Rapier's twin thrusters as they propelled him toward the point. He yawned into his headset, not realizing how loud he'd been.

Forbes appeared in his left VDU. "I guess it's the same with all you men," she said. "Give you just a little bit of action, and you're spent. Completely spent."

"Blame it on the Scotch."

"You can't keep up with me. Scotch or otherwise."

Before he could offer his own cutting rejoinder, the Rapier abruptly decreased velocity. The nav point lay just a klick ahead. He checked the radar. A single blue blip that represented Forbes's Rapier stood off to port, otherwise the zone remained clear. "Looks like we got zip here, Lieutenant. How boring is this?"

"Sometimes boring is good," she said. "Especially when your wingman's green."

"Or a woman."

"Whoa, you *are* going to pay for that."

"My credit's good."

"You know, when I joined up, they told me I'd come across some male chauvinism. I couldn't believe it. I was like, what century are we living in? Female pilots have been flying combat missions for over six hundred years."

"And we men have been harassing you for just as long. It ain't going to change, Forbes. So long as there's a difference."

"You mean as long as assholes like you keep flying."

"Look. I didn't mean what I said. I mean the woman part. I mean, yeah, you're a woman. You *really* are. But you know what I mean. I just said that to rattle you."

"Maybe you're right. You're not a chauvinist. You're just prejudiced against all other pilots because you see them as competitors."

"They're not my competitors. They're my fans."

"Oh, God. Get me to the next nav point before I barf."

"I'm good to go," he said, waving.

She switched off the video. "Autopilot. Mark."

Nav point two, a sprawling vista of outer-space real estate that yielded lovely views of more nothingness, came and went without enemy contact, as did nav point three. With the sweep completed, they started back for the carrier, passing the next security patrol pilots as they took their Rapiers out to new nav points and new heights of boredom.

Once the autopilot had disengaged at 2,200 kilometers out from the *Claw*, Forbes queried the ship and requested clearance to land. They were put on standby. Marshall's eyelids grew heavy, and he longed for a shower, for his cot.

"Hey, Marshall. I've been thinking a lot about this male-female thing. Don't take it personally. It's just a question of estrogen. Women can outfly and outshoot men. We don't manhandle our instruments, and we do better at multitasking. We can keep track of four enemy fighters."

Marshall snapped from his doze. "Hey, it takes ballsnot ovaries—to handle four enemy fighters. Nothing personal." He glanced at the opening flight deck doors. "Watch this." Toggling to the flight boss's channel, he said, "This is Delta Two. Permission to land?"

The flight boss's beefy face clicked on the VDU. "Delta Two. You are cleared to land."

Tensing every muscle in his body, Marshall fired the afterburners and banked hard, lining up with the flight deck.

"Whoa, that must've been three Gs," Forbes said sarcastically.

Taking his cue, Marshall cut the stick hard left and rolled as he gunned the throttle. "Try this." Inverted, he raced down toward the runway.

"Delta Two. You're coming in too hot," the flight boss cried, his face a survey course in fear. "Abort. I repeat. Abort. Delta Two. Do you copy? Shit!"

But Marshall held course, gazing up at the runway, now his ceiling, as, in the distance, orange-suited insects made way. He approached the energy field between vacuum and atmosphere.

"Delta Two. YOU ARE INVERTED!"

"No. You are!" Marshall shouted back, then released a cackle. The Rapier vibrated sharply as it penetrated the energy barrier and roared into the hangar, a dampened echo in its wake.

"Dammit, man. You're inverted!"

"Not anymore," Marshall told the keen-eyed flight boss. He jammed the stick left and rolled upright.

But he had misjudged his speed. Even as he fired retros, he knew he would overshoot the runway by at least twenty, maybe thirty meters.

And worse, dead ahead lay a fuel truck, strategically placed by God to punish one First Lieutenant Todd Marshall, the Confederation's egomaniac par excellence.

The deckmaster, a man named Peterson with a tax auditor's sense of humor, ran across the runway and toward the fuel truck. As he crossed in front of the vehicle, headed toward the driver's side to holler at the stunned driver, he froze, his arms extended across the truck's hood.

Marshall blasted toward him, retros wailing to the heavens, wings and fuselage rattling so violently that he thought the fighter would simply shatter across the deck before ever stopping.

Peterson's mouth opened as he resigned himself to his fate.

The Rapier slowed but kept moving.

Snap! Click! And Marshall got thrown forward, his harness

digging into his shoulders. The retros dropped from their soprano into a comforting, easy baritone. The Rapier settled onto her landing skids to reveal Peterson, still clutching the truck. The deckmaster reached out with a shaky hand and touched the Rapier's nose cannon. "Ohmygod," he mouthed.

Marshall slid aside his HUD viewer, then unlatched his helmet and O_2 mask. Sweat drenched his face, and he had apparently sublet his throat to a desert.

"I'll have your wings," the flight boss said, his eyes ablaze. "Wait until your wing leader . . ."

"What?"

The flight boss regarded something off-camera, then shouted, "Delta One!"

Marshall's VDU switched to an image of Forbes in her cockpit. "Now what were you saying?"

He cocked his head to watch her sweep over the runway, her Rapier inverted and at full throttle. She plowed through the energy field, killed the engines, then ignited retros to roll a full 540 degrees, righting herself at the last possible moment before touchdown. And she had not overshot the runway.

"Now that's how you do it," she shouted.

Marshall rushed out of his cockpit and toward her fighter. The flight crews kept their distance, not wanting to catch the rare strain of insanity that had barnacled itself to his brain.

Forbes's canopy popped, and she removed her mask to flash him a perfect grin.

"You did that to impress me," he said, leaving no room for the question.

"Just trying to redirect some of that testosterone."

He stared at her, and in her eyes he found something they now shared, a sudden and very desirable intimacy that would last as long as they lived. Military critics might call it the ill-founded camaraderie of adrenaline junkies. Marshall just called it fun. And Forbes obviously felt the same.

"You're a total maniac!" she said.

He saluted her. "Maniac Marshall at your service, ma'am."

They burst into laughter.

Then Forbes stiffened as she looked past him. "Oh, shit."

Lieutenant Commander Deveraux stood fuming on the opposite side of the flight deck, then spun and stomped out.

Deveraux's silence left Marshall even more worried. "What happens now?"

Forbes looked to where Deveraux had been standing. "I'm not sure. I'm really not sure."

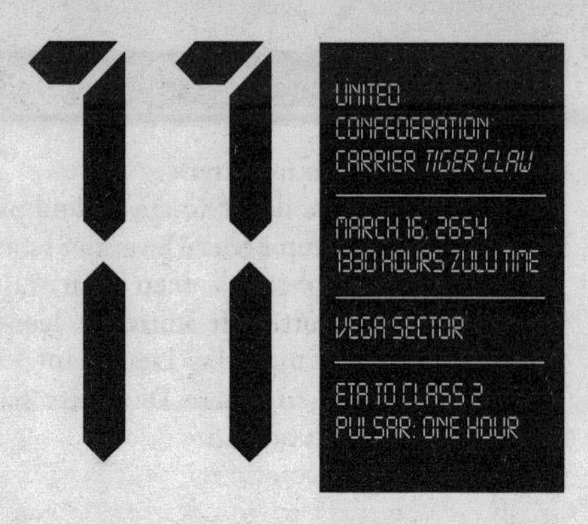

Lieutenant Commander Jeanette Deveraux, her cheeks warming, her pulse racing, double-timed through the hall adjoining the flight hangar. She had little tolerance for rebels and hotdoggers and even less tolerance for experienced pilots who succumbed to the taunts and coercion of new fliers.

Without looking up, Deveraux passed someone, then, realizing who it was, she turned back. "Hey, Boss?" she said, greeting Mr. Raznick by his more familiar name. "I was on my way to see you."

The flight boss came to her, shaking his computer slate as though it were a torch, he an angry villager. "Well, I was just on my way to talk to your people. But now that I've got *you* . . ." Raznick's shaven head glistened with sweat, and a thick vein throbbed at his temple.

"Just calm down, boss. And believe me, I know how you feel."

"Begging your pardon, ma'am, but you don't know jack. I'm going to charge those pilots with everything I can, right down to their scuffed boots. They recklessly endangered the lives of every man and woman on my flight deck—and for what? To prove they don't care about their own lives or anyone else's? I'll have those idiots busted down to spacehands."

"Just take a deep breath."

"I don't need to take a deep breath! I need to get down there and chew some butt!" He started to leave.

She held his arm. "Has Lieutenant Forbes ever given you a problem before?"

"That's not the point."

"Just . . . will you do me this favor? Let me handle this internally. If you want to go down there and let them have it, that's fine. But let me handle the discipline on my end."

He huffed. "This deserves a hell of a lot more than a smack on the hand. And Commander, your carpet's already bulging from all the bullshit you've swept under it."

"I know. But do you want to know the sad truth, Boss? If we take those two off my flight roster, I can't replace them. At least not now. And judging from the scuttlebutt I'm hearing, we'll need every able-bodied pilot we have. Hell, we might even stuff you in a Broadsword. I know you've been working off-duty on your qualification."

"Now if that's a bribe, it'll work," he said, his tone softening considerably. "I hate pilots. I love flying."

"I won't make you any promises there. But I will promise that no pilot under my command will ever pull a stunt like that again."

He squinted into a thought. "My people expect me to act. I'll lose their respect if they know I'm whitewashing this."

"They don't have to know. You go down there and say what you need to say for their benefit. Just don't follow through. Blame the delay on Confederation bureaucracy. No one will have a hard time believing that."

"I'd better get that ship assignment," he warned, then moved off.

"I'll do what I can. But Gerald will never approve it," she mumbled. "Sorry, Boss."

Back in her quarters, she sloughed off her uniform and eased into a hot shower. She closed her eyes, tilted her head back, and stepped head-on into the spray. She held that position for three, maybe even four minutes, feeling days-old knots in her neck and shoulders loosen and the tightness in her brow subside. She thought about what Forbes and Marshall had done, the absurdity of it, and imagined them laughing. She found herself laughing along, realizing that she couldn't remember the last time she had enjoyed a true, side-splitting chuckle.

After being made squadron commander at the beginning of the year, she had found little time for amusement. Her job, as she saw it, was to police a bunch of highly talented loose cannons, to collect and forge them into a single, well-honed blade that would pierce the enemy's cold heart. But the job had de-evolved into glorified babysitting, and recent events highlighted that fact. Still, how many pilots did she know who could make their final approaches inverted? The number stood at two.

She keyed off the shower, wrapped herself in a towel, then found the chair at her small desk. She sat there, staring at the statue of the little dog, a Brussels griffon, that she had ordered via a Datanet catalog. The dog's short, bearded muzzle and blond fur vividly reminded her of Pierre, a stray dog she had adopted as a child. She had felt a kinship with that dog and had loved him for ten years before he had died. He lay buried in Belgium, behind the orphanage. *Sleep well, my dear Pierre. Sleep well.*

Her hatch bell rang. "Who is it?"

"Me."

"You don't want to be here right now."

"Just let me in. *Please*."

Deveraux stood and shrugged. "You're at your own risk." She touched the keypad, and the hatch opened.

"Single malt . . . just for you," Forbes said, holding Lieutenant Todd Marshall's bottle of Scotch.

She glanced perfunctorily at the bottle, then shifted back to her chair, but couldn't bring herself to sit. "Trying to bribe me? Well, it won't work—especially with *his* liquor."

"I'm trying to thank you. The flight boss would've brought us up on charges if you hadn't said something."

"He told you we spoke?"

"Not exactly. But I could tell that you had already disarmed him. You're the only one on board who could do that. Raznick hates pilots. We get his flight deck dirty and raise his blood pressure. But you he respects."

"Do you know why?"

Her expression said that she didn't.

"Because I work with him. Not against him. That's simple math. No advanced degree required."

Forbes hid her gaze.

"What the hell were you thinking?"

Biting her lower lip, Forbes stalled. "Well, I wasn't thinking with my head."

Deveraux beat a fist on her thigh. "Goddammit, Rosie. You'll get yourself killed doing that. How could you follow *that* kind of lead?"

"I don't know."

"Well, let me tell you something. I think—"

"I *know* what you're thinking."

"I think you're one of my best pilots. I can't afford to lose you."

And that lifted Forbes's head. "Sorry. I was just showing off a bit in front of Maniac."

"Maniac?"

"Lieutenant Marshall. He's got a new call sign, although I don't think too many people will appreciate it."

"I think you're right."

Forbes went to a cabinet, removed a glass, and began pouring a drink.

"I hope it felt really good," Deveraux said, driving the point home but realizing that her tone had been too cruel.

"It felt great. Better than sex."

Forbes handed her the Scotch, and she took a healthy swig. "Bullshit."

"Well, better than sex with myself." Forbes waited for her smile before grinning herself.

"See that it never happens again."

"Never."

Deveraux took another pull on her drink as her friend, now visibly relaxed, sat on the cot and yawned.

Then Forbes stared at her. Deveraux stared back. Forbes looked away, as did Deveraux. Then it all happened again.

"What?" Deveraux asked.

"I don't want to pry, but I've noticed you've been giving special attention to Maniac's friend . . ."

She lifted the towel higher over her chest. "Oh, really? I think that's your imagination working overtime."

"He's pretty damned cute, Angel," Forbes pointed out, using Deveraux's call sign as a way to link the intimacy of combat to the intimacy of their conversation.

It didn't work.

Seeing that her Scotch glass stood empty, Deveraux said, "Just shuddup and pour."

Forbes offered her a meager fill, and with the lift of her brow, Deveraux gestured for a full glass.

Yes, she did see something in First Lieutenant Christopher Blair.

And that was why it hurt so much.

Captain Jay Sansky sat at his desk in the welcome solitude of his quarters. The antique clock hanging on the bulkhead above him ticked nearly in sync with the drums and violins of a contemporary classical theme resonating from his minidisc player. He had come here to meditate before the jump, to gather some thoughts while pushing others away.

In truth, he had come to bury the past.

He turned once more to the holopic sitting on his desk, a framed, three-dimensional doorway leading him through twenty-five years of memories. He smiled wanly at the group of young men and women posed in crisp Naval Academy uniforms, their eyes full of hope, their expressions hard and brimming with courage. Sansky had been with them that day, a brash officer with a thin face and full head of hair. Beside him, looking for all the world like an accomplice in rashness, stood Bill Wilson, former commander of Pegasus Station, now assumed dead. Bill wore his twisted grin proudly, and he had never betrayed his rebel's heart.

Every officer in the Confederation Navy played a role. Some played theirs better than others. But no one played his role more passionately, more honestly than Bill Wilson. Despite navigating through years of military corruption, Wilson had never lost sight of who he was. And he had tried for many years to make Sansky realize the same. One day, it simply dawned on Sansky that, like Wilson, he could reconcile with the universe, that he could correct years of wrongdoing. A military officer could do such a thing. A military officer wielded such power.

But Sansky still felt uncertain of his role, unsure of his future, and guilt-stricken by his past. So many people had helped him over the years. So many souls had given. Had he returned their generosity? Could he ever? Was it even right to believe that he owed them? Or was that the guilt again?

He closed his eyes tightly. "Oh, God," he whispered. "Oh, God. If I'm right, forgive me. And if I'm wrong, forgive me even more."

"This terminal has been idle for five minutes. Do you wish to continue?" came a computer voice.

Sansky looked at the small monitor, at the green navigation lines superimposed on the Ulysses Corridor. He had thoroughly studied the map, knew the region, and knew the odds of getting there. If he just had more time to better weigh his options, but was there ever enough time? Some said war represented the true enemy; Sansky knew otherwise. "Computer. Shut down."

"Shutting down."

He glanced at the hard-copy map he had printed out, took up his pen, and noted the coordinates where the *Tiger Claw* should appear after the jump.

Should appear.

Lieutenant Commander Obutu's voice boomed over the intercom. "Captain Sansky?"

"Yes?"

"Sorry to bother you, sir. You're needed in the chart room."

"On my way."

Sansky set down his pen and picked up the holopic. He stared fondly at the two young men with their whole lives ahead of them, two young men naïve of the fire that lay in their hearts. He replaced the holopic, opened a drawer, and lifted his hip flask. With an unsteady hand, he brought the flask to his lips and took several swigs before stowing the whiskey. He started for the hatch, then hurried back to the desk, where he scooped up Tolwyn's ring.

Admiral Geoffrey Tolwyn had an unspoken agreement with the universe that allowed him to take tremendous risks while managing to emerge triumphant and unscathed. Perhaps carrying a piece of the admiral would allow Sansky to do the same.

As Blair stepped into the carrier's chart room, a huge holographic display swept up his attention. Stretching from deck to overhead, the semitransparent images drew long shadows across the walls and over the navigation subterminal where Taggart sat, keying in numbers and gazing trancelike at his screen.

A red blip designated by tiny letters as the *Tiger Claw* lay at the holograph's center. The blip flashed as it moved toward a pulsating, constantly moving series of circles: a mathematical representation of the Class 2 pulsar. The databar beside the pulsar showed thousands of scrolling coordinates in space-time, coordinates being fed into the carrier's NAVCOM AI by Taggart.

"They told me you were here, sir," Blair said.

"Look at it, Lieutenant," Taggart suggested, still intent on his screen. "What do you see?"

Blair shrugged; wasn't it obvious? "That's a Class Two pulsar."

"Explain."

"Well, unlike a black hole, which is a discrete singularity, or a quasar, which has the potential of containing thousands of discrete singularities, this pulsar is a discrete singularity with an infinite number of constantly changing permutations."

"Great. You remember that academy crap. Now just look at it and read the map."

"I don't know what to say. Those permutations, they, uh, each one is capable of taking us to another part of the galaxy. The problem is, most of them are dead ends."

"With an emphasis on *dead.*" Taggart swung around and cocked a brow.

The grid surrounding the *Tiger Claw* began to deform as a long spike impaled it, then gradually pulled itself inside out to form a stalagmite with a thick, wide hole at its neck. Blair watched, fascinated, as the carrier came to a halt, poised before the gap.

"Now, Lieutenant Christopher Blair. You've told me what the pulsar is. Tell me how it *feels.*"

"I don't feel anything yet."

"That's good."

"It is?"

He gave a slight nod, then resumed his work.

With a low hiss, the chart room's hatch abruptly opened. Gerald and Lieutenant Commander Deveraux passed into the holograph's eerie glow. Blair craned his head, wanting to dematerialize into the shadows. Then he cringed as he heard Deveraux's voice. "Why aren't you at your station, Lieutenant?"

Blair faced them, their eyes like two pairs of muzzles, locked on target. "Ma'am, I—"

"I asked Lieutenant Blair to be here," Taggart interjected.

The hatch opened again.

"Why?" Gerald asked.

"I authorized it," Captain Sansky said, entering the room and double-timing toward Taggart. "Status?"

"Coordinates are laid in," Taggart said. "One keystroke, and the upload will be finished." He went to holograph and pointed to the tip of the stalagmite, letting his finger follow a trajectory across the wide gap in the quadrant. "The Ulysses Corridor. Four days' hard travel using three known jump points. By using the pulsar, we'll be there in"—he glanced to a digital clock above his station—"less than three minutes."

"If your calculations are correct," Gerald said, grinding out the words.

Back at his console, Taggart touched the final key, finishing the upload. "They're right."

Gerald steered himself toward Taggart. "NAVCOM and the

finest minds in the Confederation couldn't plot this jump. What makes you so sure you're right?"

A flicker of a grin wiped across Taggart's lips. "Because they're Pilgrim coordinates, Mr. Gerald."

"What?" Gerald's gaze swept back to the databar.

Taggart crossed into the big commander's line of sight. "We'll have a lovely view from the bridge." Then he hurried toward the hatch.

Deveraux gave Blair a frosty look before following Taggart. Gerald and Sansky left together, their voices low and tense.

Alone in the chart room, Blair stepped into the holograph and ran his finger along the same path that Taggart had marked. He strayed toward the data bar, his entire body now illuminated by millions of scrolling calculations.

Merlin sparked to life and paced along the top of Taggart's console. "If the entry trajectory is wrong, we'll be trapped in a moment outside of time and space. That is, until the ship plummets into the pulsar and we become an infinitely small part of a special singularity. My guess is there's a fifty-seven-point-one percent chance that we're doomed."

Blair looked down at his chest, now scintillating with numbers. "The coordinates are right."

"Maniac" Marshall jockeyed for a look through one of the huge portholes outside the pilots' mess. The once black and distant mass of the pulsar now dominated the view, its edges streaked by dying stars. The pulsar reminded Maniac of Scylla, though it flashed brilliantly at three-second intervals, living up to its name. The other pilots took no pleasure in the carrier's present position. Maniac would educate them. He drew back from the porthole, about to say something.

"This thing is eating suns for breakfast," Polanski interrupted.

Khumalo, who Maniac had learned went by the moniker of "Knight," turned from a porthole, a look of deep puzzlement knitting his brow. The stocky black man had Hunter's attention. "What the hell are we doing here?"

Hunter chewed on his cigar. "You know what we're not doing?"

"Turning around," Forbes answered.

Maniac regarded the pulsar with exaggerated awe, then addressed his audience. "Do you know what you people are staring at? Do you have any idea?"

With a sigh, Hunter replied, "A Class Two pulsar, mate. I've seen a lot of 'em."

"No." He cocked his thumb toward the porthole. "That, ladies and gentlemen, is the ultimate rush."

Sure, the others gaped at him as though he had gone off the deep end and had returned with gray hair and strange prophecies. He could live with that.

As long as he had Forbes smiling.

Which he did.

Blair took up a position near the back of the bridge, beside Deveraux. She noticed him and edged away. He gave a slight snort and held his ground.

An unsettling air pervaded the bridge, evidenced in the ashen faces of the officers and noncoms who dutifully and nervously ran through their prejump checklists. The casual murmuring Blair had heard during his first visit here had shifted to terse orders and even more terse acknowledgments.

An inverted triangle of consoles divided the forward bridge, with the helmsman seated at the triangle's top and gripping his wheel. Sansky and Gerald manned observation consoles at the base angles, near the bank of viewports. Taggart stood at the helmsman's shoulder, having carefully chosen his position.

Sansky touched a key on the shipwide intercom panel. "Ladies and gentlemen, this is the captain. I'll put an end to the scuttlebutt by informing you that in sixty seconds we're going to jump the Class Two pulsar directly ahead. We've been ordered to the Ulysses Corridor, and we need to get there quickly." Sansky went on to give a capsule summary of the events surrounding the destruction of the Pegasus Station. When he finished, he looked over his shoulder at everyone on the bridge, and Blair found his own trepidation mirrored in the captain's face. "May God be with us all." Then Sansky favored the helmsman with a nod. "Take us in."

The carrier lurched for a moment, then started for the pulsar. Anything that wasn't battened down—and even a few things that were—began to tremble in a cacophony that reminded Blair of the earthquakes on Nephele. He found a nearby railing and gripped it for support. Deveraux folded her arms over her chest and wouldn't join him.

As they glided closer to the pulsar, it better resembled Scylla, but this Scylla, perhaps a distant cousin, had only one head and the brilliantly flashing eye of a Cyclops. As she gobbled up stars, planets, planetoids, and smaller debris, she forged the thunderbolts of her namesake that now struck the *Claw* with massive tremors. And in her work, Blair sensed a perfect balance, a simplicity that tingled at the base of his spine.

He felt her magnetic fields.

And, in his mind's eye, he saw an avenue through space-time itself, a shiny black funnel of infinite mass that he sensed promised infinite awareness.

"Lieutenant?"

With a shiver, he looked askance at Deveraux. "Yes, ma'am?"

"For a second there I thought—"

"Attention! Attention! Course error. Adjust course immediately," came the NAVCOM's automated voice. An alarm squawked.

"Ignore that," Taggart said confidently. "Helm. Hold steady as she goes."

"Captain," the NAVCOM began, its tone waxing persuasive. "The ship is headed into the PNR zone of an uncharted Class Two pulsar. One minute before gravitational pull is one hundred percent."

Sansky spun toward the helm, his voice freighted with tension. "What about it, Taggart?"

"The readings are wrong. Your AI's sensors are not calibrated to the pulsar. They've already been warped by the gravitational field."

"I must insist that we change course immediately," the NAV-COM said. "Initiating AI override."

"No!" Taggart screamed.

The *Tiger Claw* suddenly bucked, and Deveraux came crashing forward into the railing, near Blair. She found her grip as the ship began pulling to port, throwing them parallel to the rail.

Taggart, who now held fast to the helmsman's console, shouldered his way to a touchpad. "Manual override! Now! Disregard your artificial intelligence—or we're all dead."

"Captain," Gerald said through clenched teeth. "I believe you should reconsider."

Sansky cocked a brow. "I already have. Steady as she goes, helm."

Like a cosmic predator with talons of gravitational force, the pulsar reached out and clutched the carrier. Fighting to stabilize the ship's pitch and yaw, the helmsman's face locked in a grimace as the *Tiger Claw* convulsed, her bulkheads writhed, and her overhead threatened to cave in.

"This is the captain," Sansky said over the intercom. "Brace for jump point interphase. Fifteen seconds to jump point."

"Jesus . . ." Deveraux said as the ship released a ghoulish bellow.

But Blair scarcely heard Deveraux, scarcely saw the bridge or felt the rail. His senses began shutting down as they had when nearing Scylla.

And the feeling, the awe-inspiring feeling, lived in him, a vital, unstoppable force that placed the moment inside a subatomic particle, in a universe whose boundaries he longed to explore. He glimpsed the entire Ulysses Corridor and beyond, saw Nephele, the Sol system, whatever he wanted to see because distances no longer held meaning. Time no longer held meaning. He thought of his mother. And there, before him, she gave a mild frown, her hair and complexion as smooth and dark as he remembered. "You shouldn't do this to yourself, Christopher. You weren't meant to see me. This is not your continuum."

"It is mine. I chose it."

"You don't have the right to choose. Only one does."

"What do you mean? There aren't any rules. I feel this. I can do what I feel."

"Then you'll fall. Like the others."

"You're not my mother, are you?"

"I'm everything your mother was, is, and will be. I'm in every part of the universe at once, as you are now, as you shouldn't be."

"Why?"

"I wish you could understand. I wish that more than anything. But I've seen your path. And there's nothing I can do to change it." Her features grew younger, more narrow, until Blair stared at Lieutenant Commander Deveraux, who said, "Didn't you hear him, Lieutenant? Fifteen seconds to jump. Better hang on."

He reached with trembling hands for the rail and blinked as a burst of light shot from the pulsar.

Then he found a bewildered Taggart staring at him. Blair could only imagine how strange he looked. He had not just seen a ghost.

He had seen the universe itself.

And the experience had left him frightened of who he was and might become.

No warning had stunned him more.

Spacecraft Ordnance Specialist Justin Jones jogged across the carrier's shaking flight hangar toward a long, high row of missile racks, where Specialist David Olivia slammed down pairs of bracing arms, locking the projectiles into place.

"Where the hell have you been?" Olivia asked, then grunted as he slammed down another set of arms. "Do you wanna be on or off this arming crew?"

"C'mon," Jones said, then ran ahead of Olivia to reach another brace. "You know I've still got my problem."

"Well, you'd better do something before it winds up in my report."

Jones's mouth fell open. "So how are you gonna write that up, anyway?"

Olivia paused, holding a brace, his face glistening with sweat. "Easy. I'll just tell them the truth."

"You wouldn't . . ."

He wiped sweat from his mouth. "Oh yeah, I would."

"I thought we were friends."

"We are. But now you're screwing with my career. I'm not covering for you anymore."

"Just give me some more time," Jones pleaded, dashing ahead

to seize another brace. "I think I'll have it solved in a couple of days."

"That's what you said last week. I don't got any more time. You either get to a doctor, or I'm getting you off this crew."

"All right. All right. But do you think they can do anything for me?"

"For God's sake, man. It's just diarrhea."

"Not this. No way. This is a curse. I wouldn't wish this on my worst enemy." With that, Jones sprinted off.

"Where are you . . ." Olivia began.

Then it was obvious.

In the flight control room, Boss Raznick buckled himself into his seat, took a sip of his coffee, then placed the mug on the vibrating work surface of his console. He stared down through the Plexi at his flight hangar. His department heads seemed to have everything under control. Their crews battened down ordnance, tools, rolling carts, moorings, and scores of fighters and bombers.

The readiness reports came funneling back to him, and, as usual, the arming crew was last to check in. "Specialist Olivia here, sir. My weapons are tucked in."

"Then move your ass, Spaceman. You've got all of eight seconds to get to your jump station."

"Yes, sir!"

Raznick dialed up the two pilots who would fly the first security patrol once the *Tiger Claw* made the jump. They sat strapped in their idling fighters. "Knight? Spirit? Report?"

"Systems nominal here," Spirit said, then she muttered something in Japanese that Raznick couldn't decipher.

"What was that, Lieutenant?"

"Oh, nothing sir. It's just a little prayer."

"Knight?"

"We're good to go, Boss. That is, if this old lady survives the jump."

Raznick nodded grimly. "I hear that."

Spaceman 2nd Class Miguel Rodriguez checked for the third and final time that the missiles in his section of the *Claw*'s secondary ordnance room were locked and that all laser batteries held steady at full charge. With that done, he hurried to his seat and belted in next to Spaceman Ashley Galaway, her smile as transparent as his. She let out a tiny cry as the carrier shifted suddenly, and the conduits rattled like metal tubes striking a tiled floor.

"Don't worry, *mi amiga*," Rodriguez said, summoning up a false bravado perfected by neighborhood skirmishes in his youth. "When God created *Señor* Miguel Rodriguez, he thought, Damn! Now that is a good-looking *hombre*. So there's no way he'll tamper with perfection."

"Or when he created you, he thought, Hmmm. This young man loves himself too much. When I have the time, I'll stomp him out of existence. So I guess God's got some time on Her hands . . ."

Rodriguez looked at her and *tsk*ed.

The ship suddenly rolled a few degrees, shoving them against their seats.

Galaway began whispering to God, making her peace. Rodriguez blessed himself, closed his eyes, and joined her.

"You know, somebody told me about a time when government didn't control your personal life, when you could, say, get into a ground vehicle and drive as fast as you want without wearing a seatbelt. You didn't have some government regulating your personal freedom, defining for you what's safe and what isn't. When it came to stuff that you wanted to do, good old-fashioned common sense was the law. What ever happened to that?" Maniac searched the faces in the mess hall, but most of the pilots were too busy adjusting their jumpseat harnesses to listen. "Hey, I asked you people a question."

Polanski rose and paraded up to Maniac, using his index finger to poke Maniac's chest. "You wanna know what happened to our personal freedom? Idiots like you ruined it. You abuse every bit of freedom you get. And so to control you idiots, the

Confederation steps in. So, I'm you, I plant my ass on a jumpseat and buckle it down. You wanna live to abuse more of your freedom, doncha?"

Maniac eyed Forbes. She shook her head. No, both of them would ride this out naturally, unfettered by the convention and cowardice that ruled the others.

Staring up some twenty meters at the overhead, Engineer Davies swallowed as a quake passed through the durasteel, making the engine room's ceiling look like gray waves fanned by a north wind. He slapped his palms on a handhold, then leaned out to look at his crewmates, wondering if the other eighteen-year-olds felt as scared as he did. One new recruit, Engineer Oxendine, a tall blond boy with big arms but a bag of gelatin for a gut, crinkled his nose and said, "You smell that? Hey, everybody? You smell that?"

Murmurs erupted, and Davies said, "What? What is it? Fire?"

Oxendine took a few exaggerated whiffs of the air. "No. I think it's you, Davies."

"What do you mean?" he asked, lowering his nose to his armpit. "I don't smell."

"Are you kidding? Your fear is stinkin' up the place."

"Shuddup, Oxy," someone ordered.

"Five seconds to jump," the captain said on the intercom.

Davies leered at Oxendine, then tightened his grip on the handhold.

With the vibrations increasing by what felt like a factor of ten, Blair envisioned his arms as sticks of durasteel and hung on to the bridge railing, his feet occasionally leaving the floor. Deveraux, too, struggled to keep standing, her poker face faltering as the pulsar tightened its grip.

Taggart, whose cool remained unruffled, clung to the helmsman's chair and shifted behind the officer, alternating his gaze between screens and viewports. "Steady now. Steady . . ."

Apparently bored with simply tugging on the carrier, the pulsar decided to jerk the *Tiger Claw* in as though she were a sailfish on a line. The force sent Deveraux crashing into Blair. They fell away from the railing and rose to grab the bulkhead.

"What the hell was that?" Deveraux asked.

"The ship's trying to tear itself free of the space-time fabric," Blair said, his stomach acting out a similar battle.

Growing in pitch, the vibrations continued until Blair's ears filled with a single, deafening hum. The pulsar coruscated again, momentarily blinding him. As his vision cleared, he looked down to see Deveraux's hand reaching toward his shoulder—

And at that moment, the *Tiger Claw* plunged into the pulsar, into the gap in the space-time continuum calculated by Taggart.

The hum, the vibrations, and the taste of bile at the back of Blair's throat fell off into nothingness. He should feel more comfortable in the moment, knowing what to expect. But the feeling had returned, and like a siren, it sang a bewitching song, trying to lure him out to explore the universe, to move beyond the corporeal, to comprehend eternity in a billion-year second, to live an entirely different life in which he knew his parents, really knew them.

Then you'll fall. Like the others.

Such power. And only a thought away. How could he control it? How could anyone control it? The only thing that kept him in place, bound to a minute portion of the universe, was the fear evoked by his mother. Yes, he could refine the feeling, hone himself into a true Pilgrim, he sensed that. But even with a perfect sense of direction and the power to achieve infinite mass and infinite awareness, he would still struggle to find happiness, love, friendship, hope, wisdom, all of the things that defined being human.

Or he could choose to abandon them.

Christopher Blair stood at a cosmic crossroads, and he refused to make a decision, refused to surrender to the intoxication of the feeling. If he did that, he felt it would forever control him. There had to be a way to achieve balance, to preserve his humanity while sharing a relationship with the universe more intimate than he had ever known.

He searched his thoughts for a way to contend with the feeling, but a powerful shudder passed through his body, wrenching him from his introspection. His senses returned with an electrifying vengeance. He gagged as the atonal roar of the carrier's passage echoed through the bridge. Sansky, Gerald, Taggart, and the helmsman, once pillars of salt, now fought to maintain balance.

Deveraux's hand finally settled on Blair's shoulder, and as he turned to look at her, the deck buckled and tossed her into him. They fell back toward the bulkhead, and Deveraux's forehead struck the merciless durasteel with a thud that made Blair grimace. She dropped to her knees, and he grabbed her shoulders, shifting her back to observe a bleeding laceration on her forehead. "Are you all right?"

Her eyes seemed vague, her head swaying. "We make it?"

A glance to the bank of forward viewports gave Blair his reply. The pulsar had slid back into her gloomy cavern of gravity that lay four days and three jump points away. In the distance loomed a massive planet, a gas giant banded in mauve, yellow, and orange. Several large spots blemished its surface, and tiny points of light hovered about it, moons gliding peacefully in their orbits. Beyond the Jovian-like system lay the quiet and dark vacuum, bejeweled by ancient starlight. "We're through the jump point."

Even as Blair finished telling her, the carrier's alarms clicked off, and the rumbling deck and bulkheads grew still, giving way to the routine din of the bridge's instrumentation.

Taggart considered the helmsman's screen, then glanced through the viewport. "Ladies and gentlemen, welcome to the Ulysses Corridor."

Lieutenant Commander Obutu craned his head toward Captain Sansky, one hand on his headset. "Launching Rapiers. Now."

After a few seconds, two fighters shot by the viewport, their afterburners aglow. Blair followed their path until they ascended out of view.

"Shields up," Sansky ordered, getting to his feet. "Mr. Obutu, stealth mode, please."

Obutu threw a toggle. Every console grew dim. "Going to stealth. Seven percent electronic emissions, zero communications."

Arriving at the radar station, Sansky leaned over the beanpole of a boy seated there. "Status?"

"Scanners picking up strong electromagnetic signature at one-eleven mark four-three. An asteroid field. I'd say she's a Kilrathi, sir."

Sansky nodded, then brought himself to full height to consult with a dour-looking Gerald.

Meanwhile, Blair struggled to his feet. "Don't move," he told Deveraux. "I'll be right back." He hustled to the rear of the bridge and unclipped a first aid kit from the wall. He returned with the kit and removed a laser pen from its holder. "Don't move," he said, then lifted the pen to her forehead.

"You already said that."

"This time I really mean it." He thumbed on the power and began sealing the laceration. "You're a good patient," he said softly, then his aim shifted.

"Ouch."

"Sorry." He finished the seal, lowered the pen, and edged closer to her, studying his handiwork.

"It's all right," she assured him, drawing back. She lifted her brow, breaking the seal.

He quickly shook his head and brought the laser pen toward her. "It's still bleeding. If I—"

"It's all right," she insisted, then grabbed his wrist, forcing the pen away.

"Yes, ma'am." He stood and proffered his hand.

She dismissed the offer. Using the bulkhead for support, she clambered to her feet, wavered a moment, then found her balance.

Blair opened his mouth, wanting to tell her he was sorry, that he didn't mean to move so close to her, that all he had wanted to do was help. He also wanted to say that her perfume made him lightheaded, that her skin seemed like the smooth surface of some ripe, exotic fruit, and that he would like to explore the secrets in her hair. He wanted to tell her most of that, well, some of that, but Captain Sansky suddenly came between them. "That head all right?" he asked Deveraux.

"Little scratch. I'm fine."

"Good. Security patrol's been launched, but I'm keeping them in tight. I want you to prepare a recon. I want to know what's out there."

"Yes, sir." She started for the corridor.

"And Deveraux," Sansky called after her. "No contact with the enemy. Not yet."

She looked over her shoulder and nodded, then faced Blair. "Let's go, Lieutenant."

Twenty decks below the bridge, in a dank, cramped latrine, Specialist Justin Jones struggled up, gripped his stomach, then released a moan. He was, he suspected, the only man alive who had jumped a pulsar while seated on a toilet.

Then again, some feats were better left unreported.

Flight Boss Raznick swore as he removed the coffee mug from his lap. A large stain darkened the front of his uniform. He vowed to find the idiot responsible for convincing the captain to jump a pulsar. And when he did, he would have that idiot busted down to spacehand. The laundry detail repeatedly did a poor job of cleaning his uniforms; they could never remove a stain of this magnitude. He looked up to the heavens and demanded a refund for the day.

He thought he heard God laugh.

Miguel Rodriguez reached into his shirt and withdrew the St. Christopher medallion hanging from his neck. He kissed the patron saint of travelers and whispered a thank you.

"I think we made it," Ashley Galaway said, removing her seat straps.

"We did, *mi amiga*," Rodriguez said. "Come. Give me a hug."

"Yeah, right."

"No, really. On my world it's customary to hug the nearest person after a dangerous situation."

"On my world, the men don't lie to get close to their women."

"Oh, come now, *mi amiga*. Do you see a lie in this face?" He mustered his most sincere look.

"No. I see lust." She stood and abruptly kissed him on the cheek. "Don't try so hard. If we're going to violate regs, let's make it worth it." She strutted off, leaving him to contend with his runaway pulse.

"That'll be a nice bruise, mate," Hunter told Maniac as the older pilot inspected Maniac's forearm. "Have you found your manhood yet? Or does the quest continue?"

Rubbing his swelling arm, Maniac smirked and left Hunter, weaving his way through the mess to join Forbes, who had gone to fetch a drink.

As she spotted him, her eyes lit over the rim of her glass. "That was good. Very, very good," she cooed.

"Some men know how to show a lady a good time"—he scowled at Hunter—"and some don't."

"And speaking of time, have you noticed the shift?"

"What time is it?"

"It's nearly oh-three-hundred Zulu."

He checked his watch; it read 1434. "It only took a few minutes to make that jump."

"But we still lost over half a standard day."

He lifted his brow. "Then we have some time to make up."

She began to answer, but the intercom speaker emitted a short beep. "This is the captain. As most of you have guessed, we just made one hell of a jump."

"Is that what that was?" Polanski groaned.

"Actually, we've just taken a little short cut into the Ulysses Corridor, where, as I told you, the Pegasus Station was attacked and destroyed. The main Kilrathi battle group is in the quadrant and headed for the Charybdis Quasar. In just over ten hours it'll be in position to jump into Earth space. Our mission is to find the Kilrathi, assess their capacities and plan of action, and if necessary, stop them."

Maniac exchanged a look with Forbes: Action! Yes!

"We're the only Confed ship within range, people," Sansky continued. "We'll have no help and no rescue. We can only count on each other. That is all."

The stars, once distinct points of light, had shifted into a swirling eddy of glistening claw marks. Admiral Geoffrey Tolwyn sat at an observation console, pondering those marks and what lay beyond them. He imagined the future, imagined his battle group arriving in Earth space two hours too late. The once-blue planet had grown dark. Kilrathi bio-missiles exploding in her atmosphere had whipped up thick clouds of a toxin that would descend upon her citizenry for several months, killing the millions who couldn't make it to shelters and decimating all flora and fauna. It would take several millennia for the planet to recover. Tolwyn smote a fist on the console. Two hours. One hundred and twenty minutes. The irony had worn into a deep-rooted sense of helplessness and frustration that had turned his dreams to nightmares.

Someone approached from behind, and Tolwyn considered turning around, but he recognized the tentative footsteps. "What is it, Commodore?"

"Message from Earth Command, sir. Their defenses are on line, but—"

"They don't believe they can withstand a Kilrathi battle group without fleet support."

"No, sir. But they will fight. Earth will never surrender."

"Surrender? That's not an option with the Kilrathi. They believe they're the supreme race. The rest of us are just here to do one thing."

"What's that?"

Tolwyn snickered. "To die." He swiveled his chair to take in Bellegarde's somber countenance. "Our status?"

"We're still running at one hundred and ten percent. But we've already lost three ships, two at jump points, one from a reactor meltdown."

"Run at one-twenty."

"We'll lose more of the battle group."

"One-twenty, Commodore."

"One-twenty. Aye-aye, sir."

Tolwyn leaned back and folded his hands behind his head. "Before you go, Richard, have you had time to consider, well, how should I put this . . . your past?"

The commodore thought a moment, then said, "As you know, sir, I've been busy."

"Do you feel somehow put out because we're rushing to save a planet that doesn't concern you?"

"Earth represents a valuable commodity to the Confederation, sir. Its strategic importance—"

"But as you said, you have no ties to the planet, no desire to recognize your ancestry. I thought we came from the same generation. I thought we placed some value on our history, our heritage."

"We do, sir. We just go about it differently. If that makes you feel uncomfortable—"

"I don't question your loyalty. I question your identity. Who are you?"

"Sir?"

"Tell me who you are."

"Bellegarde, Richard. Commodore. Terran Confederation—"

"No, Richard. That's all grandeur and bullshit. You were born in the Eddings system, Vega sector. But you can trace your ancestry back to Earth, to Scotland."

"I can do that, sir. But I'd rather not."

"Why?"

"I'd just rather not."

"I'm sorry, Richard. But I order you to tell me why you would rather not."

The commodore set his jaw, turned away, about to leave, then stopped. "My ancestors were thieves, murderers, and rapists. We took the name Bellegarde after systematically exterminating an entire family in order to gain their power and wealth. We assumed their identities through surgery and legal maneuvering, and continue to live a centuries-old lie. It was an amazing feat. And a tragic one." He gathered the courage to face Tolwyn. "Do you have any idea how many people died because of my family? Some of us were assassins who went off-world, found more of the original Bellegardes, and killed them, too. We didn't stop until every last one was dead."

That gave Tolwyn pause. He appreciated Bellegarde's forthrightness and now felt guilty over ordering the man to confess. "You had no control over what happened. We deal with the past we've been handed. It's in the dealing that our true identities are born."

"Or we bury the past, sir. Bury it very deeply. If Earth burns, maybe that's not such a bad thing. Terrible people have come from that place."

Tolwyn unclasped his hands and stretched. "Well, Richard. This has been a very *enlightening* conversation."

"If I'm nothing else, sir, I'm honest."

"I appreciate that. Now I'd like you to return to your quarters, flush your liquor, and send mail to your mistress, breaking it off. *Then* you'll be honest. Dismissed."

Utter shock gripped Bellegarde's face. Then he shook it off and saluted. "Yes, sir." He fled the bridge.

Shifting his chair back toward the viewport, Tolwyn wondered whether he had crossed the line with Bellegarde. Of course he had. But no simple tongue-lashing from him would solve Bellegarde's problems. In a few weeks, Richard would return to his mistress and his bottle. Despite that, Tolwyn sensed that within the commodore lay one of the Confederation's greatest officers.

Or one of its greatest traitors.

With a drumming heart and shaky hands, Blair zipped up his scarlet flight suit, concealing his cross. He removed the helmet from his locker, tucked it under his arm, and bolted out of his quarters.

Lieutenant Commander Deveraux had chosen him to be on her wing for the recon, and the surprise of her decision wouldn't leave Blair any time soon. She could have chosen a far more experienced pilot like St. John or Khumalo, but she had opted for him. Blair doubted that she actually trusted him, so her choice posed a mystery that he decided to solve by going to the source. When he got the hangar, he would simply ask her.

He elbowed his way into the crowded lift and waited impatiently for the doors to close.

"Hey, Blair. Where are you going?" Maniac stood at the back of the lift, his face a red globe of sweat.

"Better question. Where have you been?"

"They're testing out a new Zero-G wataerobics pool. Thought I'd kill time and volunteer as guinea pig."

"So how was it?"

"It's still got problems. Threw me around pretty hard, but as you know, I'm the master of recoveries. Rosie got pretty sick, though."

"Who?"

"Rosie. Forbes."

"Oh, *Rosie*. Just be careful."

Maniac chuckled. "Can't help you there, Ace."

When he arrived on the flight deck, Blair found Deveraux standing near the lift doors, waiting for him. She gave a curt nod and turned toward the Rapiers. Blair crossed in front of her to check her wound.

"Would you cut that out?" she said, flustered by his concern.

"Sorry. I think it'll heal okay. I don't want you to have a scar."

"Too late. I've cornered the market on those. C'mon."

They walked down the flight line, past a row of Broadsword bombers. Scores of techs stood atop, below, or beside the bombers, some in the blue glow of torches, some on rolling ladders, all wreathed in the fumes of fuel and heated metal. The flight crews would never run out of work because every time they fixed a fighter, some pilot would take it out and get shot up again. Were Blair among them, he would find the job exceedingly aggravating and probably voice that feeling to the pilot who had ruined his work. Consequently, Blair wholeheartedly respected these people who pushed the rock of their repairs up an endless mountain.

"Any standard operating procedure I should know about?" Blair asked as they neared the first line of Rapiers.

"No SOP out here," Deveraux said. "There's only one rule."

"Don't get killed?"

"Don't get *me* killed." She broke off toward one of two fully armed Rapiers, their short wings slightly bowing under the weight of Dumb-fire, Spiculum IR, and Pilum Friend or Foe missiles locked to over- or underwing hardpoints.

Blair followed her, taking a closer look at her fighter. He noted her call sign: "Angel."

But that hardly surprised him.

The many rows of kill marks shortened his breath. He counted them. "Twenty-six. Jesus."

"That puts me ahead of the law of averages," she said, mounting her cockpit ladder. "Well ahead. The curve'll catch up to me sooner or later." She tipped her head toward the Rapier next to hers. "Your bird, Blair. Treat her well."

Only then did Blair recognize the Rapier's number: thirty-five. They had given him Bossman's old fighter. Chen's name had been removed, along with his kill marks. The yellow paint used to stencil LT. CHRISTOPHER BLAIR below the cockpit seemed too new, too perfect against the Rapier's battered armor.

Although he had never known Vince Chen, he felt a tinge of guilt over taking the man's fighter, as though he were desecrating Chen's memory. But he shouldn't feel that way. Taking the fighter out again would be in tribute to Bossman's life, to what he held most dear. If Chen were like most pilots, he would want it that way.

Blair gently touched the mighty nose cannon. "She's all mine," he told Deveraux, beaming.

"And she'll probably be someone else's. Mount up. The clock is ticking."

"One more question. Why me for this recon?"

"Why not?"

"Yeah," he said, only half-buying her reply. "Why not." He jogged up the ladder and lowered himself into the pit.

Once tight in his harness, he ran though the preflight check. Meanwhile, ground crews below made their final walkarounds of both fighters, running scanners and their own gazes over every seal and double-checking the loadout. Blair threw a pair of toggles, powering up the thrusters, as Deveraux did the same. The engines purred and made Blair feel as though he were flexing his muscles. He slipped on his headset, helmet, and O_2 mask, then dialed up Deveraux's comm channel. "Maverick to Angel. Comm check. Roger."

"Comm established," she replied, flashing him a thumbs-up on the left VDU. "Lieutenant, your call sign is Maverick? Where'd you get that? From some old movie?"

"Actually, ma'am, it's been a standing joke for a while now. Back at the academy, I had a rep for being a by-the-book flyer. So, of course, they called me Maverick. And yeah, I did see that old movie. They flew those big, heavy atmospheric fighters. Must've been fun back then."

"We'll never know," she said curtly. "All moorings are clear. External power disengaged. Internal systems nominal, roger."

"Roger. I'm fully detached and ninety-five into the sequence," Blair said, reading his panels.

The deckmaster waved Deveraux toward her launch position.

Her Rapier ascended several meters, then floated forward as the landing skids folded into the fighter's belly. She lined up with the runway and the shining energy field beyond.

"Lieutenant Commander, you are cleared to launch," Blair heard the flight boss tell Deveraux.

"Roger, Boss. See you on the flip." She punctuated her sentence with a blast of thrusters that cast Blair's Rapier in a tawny sheen. Like a finned bullet, she blew out of the hangar.

"All right, Lieutenant. Let's see if you remember how to do this," the flight boss said tiredly.

Without a word, Blair took his Rapier into a hover and, following the deckmaster's signals, lined up for launch. He would perform a textbook takeoff that would shut the boss's mouth.

"That looks good, young man," the boss said, as though inspecting Blair's coloring book. "You're all clear."

Throttling up to exactly eighty percent thruster power (the textbook's suggestion), Blair tore off toward the energy field, bulkheads whirring by, the stars clouded by what looked like a wall of water. The Rapier shimmied as he passed through the field and burst into open space. He climbed away from the *Tiger Claw*, accelerating to full throttle, then flicked his gaze to the radar display, finding the blue blip of Deveraux's fighter. He banked sharply to form on her wing. With his free hand, he unzipped his flight suit, dug out his Pilgrim cross, and gave it a squeeze for luck. A signal from Deveraux lit up his right display: KEEP RADIO SILENCE.

Ahead lay a small, rocky world, draped in shadow and orbiting a distant and dimly burning brown dwarf star. Blair targeted the planet, and data spilled across his right display. Officially catalogued as Planetoid SX34B5, it bore an uncanny similarity in both appearance and composition to Earth's moon. Blair targeted the brown dwarf and quickly scanned the information on the star's size, age, and something about it not having enough mass to convert hydrogen into helium via nuclear fusion. He stopped reading when the data became too technical but still felt satisfied with his cursory inspection. Some pilots like Maniac flew into the unknown relying only on their eyes. Blair had been taught that a physical understanding of his combat environment would allow him to use it as an ally, not an obstacle.

He switched his targeting cross-hairs to a field of asteroids encircling the brown dwarf. Jagged chunks of ice-covered rock tumbled slowly and occasionally collided with others to emit spates of smaller rubble.

Deveraux's Rapier jumped a little ahead of his, and Blair noted the cue. They would move into and sweep the field. He slid over the Heads Up Display viewer on his helmet, then, with one eye, studied the digitized tactical schematic. Dozens of reticles singled out targets, outlined them, and flashed, then sensors gave him an instant report of their position. Green lines formed into a glide path through the thousands of spinning rocks.

But not all of the debris appeared natural. Shiny objects began peeking out from behind the rocks, objects that became more distinct—pieces of durasteel shredded like paper.

A particularly huge plate, twisted and scorched, spun by his canopy. He recoiled a little as he spotted the letters ASUS painted near its edge.

"Angel? Did you catch that? That's from Pegasus."

She appeared on his left display. "You just broke radio silence, Lieutenant."

"I'm sorry. I just—"

"Forget it." She shook her head, then looked up, taking in more of the asteroid field. "Concussion must've blown pieces of the station all over the sector." Her tactical computer chirped.

Blair's computer answered with a chirp of its own. A blip flashed across his radar, then another, then both disappeared. "I just picked up multiple contacts, bearing—"

"Pipe down. I'm getting something . . ."

And Blair spotted them, too: six blips burning brightly in his radar, headed directly for their position.

"Angel—"

"Radio silence. And let's get deeper into this field. Low power. We'll see if we can wait 'em out."

"Roger."

She dove ahead, following the digitized glide path through the asteroids. Blair kept tight on her six o'clock until she veered sixty degrees to port and settled in the lee of an oblong-shaped rock nearly one hundred meters long. Blair raced by her, finding cover of his own below a similar rock about five hundred meters away. He frantically switched off everything save for life support and sat there a moment, the oxygen whistling softly into his mask, the sweat beading on his brow. His gaze traced the thick veins of ice that fanned out across the stone. He tried to concentrate on something as mundane as the rock, but the suspense had his skin crawling.

"My scanners are blind, Merlin. Talk to me."

The little man knew better than to appear in Blair's cockpit, perhaps creating a detectable energy source. Instead, he transferred himself into the Rapier's main computer, where he could speak sans his holographic form. A dim light flashed in the right display as he replied, "Crosstalk between a large Kilrathi vessel and the brown dwarf down there. I can't decipher the code."

"They know we're here?"

"Possibly. From the sophistication of the equipment on board, I'd say the vessel is a Command and Communications module, probably a Thrakhra-class transport retrofitted for the job."

"So what's it commanding?"

"At least six other ships near the brown dwarf are communicating with it. Interesting. I'm picking up an Ultra Low Frequency signal. The Rapier's scanners aren't equipped to receive or detect ULF."

"But *you* are?"

"Don't tell me you've downloaded my sarcasm program?"

Blair waved his hand. "Forget that. What's it mean? This frequency?"

"It's a primitive pulse technology, Ultra Low Frequency. Very slow, but it carries over extreme distances, not unlike tom-toms. Pilgrims used ULF during the war."

"So why would the Kilrathi—" Blair caught himself. "Did you say *Pilgrims*?"

"Yes. I believe I did."

"Then you know more about the Pilgrims? You told me my father wiped your flash memory."

"I . . . I don't know how I know about the ULF signals," Merlin stammered. "I just do. Perhaps that data is buried in my suboperating memory, left over from the war. Maybe it's intuition."

"Intuition?" Blair fought off a chill. He could deal with Merlin's sarcasm. But a PPC with intuition? The prospect unnerved him. "Well, do you have signal source?"

"It appears to be coming from quadrant thirty."

"Thirty. That puts it near the *Tiger Claw*. Can you translate it?"

"The code isn't in my . . ." Merlin broke off.

"What?"

"They're scanning the rocks."

"Merlin off."

Emerald light flickered above, and Blair could almost feel the scanning beam as it passed over the rock.

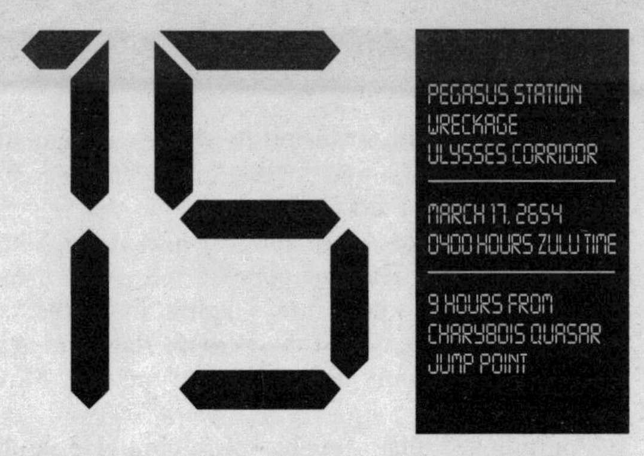

"Go on," Deveraux whispered to herself. "There's nothing in this mouse hole. Beat it."

The Kilrathi ship continued probing, its beam throwing a green halo over the asteroid.

A thump from the port side caught her attention. She shuddered as a figure dressed in Confederation Marine Corps armor floated near her wing. She looked away before the face rolled into view, but her stomach dropped anyway—and not from nausea. The Rapier had begun drifting.

Unable to fire retros that would reveal her location, she watched as the starboard wing brushed against an uneven valley of ice and rock with a sickening creak. She shushed her fighter and looked up. "You didn't read that," she told the Kilrathi. "And if you did, it was just two rocks colliding."

She waited. Waited some more. Became an authority on waiting. Knew the details. The frustration. Could tell you all you wanted to know about it. Could tell you that in the end there was, of course, nothing to do but wait. And react. And sitting in the cramped cockpit felt very much like hiding in her old closet, back at the orphanage. Sister Fleurette would come with her red and swollen eyes, with her wooden paddle, and with her breath that reeked of alcohol. The door would swing open. The light would rush in. Squinting, Deveraux would watch the paddle eclipse the sun.

She shook off the memory, seeing now that the Rapier floated away from the rock, widening the distance by a meter every two or three seconds.

The asteroid's halo grew brighter.

Far to port, past teeming knots of rubble, something glimmered. Was it just more durasteel from the Pegasus Station? A second look proved Blair's suspicions. The Kilrathi ConCom ship had paused near Deveraux's position. "What do they see, Merlin?"

"They don't *see* anything. Switch on your thermal scanner. They're out of range to detect it."

He slid the HUD viewer over his eye and tapped on the scanner. Not much of a view: the glimmer once more, the asteroids among twinkling shards of metal . . .

There. A fading red glow shone through the massive rock shielding Deveraux. "They've spotted Angel's heat corona."

"Two more Kilrathi closing fast," Merlin said anxiously. "Probably fighters."

Blair's gloved fingers traveled quickly over his instrument panels. Displays rose from darkness. Scanners flashed data to him. Engines hummed in their warming sequence. The communications system gave a readiness beep. "Angel. They've spotted us. Two more bogies coming in hot. Six o'clock." He stole a glance at his radar display. No, the Kilrathi weren't changing their minds.

Deveraux's wide eyes filled his display. "Can't spot them, Blair. Call it."

The blips moved closer.

"Jack in the box," Blair instructed. "On three. One . . . two . . . three!"

The Rapier's engines ignited with a thundering roar. Jagged stone wiped past him as he skimmed along the asteroid's surface. Once clear of the rock, he corkscrewed straight up, out of the field and into a starry sky.

"Form on my wing," Deveraux ordered.

"Yes, ma'am!" Wheeling around, Blair rocketed toward her fighter, strangling more thrust from his Rapier. As he neared her position, he spotted two Dralthi fighters escorting the ConCom ship.

Without giving the enemy pilots time to blink, he and Deveraux squeezed off Dumb-fire missiles. Her rocket tore past the left Dralthi's shields to swallow the fighter in a fireball. His missile caught the other Dralthi as it began veering off. The explosion tore away the ship's engine housing to send it spiraling out of control. It glanced off the asteroid Deveraux had used as cover, shedding plastisteel like a cybernetic snake, then splayed itself over a valley.

Charging through the still-lingering blast waves, he and Deveraux targeted the ConCom ship. Even as his sensors indicated that she had ignited her missile, Blair jammed down his trigger. Their projectiles trailed ribbons of exhaust as they traversed the thousand-meter gap. But they stopped short, detonating in useless ringlets of energy as the ConCom's powerful shields absorbed them.

"Well, they're awake now," Blair said. He checked his radar display. "I've got two more bogies coming up from the brown dwarf. Engaging."

"Negative! I count fourteen unfriendlies inbound. Looks like two destroyers. We are out of here!" Her exhaust ports flared as afterburners engaged.

Blair lit his own burners and banked suddenly, following her back toward the *Tiger Claw*. He switched his left VDU to the rear turret display. A swarm of glowing specks descended upon the asteroid field.

Standing in the center of the *Grist'Ar'roc*'s bridge, Captain Thiraka nar Kiranka reflected on the report from his tactical officer. Bad news regularly turned him inward, in search of a response. Oh, yes, he knew what he wanted to do now. But he also considered what the admiral would do—another response altogether. In the unlikely event that Thiraka and Bokoth agreed upon their next action, then Thiraka might honestly believe that he did have a future with the Kilrathi military. But as the past had already proven, he did not think like his superiors, and he suspected that recent events would not change that.

He moved cautiously toward the rear of the bridge, where Kalralahr Bokoth crouched on bent knee below a meter-high statue of Sivar, whose fearsome personage stood on a pedestal and loomed over the bridge like a brooding rain cloud. Banners of the Kiranka clan hung behind the candlelit effigy in testament to fallen and future glory. The banners' asymmetric symbols told stories of death, conquest, and domination; stories of sterilized worlds and territorial ambitions; stories of civil wars so heinous that humans could never comprehend them.

Waiting at the proper distance, Thiraka hoped the admiral would notice him soon. Bokoth could choose to meditate for another hour, and Thiraka would have to remain, neither able to interrupt Bokoth nor retreat. Death awaited any Kilrathi who violated that precept.

But Bokoth had heard his approach. As though emerging dizzy from a vision, the admiral craned his pale, oblong head toward Thiraka. "Kal Shintahr?"

"Sir, our lead ConCom ship has engaged a Confederation reconnaissance flight in sector seven. Fighters from two of our destroyers were dispatched to intercept."

"And the reconnaissance patrol escaped."

Thiraka nodded and ground his long teeth. The admiral had not listened to Thiraka's wish and continued to have intelligence beamed directly to his quarters, overstepping his authority. Thiraka considered Bokoth's quick murder followed by his own suicide. He breathed deeply, trying to quell the thought.

With a slight growl, Bokoth forced himself to his feet. "So the *Tiger Claw* is here."

"Yes, sir. The merchantman we tracked earlier jumped into

this sector by using a gravity well. And the carrier jumped here through a pulsar."

"Do we have a fix on her signal?"

"Yes, sir."

The admiral turned to the command chair, where, cloaked in shadows and nutrient haze, a figure stirred. "Your friend is dedicated," Bokoth said, his words translated into the hoots and squeaks made by humans.

Stepping forward, the hairless ape in the atmospheric suit raised one of its stubby, glove-covered fingers and replied, "My friend is a Pilgrim. This is what he trained for. Prepare the ambush."

"In time," Bokoth said, raising his own paw and withdrawing a nail.

"That ship is the only thing that stands between us and the success of this mission. It's yours for the taking."

Bokoth absently tugged on his whiskers, purring into a thought. Then he abruptly answered, "That ship is insignificant. That hate of your kind blinds you. All things pass. Let it go."

The ape took a step closer. "You're wrong, old man. Most things pass: love, passion, anger, life. One is eternal: hate."

"What's the matter?" Blair asked Deveraux as they walked swiftly down the corridor. "Are we in trouble?"

She wouldn't answer as she made an abrupt ninety-degree turn to march onto the bridge. She went to the viewports and came to attention as Gerald and Sansky left the radar station. Blair arrived at her side, held his shoulders high, and saluted his approaching superiors.

The captain and commander simply eyed them a moment, then Gerald, firing up his usual implacable glare, said, "We read your After Action Report. And I, for one, am unimpressed. You knew what the orders were. No contact with the enemy. Now you've compromised the mission and this ship."

"Sir. I had no choice. The enemy had spotted Lieutenant Commander Deveraux's heat signature, sir."

"Really," Gerald said, half-singing the word. His gaze shifted radically. "Angel, how sure are you that the Kilrathi had you targeted? Given the lieutenant's background . . ."

"Excuse me?" Blair bristled.

Gerald's head slowly shifted like the turret-top cupola of a tank, bringing its weapon to bear. "It's well documented that Pilgrim saboteurs have been responsible for much of the Confed's problems in this war. I'll be sure to download that information to your account, Lieutenant."

"Did they have me targeted?" Deveraux demanded, turning to face Blair. "Or did you just get trigger-happy?"

"Trigger-happy? What kind of an operator do you—"

"Enough," Sansky said. "This is sterile conjecture. The Kilrathi are aware that Rapiers are short-range fighting craft assigned to cap ships. They know we're close by." He focused on Blair. "Tell me again about this communication you claim to have heard."

With a flagrant turn of his head, Blair flicked Gerald a look of raw repulsion. "It was a ULF signal emanating from the vicinity of the *Tiger Claw*, sir."

Sansky swung toward the navigation station, though the computer would detect his voice no matter where he projected it. "What about it, NAVCOM? Were any communications sent from this ship?"

"Negative, Captain. There were no communications sent by the *Tiger Claw*."

Gerald smirked and gave a nod.

"Sir, I tell you—"

"You tell me nothing, Lieutenant," Sansky said. "Nor does your flight recorder. A Rapier's scanners are not equipped to detect ULF transmissions. Your reliance on your PPC—unauthorized equipment, I might add—does not convince me that the signal exists. PPCs are not standard military issue and are vulnerable to a number of viruses. What you thought you heard—"

"But sir—"

"—could've come from any number of natural sources."

"This was not a natural—"

"Dismissed, Lieutenant."

Blair saluted and rushed off the bridge before foul language landed him in the brig.

Granted, Sansky and Gerald didn't want to waste time chasing down false leads, but to ignore something of this importance seemed absolutely foolish. Then again, trusting in a half-breed and possible saboteur without proof of his loyalty would be equally so. Deadlock.

Captain Sansky took a moment to recover from his argument with the insistent boy. He admired Blair's courage in holding his ground, even on the bridge. Yet he also began to fear the boy, perhaps as much as Gerald. With little time to further speculate on Blair's potential damage, he glimpsed the distant asteroids through the viewport. "Your assessment, Mr. Gerald?"

"That ConCom's running point for the battle group. Their fleet won't be far behind. As you said, they know we're here, so I say we send them a message. I can have my fighters up in thirty minutes."

"Twenty," Deveraux corrected, her self-confidence revving even higher than Gerald's.

"That would be a mistake," Taggart said, lifting his head from the helmsman's screen. "Without her fighters, this ship's vulnerable." He stood, approached Sansky, and began shaking his head.

Pursing his lips, Sansky contemplated the pros and cons of a first strike, the mental list beginning to blur as he tried in vain to spot the longer side.

"You're a civilian scout," Gerald reminded Taggart, "not a naval officer. Tactical operations are our concern."

Taggart's face grew rigid, and his tone plunged to warning depths. "There's a great deal more at stake here than you seem to understand, Commander."

Sansky threw up a hand. "The XO is right. I'm sorry, Mr.

Taggart. Destroying that ConCom and its escorts will slow the Kilrathi. Deveraux will lead a strike force. You will accompany her." He crossed back to Lieutenant Commander Obutu, who kept vigil over his screens. "Con, plot a course for the rings of Planet Four-fifteen. We'll find good cover there."

"Before every battle, all pilots should spend a quiet moment of meditation. Within each of you lies the ability to transcend what you believe you can do. Within each of you lies a tiger's heart. To find it, you must begin at peace, comfortable with the world around you, with the future as you see it, with the thought of killing. There is no emotion. Only the job. You sight the target, terminate it with impunity, and move through it without looking back."

Deveraux's academy instructor had said those words to her graduating class, words that lived in Deveraux with the same vitality as the day she had first heard them. She could repeat every sentence, every cadence of his speech, having turned a heartfelt reminder into a personal pledge and prayer that she repeated before every mission.

When she had left the bridge with orders to lead a strike force to take out the Kilrathi ConCom ship, she had headed directly to her quarters to shower, change into a clean flight suit, and sit at her desk to meditate.

No one had ever taught Deveraux how to meditate; in fact, she wasn't sure if she did it correctly. She had read that proper meditation can lessen levels of cortisol, a hormone released in

Top: Todd "Maniac" Marshall (Matt Lillard), Christopher Blair (Freddie Prinze, Jr.), and James Taggart aka Paladin (Tcheky Karyo).

Right: Jeannette "Angel" Devereaux (Saffron Burrows).

(Top) The Kilrathi attack on the Command Center at Vega Sector Fleet Headquarters.

(Bottom) Confederation Broadsword bomber attacking a Kilrathi Dreadnought.

(Top) Kilrathi Dralthi being fired on by Blair while Devereaux (upper left) tries to escape.

(Bottom) Captain Sansky (David Suchet) on the deck of the *Tiger Claw*.

(Above) A Kilrathi pilot.

(Right) Blair in a Marine combat suit entering Kilrathi ship.

(Opposite page,Top) Confederation Marines on board the *Tiger Claw*.

(Opposite page,Bottom) Kilrathi general (with beard) facing Kilrathi soldier.

(Left) Maniac being "questioned" by Devereaux.

(Bottom) Rapier plane under attack on the flight deck of the *Tiger Claw*.

(Opposite page, Top) Kilrathi soldiers on the attack.

(Opposite page, Bottom) Kilrathi Cruiser (on left) attacking the *Tiger Claw*.

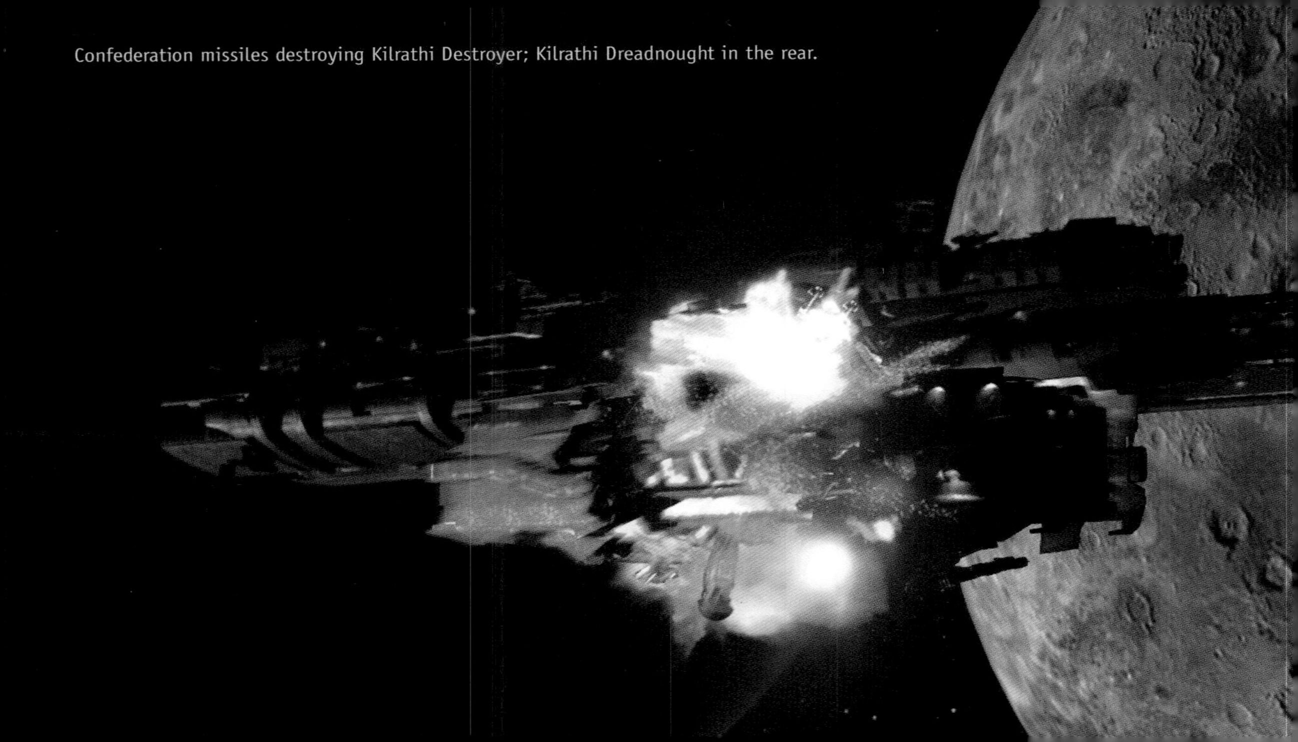

Confederation missiles destroying Kilrathi Destroyer; Kilrathi Dreadnought in the rear.

response to stress. She also knew that meditation enhanced the body's recuperative functions.

But what she really searched for, what remained at the fringe of her thoughts, was a sense of true identity. A sense that she wasn't just the product of an orphanage, that her parents' lives meant something to hers, that the feeling of emptiness would not lie locked in her heart forever, that somewhere inside lay a key.

Deveraux had yet to find that key. Perhaps she did need lessons in meditation. And she didn't ask for much. She had no aspirations to attain conscious union with the divine or experience divine grace; she simply wanted to feel good about herself. She opened her eyes, reached across her desk, and switched on the holovid player.

A small girl seated on the edge of a picnic blanket glimmered at the foot of her bunk. A young man rolled a pink ball toward the girl, while a young woman looked on with a proud grin. Intermittent buzzing resounded over their voices, and the picture flickered with static. Deveraux swore over the disc's age. She would have to mail it off to a company for restoration, but she would hate parting with the vid, even for a second. That family, sometimes looking so distant, so unfamiliar, sometimes looking like her exposed soul, remained the only visual record she had of a life that had suddenly ceased. Sure, she could make copies of the vid, but knowing that her parents had touched the same disc rendered it irreplaceable.

A ring from her hatch bell startled her. She stood, paused the holovid, then moved to greet her visitor. Not many people came to see Deveraux, owing to her admonishments about the value of privacy during stand-down. She touched the open key.

And lost a heartbeat.

"I need to talk to you." Blair leaned on the doorjamb, his face long, his eyes reflective pools.

She forgot to breathe. She glanced to the holovid, the figures frozen—

Blair pushed his way past her.

"Hey. You can't barge into my—"

He spun and tossed something to her. "I wear it for luck."

She caught, then examined the cross.

"It was my mother's," he explained.

"Is your luck at odds with our mission?"

That drew a long sigh from him. He shifted away, surveying the rest of her quarters, his gaze falling on the paused holovid. "What's this?"

"Nothing," she said, then practically dove toward the holovid and shut it off. "You should leave."

"You worried about gossip? I'm not. I already know what they're saying about me."

"You give them reason to talk."

He searched the ceiling for a reply, then finally said, "You think he's right about me?"

"Who? Gerald?"

"Yeah. I mean, in his mind I started selling out the *Tiger Claw* the moment I stepped on board."

Her gaze flicked to the cross. "I don't see how you can be a Pilgrim and fight on our side."

"I'm not a Pilgrim. I don't even know what a Pilgrim is."

"You're not that naïve—otherwise you'd keep this thing in a box."

"I guess you're right. My mother was an off-worlder who grew up hating Earth, hating humanity. My father fought for the Confederation. Somehow, despite all the hate, they found each other."

"How?"

"I don't know. They died before I was five. He was killed trying to save her in the Peron Massacre. That cross is all I have. I'm not sure where I belong, Commander, except here, fighting and flying."

As she turned the cross over in her hands, Deveraux felt a chill spidering across her neck. "Sit down, Lieutenant."

He moved toward her bunk, but she directed him to the chair at her desk.

"Why do you think they call me Angel?" she asked.

His shoulders lifted in a half-shrug.

"It's a real weeper. Headlines: My parents died in the same war. I grew up in an orphanage on Earth, in Brussels."

Their gazes met, and Deveraux sensed an even stronger connection.

"At night, I'd cry for them," she continued. "The sisters told me they were angels. I kept crying for them to come and take me to heaven. But they weren't angels. They were dead. Gone. It was like they had never existed."

"Like Bossman?"

Deveraux held herself for a moment, forcing her breath to steady, her hands to stop trembling. "Emotion gets in the way of our mission. There is no emotion. Only the job. You sight the target, terminate it with impunity, and move through it without looking back."

"Commander, emotion is what separates us from the Pilgrims. And the Kilrathi."

She leaned back on the bulkhead and shut her eyes, seeing Chen's smile, listening to him joke about being "Ripper" in his younger days and how he had changed his ways to become a model pilot revered by the younger jocks who sought him for advice. They began to call him Bossman. And Bossman had left his wife and baby daughter behind. That little girl would never know her father, and the thought enraged Deveraux. She opened her eyes, felt the sting of tears, and said, "Lieutenant Commander Chen was . . . Bossman and I got close. Too close. And then he got himself killed." A tear slid down her cheek, damn it.

Blair rose, reaching out to comfort her.

She motioned him off, then backhanded the tears away. "Consider what you just saw classified."

He lowered his hand and smiled just enough to make her feel better. "Yes, ma'am. And can I ask you something?"

"That depends."

"You said that your parents were killed in the same war. Were they killed by Pilgrims?"

Her gaze searched his. "You want to know what side my family was on, is that it, Lieutenant?"

"Actually, I was wondering more about you." He looked at the cross.

"I don't know how they were killed. So the point is moot."

"Wouldn't you like to know?"

"I've already tried to find out. Those records were lost."

He looked to the holovid player. "Is that your cross?"

"Lieutenant, we're square. You saved my ass today. And I have a few things to finish here." She handed him the cross.

With a curt nod, he headed for the hatch.

"And Blair," she called after him. "Gerald's a clown."

His eyes thanked her.

Maniac lived to eat, to fly, and to have sex. Nothing profound about it. The food aboard the *Tiger Claw* wasn't half bad, the fighters, though patched up even more than some of his father's ships, weren't half bad, and the women, well, that was where the *Claw* really excelled.

"Are you *sure* he's not coming back?" Forbes asked, laying naked and sweaty beside him.

"Even if he does," Maniac said, still catching his breath, "I changed the hatch code. Besides, Blair's a bright boy. He'll find a place to sleep and leave us alone."

"But will he talk?"

"Blair?"

"I guess you're right." She rolled over and began sucking on his earlobe. "Come on, fire it up one more time."

He placed a palm on his bare chest, feeling his heart pumping overtime. "I think the Big Maniac needs time to refuel."

Forbes *tsk*ed. "C'mon, baby. Don't I take care of you?"

"That is a big yes, ma'am."

"Well, don't you care about my needs?" She climbed on top of him and finger-combed his hair.

"I'm all about your needs."

"Really?"

"Yeah. And right now you need to shut up and go to sleep."

She looked wounded, rolled off of him, then draped an arm over her eyes.

"You make it all worthwhile," he said earnestly.

"Make what worthwhile?"

"Busting my ass at the academy. Coming out here to fight. Saying good-bye to everyone back home."

"Yeah, I remember the briefing," she began, then dropped her voice to quote some Confed noncom. "By the time you return, everyone you know will be dead and buried."

He frowned. "I don't care about any of that."

"You lie. What about your family?"

"What about yours? In fact, you haven't told me anything."

"You haven't asked."

"Touché. So what's your story, uh, what did you say your name was?"

She slammed him with her pillow. "Like you want to know."

"Really. I do. Tell me about your parents. You got any brothers or sisters?"

"I'm an only child. When I left for the academy, my parents stopped talking to me. It was like I was dying, and they couldn't take a long illness. So they cut me off from the start. I haven't spoken to them in six years."

"Sorry. I was better off not asking."

"No, it's all right. I've come to terms with it. I understand why they did what they did. I think they're cowards, but I understand. Some day I am going to die out there. I've had premonitions for years. So I don't blame them anymore. I'm their baby, and there's nothing more painful than losing a child. Sometimes I wonder how they're doing. I wonder if my mother's still yelling at him for drinking too much beer and if he's still yelling at her for complaining."

"I don't think that'll change." Maniac rubbed the corners of his eyes. "Man, this conversation has gone all weepy on us. But thank God there's good news."

Her brow lifted.

He cupped his mouth and leaned into his shoulder. "Roger, Whiskey Halo Three. Refueling complete. The Big Maniac is back in business." He grabbed her shoulder and zeroed in for the kiss.

A rapid beeping sounded from the intercom, a tone Maniac recognized as the alert call.

"Shit," Forbes groaned. "This war's really starting to piss me off."

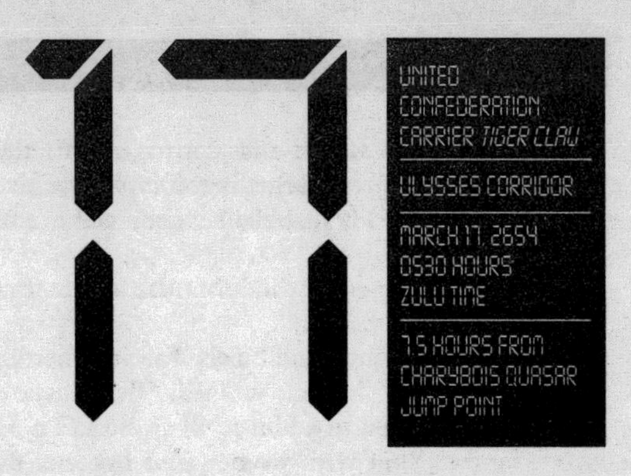

Blair finished a walkaround inspection of his Rapier, then joined the other pilots milling about the flight line, waiting for Lieutenant Commander Deveraux.

The nearby lift doors opened, exposing Maniac and Forbes, both still pulling on their uniforms. They hustled out of the lift as the others guffawed—all except Blair.

"Targets locked," he muttered, then set his jaw and marched toward Maniac. "Did you change the lock code?"

"What are you talking about?"

"The lock code on our hatch? I couldn't get in." He scowled at Forbes. "And I heard laughing from inside, but no one would answer."

Maniac slapped a paw on his shoulder. "Someday, Blair, you're gonna look back and say, 'God, I wish I'd been him.'"

"Some day, I'm going to look back and—"

"Ten-hut!" Knight shouted.

Blair abandoned his retort and scrambled to the line with the other jocks. They assumed the pose as Lieutenant Commander Deveraux walked down the row, her face unreadable. "All right, ladies, listen up. We have a ConCom with escorts. That means two, possibly three Ralari-class destroyers with their fighters and support ships. Primary target is the ConCom. Everything else is gravy." She paused before Blair. "Let's make 'em bleed. Mount up!"

The group dispersed, and Maniac said, "I'm feeling good today!"

"Try to keep your mind on the Kilrathi there, *Maniac*."

"C'mon, Blair," Maniac whined. "Be realistic . . ."

Though he hated to admit it, Blair did feel a pang of jealousy over Maniac's skill with women and fighters. But he felt even more jealous over Maniac's ability to turn fear into a source of amusement. Maniac flitted blithely through his life, neither suffering it nor apologizing for anything he did. People loved him. People loathed him. He couldn't care less.

Blair started for his fighter, passing Hunter, who, as usual, champed his cigar and brushed that long hair out of his face. Blair thought of wishing the man luck, but as he looked up, he saw how Hunter made a point of ignoring him, so he headed straight for his cockpit ladder.

"Blair," Deveraux called out. "Take Hunter's wing."

"I got his wing, ma'am."

Failing to remove his cigar, Hunter said, "Ma'am, I'd just as soon you assign me another wingman."

Deveraux came toward Hunter, who had inadvertently stoked the fire in her eyes. "You have some problem I should be aware of, Hunter?"

The big Australian sneered at Blair. "Yes, ma'am, I do. I don't fly with Pilgrims."

"Then maybe you don't fly at all."

"Ma'am, there might be over a hundred pilots assigned to this bucket, but I think you want me for this op. We both know that."

With disgust all but dripping from her face, Deveraux thought a second, then said, "Blair. You'll fly *my* wing."

"Are you sure about that?" he asked.

Her eyes snapped wide. "Did I just give you a suggestion or an order?"

"I got your wing, ma'am."

She tossed an ugly look in Hunter's direction, then left.

"Hey," Hunter said.

Blair hesitated.

"You put me or my shipmates in danger, half-breed, I'll kill you."

"You'll try." He stared unflinchingly at the man, then pounded up his ladder. "It's all one big lovefest," he said through a sigh.

Once everyone had preflighted, the comm check commenced. When Taggart's voice came over the channel, Blair couldn't help but dial up the captain's private frequency. "Sir, I didn't know you'd be flying this one. In fact, I didn't know you were qualified to pilot a Broadsword."

"Yeah, well, this mission needs a conscience, and I'm it. You keep your head low and your eyes bugged, Lieutenant."

"Count on it."

Wondering if there were any more surprises on the roster, Blair listened in as Knight, Hunter, Forbes, Polanski, Maniac, and Deveraux exchanged status reports. Knight flew the other Broadsword, and Polanski now took Hunter's wing. Maniac would, of course, fly with Forbes.

The launch went off without a hitch, save for Polanski's report of a hydraulic leak too insignificant to ground him.

Blair held a steady course at Deveraux's four o'clock low. They, along with the other Rapier pilots, escorted the two Broadswords. Originally designed as an attack bomber for Kilrathi capital ships, the Broadsword held its own as an all-purpose fighter, equipped with port, starboard, and aft turrets as well as four missile and four torpedo hardpoints. If a Broadsword got close enough to a capital ship (or in their present situation, a Kilrathi ConCom ship), its torpedoes would successfully penetrate phase shields. Thus, getting Taggart and Knight in close enough to the ConCom ship remained the foremost objective. Accomplishing that meant punching a hole through the Dralthi fighters surely awaiting them.

They came up fast on the ring of asteroids and debris orbiting the brown dwarf. Blair slid his HUD viewer into place and surveyed the zone with thermal scanners, finding it cool and clear. The strike force wove into the field, huge rocks and splintered durasteel tumbling by, some pieces just meters away.

"Picking up any comm traffic, Baker Seven?" Deveraux asked Taggart.

"Nothing."

"Let's get in a little closer."

"My words exactly," Maniac said.

"Shuddup," Polanski groaned. "Pervert."

"Secure that, ladies," Deveraux ordered.

"Com traffic still at zero," Taggart reported.

"They're observing radio silence," Deveraux said. "Except for short-range frequencies."

"Or they aren't here anymore," Taggart warned.

"Baker Two, Three, and Four," Deveraux called. "Anything?"

Blair scanned his radar display. "*Nada*, Chief."

"Nothing happening, Boss," Forbes said.

Maniac released an exaggerated hem. "My scope's clean, Commander."

"Dammit!" Hunter cried.

"What is it?" Deveraux demanded.

"Big piece of something just glanced off my canopy. Computer didn't course-correct in time."

"He's probably going nuts without his cigar," Polanski said. "He's having hallucinations of little dancing cigars."

Several pilots chuckled into the comm, but Blair knew better than to join them.

Then Maniac's masked face and big, round eyes lit up Blair's VDU. "All right, losers, listen up. I got three confirmed targets at five o'clock, near the brown dwarf."

"Confirm that," Forbes said. "Middle one has a massive electromagnetic signature."

Blair switched the radar report to his HUD. A grid formed at his twelve o'clock, with coordinates scrolling at its corners. The three blips advanced slowly through the lines. "Target number one, bearing one-two-five by three-four-five. Target number two, bearing one-two-six by three-six-six. Target number three, bearing one-three-zero by three-seven-seven. Intercept course locked and disseminating, roger."

"It's the ConCom," Deveraux said. "All right, ladies, deploy for attack. The clock is ticking."

"You all can hold back if you like," Maniac said as he leapt past the other Rapiers. "Maniac'll put these cats out for the night."

"Do *not* abandon your wingman," Deveraux said.

"Don't worry, Commander," Forbes said. "He's just having trouble keeping up with me." Then her Rapier shot off and razored past Maniac's, narrowly missing a long pipe that rolled end over end.

"Blair. Stay close. Here we go," Deveraux said.

"That's no ConCom," Taggart muttered, his voice barely perceptible. "Abort!"

"You're kidding," Maniac said.

"Baker Seven, you have no authority over this mission or its personnel," Deveraux barked. "You will obey my orders."

"Forget it. I've already analyzed those targets. They're Dorkir-class supply ships. They were deliberately left behind and out of harm's way."

"You're saying they want us to attack those freighters, then they'll ambush us?"

"Not us, Commander. The *Tiger Claw*. She's at risk. We have to get back."

"You're a civilian scout. Why should I—"

"Commander, I'm not a civilian."

"Mr. Taggart. I don't have time for—"

"I hold the rank of commodore in Confederation Naval Intelligence, reporting directly to Admiral Tolwyn. My call sign is Paladin."

"Yeah, right," Forbes said. "And I'm Admiral Nelson."

"Shuddup!" Blair said, intent on Taggart's revelation.

"My security verification code is Charlie Six Alpha Zebra Niner. Try it, Commander. Now."

Blair couldn't wait for Deveraux. He plugged the numbers

into his own computer's touchpad, attempting to tap into the Confederation Navy's Datanet. The left VDU blinked for a moment, then a message rolled across the screen:

> COMMODORE JAMES TAGGART
> CALL SIGN: PALADIN
> FOURTEENTH FLEET
> SECURITY ACCESS GRANTED

"Holy . . ." Blair lapsed into astonishment.

"Lucky guess," Deveraux told Taggart. "For all I know, you could've killed the real commodore and assumed his identity."

"Listen to me, Angel. That's all I ask. If I'm wrong, you'll have missed out on destroying a couple of freighters. If I'm right, the *Tiger Claw* could already be under attack."

"The *Claw* is already in the radiation belt, boss. They couldn't contact us if they wanted to," Forbes pointed out.

"Well, I ain't for turning tail," Hunter said. "I say we take out the freighters, *then* go back for the *Claw*."

"So we can pick through her rubble for survivors, Mr. Hunter?" Taggart asked.

"We're not taking a vote here," Blair said. "It's up to the commander. What do you say, ma'am?"

As Blair waited for her reply, he pictured the others doing the same. Forbes rubbed her eyes and wished she had spent more time sleeping. Polanski threw his head back and swore. Hunter damned regulations to hell, unclipped his O_2 mask, and stuffed an unlit cigar between his lips. Knight imagined with a shudder that a hundred fighters now buzzed over the *Claw*. Maniac itched with the desire to race forward and kick some Kilrathi butt. Taggart muttered a half-dozen "come on's" as precious seconds ticked by.

And Lieutenant Commander Jeanette Deveraux heaved a sigh and felt the absolute loneliness of her rank.

UNITED
CONFEDERATION
CARRIER *TIGER CLAW*

ULYSSES CORRIDOR

MARCH 17, 2654
0600 HOURS
ZULU TIME

7 HOURS FROM
CHARYBDIS QUASAR
JUMP POINT

Rolling Admiral Tolwyn's ring between his fingers, Captain Jay Sansky transported himself 700 light-years away from the bridge of the *Tiger Claw* and the Jovian-like system it now approached. He put himself back in his holopic, back on graduation day from the academy in Houston. He and Bill Wilson had driven out to the desert preserve with two bottles of champagne and four years' worth of memories . . .

"Was it really worth it?" Wilson asked, leaning on the hood of their borrowed military hover.

"For once the years didn't go by fast. God, the exams. The sacrifices. What did we do, Bill? Sell off our youth?"

Wilson roared with laughter. "I was talking about driving out here. We could've drank and said our good-byes at my place. But no, you wanted to come all the way out here to see your desert one more time. Well, here it is." He waved his bottle over the wind-swept sand, then took a long pull.

"Truth is, this might be the only thing left when I return. The people? They'll all be gone—and maybe the academy with them. I need something to come back to."

"Hang on to your memories. This planet might be gone." He raised his bottle to the sky. "There's a force out there much greater than our experience. And we think the stars are our destiny, Jay. I think we're wrong."

"Then why are you going?"

"I don't know. Maybe it's already too late to say no. Or maybe I just want to prove that we don't belong there."

Sansky lifted his own bottle in a toast. "Then here's to going—for whatever reasonand coming back."

"We're going to change the universe, Jay. I know that."

"Okay. But let's get drunk first."

A bead of sweat trickled down Sansky's forehead, as though he still stood in the desert's unforgiving heat. The mottled gas giant returned to view, two of its moons floating to port, a third peeking out behind the planet. A wing of Rapiers flew point, escorting the *Tiger Claw* through a broad series of rings composed of billions of water-ice particles and rock fragments ranging from 5,000 to about 79,000 kilometers away from the planet. Two other tenuous rings orbited much more distantly.

"This is Black Lion Seven to Pride One. Getting a lot of interference from the belt. Scope's clear, but I don't trust it, roger."

Sansky shifted to the comm console, where Lieutenant Commander Obutu stood at Comm Officer Sasaki's shoulder. The screen showed the reporting pilot, Major Jennifer Leiby, her eyes narrowed, her face cast in the blue glow of display units. "Copy that, Seven," Obutu said into his headset. "Continue the sweep, manual as necessary."

"Aye-aye, sir. Think I see something now. Wait a minute. Is that . . . Bogies inbound. I say again—" A burst of static stole her words. "I'm hit! I'm hit! Mayday!"

Through the viewport and out past the Jovian-like planet's third moon, a speck of light burned briefly.

"Who's reporting in?" Gerald asked, bursting onto the bridge.

"Major Leiby," Obutu answered. "But we've lost contact."

Gerald's lip twitched. "What?"

"I read multiple targets inbound!" Radar Tech Harrison Falk said. The twenty-year-old stood before his tall, transparent screen and looked to Sansky, his face stricken.

Sansky regarded the viewport as Gerald and Obutu strained for their own view.

Dozens of small, glinting dots—and three larger ones—materialized from the cover of the third moon.

As Sansky turned back, Falk had already begun plotting the enemy's course. Obutu shouted commands to the security patrol pilots. The helmsman pulled up an evasion course on his screen. Then Gerald bolted to his command chair, dropped into it, and, after a nod from Sansky, shouted, "Battle stations! Battle stations! Launch all fighters!"

Despite the bridge's frenetic energy, Sansky felt a strange calm settle over him. The enemy attack force charged toward them with only a wing of Rapiers to stop it, but his calm would not yield to fear. And that wasn't so strange, after all. It was the calm you feel while lying on the ice at the moment before freezing; the calm you feel while staring into the headlights of a massive transport about to strike you down; the calm you feel while surrendering to fate after too many years of fighting it. *Bill was right . . . Bill was right.*

"Get those goddamned flight doors open," Flight Boss Raznick shouted into the comm. He stood at his desk, glaring down through the Plexi at the techs running frantically about his deck.

"I'm on it, sir," a jittery Specialist Mistovski replied. "But the pressure's low on the left side. Once it's open, I don't know if we'll get it shut again."

"If we don't get it open, you won't . . . never mind! Just prioritize, young man. Prioritize!"

"Yes, sir."

"Peterson!" Raznick called.

"Here, sir."

"Are we clear yet?"

"I got one more tanker and another plow to move."

"Then why are you talking to me? Get on it!"

"Yes, sir!"

"Raznick? Where are my fighters?" Commander Gerald asked through the comm.

"They're hot. Ten seconds to clear."

"What's the delay?"

"Problem with one of the hangar doors, sir." Raznick looked to the doors, now yawning open. "But it's been resolved."

"Good. Let's see if you can beat your record."

"Aye-aye, sir!"

Raznick's record: six launches per minute. But that included preflighting. He flipped on the deckwide intercom. "Attention pilots. Quickshot launch procedures are now in effect. I want seven birds off my deck in one minute. Do you read me!"

"We read you, sir!"

Sansky took one more look at the wave of enemy ships, then retreated to the captain's console, where he watched the attack as though it were a holo. The security patrol engaged the incoming fighters, converting the gas giant's ring system into a furball more deadly than any he had ever witnessed. Dralthi fighters double- and triple-teamed Confederation Rapiers, while the enemy's Krant medium fighters darted like furtive wasps between ice and stone, vectoring toward the *Tiger Claw*. The viewports soon flooded with the images of individual dogfights, of fighters from both sides being run off-course to collide with asteroids. The carrier's eight dual laser turrets oscillated and sent shudders throughout the ship as they fired upon swooping targets while intermittently throwing up clouds of scintillating flak. Rapiers and Broadsword bombers arrowed away from the flight hangar to join the explosive fray, some torn to ribbons less than a kilometer from the ship and chain-detonating others.

Beyond the launching counterassault, on the fringe of the hastily drawn battle line, awaited the still-indistinct Kilrathi capital ships. Paused now so that their fighters could soften up the

Claw, they would soon spring for the kill.

"All fighters launched, sir," Obutu announced, his voice sounding hollow and several lifetimes away.

Someone touched Sansky's shoulder. "Sir?"

Gerald's concern, an emotion he rarely displayed, brought Sansky back to the bridge, to the memory of his rank, his job. All was not lost—or gained—yet. "Shields up!"

Obutu looked at him, puzzled. "Sir, shields already standing at maximum power."

"Good," Sansky said, unmoved by his redundant order. "Torpedo room. Prepare all tubes!"

"Got her down?" Spaceman Rodriguez asked, lifting his voice over the squeal of alarms that still echoed through the secondary ordnance room.

"Weapon is set," Galaway answered as he jogged toward her.

The torpedo sat on its loader, ready to slide smartly into its tube. Rodriguez threw open the hatch, then thumbed the autoloader switch. The loader hummed as it delivered its cargo. Once the weapon clicked into place, he closed the hatch and waved Galaway on to the next tube.

Rodriguez had been taught that the manual loading of torpedoes on capital ships, while seemingly archaic, not only resulted in an unparalleled level of safety but also upheld a centuries-long tradition of naval teamwork. And, Rodriguez thought, touching the torpedoes before they went out personalized the war; it put him on the front line instead of in the ship's bowels.

"Tired yet?" he asked Galaway.

"No way."

"Good. After we win this battle, let's you and I celebrate. We're going to salsa."

She grinned slyly. "You just want to dance?"

An automated voice rattled through the bridge's speakers: "Torpedo launch status: nominal."

"I count three dozen Kilrathi starfighters, two Ralari-class destroyers, and one dreadnought," Falk said, studying the holographic images on his display. "The cap ships are advancing at one hundred and twenty KPS. They'll be in firing range in four seconds."

Sansky glanced obliquely at Gerald. "That damned Taggart was right."

"Maybe he knew something that we didn't. And if he did, then I'll brig him for withholding information."

"Worry about your bruised ego later, Mr. Gerald. Helm. Come about."

"Torpedoes incoming!" Falk cried.

A pair of Kilrathi torpedoes trailing thin plumes of exhaust followed a lazy curve, then shot headlong at the carrier.

"Launch countermeasures," Sansky said.

Falk nodded as the chaff clouds illuminated his screen. "Countermeasures away and . . . shit, sir. Sorry, sir. Torpedoes still on course, targeting port bow."

"Sound the collision alarm," Sansky ordered Gerald. "Rig the ship for impact."

Slashing through shards of ice and fluttering rock chips, the projectiles increased velocity as they came within fifty kilometers of the ship. Forty . . . thirty . . .

"Oh, God," Falk moaned. "Impact in three seconds."

The first missile exploded over the carrier's phase shields, tossing up lightning-laced rainbows of energy and debris that fell mercilessly upon her superstructure. Sansky clung to his chair as the second torpedo hit, and the bridge seemed to wheeze as the bomb throttled it. Falk shouted something unintelligible. Gerald grunted. Obutu demanded a damage report even as the blast wave persisted.

Down on the flight deck, Specialist Jones rushed to his feet, then he and Olivia sprinted toward a half-full missile rack that had broken free from its bulkhead straps.

A second impact tossed them back to the deck, and the bulkheads seemed to clap with the volume and vigor of an enormous god. The rumble gave way to a piercing screech.

"Watch out!" Boss Raznick screamed over the intercom.

Jones stared into the faces of dozens of missiles as the entire rack that housed them fell forward. He threw himself back, fleeing crab-like as the three tons of explosives and durasteel hit the deck, missing him by a half-meter. The resulting concussion tossed him nearly as far away.

He looked around, chills rippling, heart slamming his ribs. Where was Olivia? *Ohmygod. Ohmygod.* "Olivia!"

"What?"

After a glance over his shoulder, Jones sighed.

"Gentlemen! I want a crane in there now!" Raznick said. "I want that rack up and battened down in ninety seconds!"

Jones gave Olivia a nervous stare, then got to his feet. "I'll be right back."

"You're kidding me. No way. Not now."

He charged toward the lift doors. "I'll be right back!"

Aftershocks reverberated through the bridge. Sansky caught his breath and said, "Do we have a reply, Mr. Gerald?"

"We do, sir. Give me a target, Mr. Falk."

"Target acquisition imminent," Falk said, his voice cracking. "We have a lock!"

Gerald beat a fist on his palm. "Fire tubes one and two!"

Like unleashed bloodhounds, the two torpedoes sped away from the carrier, drawing chalk lines across the Jovian rings.

"Captain, I have visual from a Rapier near the destroyers," Comm Officer Sasaki said.

"On my screen."

The Rapier pilot spiraled through an incredible hailstorm of flak and laser fire, hurling himself toward the enemy destroyer, then pulling a six-G climb to break away. The image switched to his aft turret as two torpedoes slammed into the destroyer's weak shields and penetrated her hull armor. Twin shock waves undulated through the ship's port side, dividing her amidships with underwater slowness. She spewed a huge, debris-laden gas bubble into the vacuum as hundreds of smaller explosions dotted her plastisteel innards. For a moment, Sansky thought he saw the Kilrathi themselves, giant bodies floating free and clawing for that green fog they breathed.

"Two direct hits, sir," Falk reported to cheers from the bridge crew.

The Rapier pilot kept broadcasting images, and Sansky slipped back into his alluring calm as the dreadnought turned parallel with the remaining destroyer.

Her tubes opened.

A pair of torpedoes lanced out.

There would be no stopping the Kilrathi now. *And a man*, Sansky thought, *must be true to his heart, especially at the end.* If he could manage that, then an apparent defeat would become a resounding victory. No one else would understand, but he would. And that was all that mattered.

Voices grew faint, muffled. Gerald shouted something about countermeasures. Falk's reply lacked hope. Then everyone screamed in unison as the enemy torpedoes struck a one-two punch across the phase shields.

Sansky rode the first shock wave, then fell to the deck as consoles crackled and smoked above him in a sudden choreography of chaos.

"Comm is off-line!" Sasaki exclaimed. "Rerouting bridge to secondary."

"The phase shield is suffering a forty percent failure," Obutu added. "Battery room reports a fire. Torpedo room reporting damage. Unable to launch."

Sparks danced on Sansky's shoulders as he climbed back into his chair. Just outside the viewport, the remaining Rapiers struggled to lure the dozens of Dralthi and Krant fighters away from the *Tiger Claw*.

"I'm reading eight more targets from behind the dreadnought," Falk said.

Gerald made a lopsided grin. "They're sending in reinforcements."

"We should be flattered," Sansky said. He opened a comm channel. "Torpedo room. Report."

Spaceman 2nd Class Rodriguez, his eyes red from the smoke pouring into the station behind him, leaned toward the camera. "Tubes three and four damaged, sir. Autoloaders not operational. And we can't get back to one and two. The bulkhead's collapsed."

"Get me one tube back online, son. Can you do that?"

"I'll try, sir."

"Jesus . . . we can't fire?" Gerald said, springing to his feet. "Mr. Obutu. See if Mr. Raznick can spare some people to form a damage control crew in Secondary Ordnance."

Obutu nodded and spoke quickly into his headset.

"Captain, scanning the cruiser," Falk said. "She's opening tubes."

"Of course she is," Sansky said calmly. "Of course she is." A shadow fell over him. He gazed into Gerald's solemn face. "Commander?"

"The situation is dire, sir. If we're going to die, I suggest we ram this ship straight up their asses."

"That's a brave if not eloquent thought, Mr. Gerald. But we'll never get in that close."

"So we wait here to die?"

"Watch that tone, Mister."

"For God's sake, Captain. *Jay*. Let's go down fighting."

"I agree, sir," Obutu said, then looked to Gerald. "Damage control crew on its way to the secondary ordnance room."

"Gentlemen. I have no intention of dying. Rolling over and playing dead . . . maybe."

UNITED
CONFEDERATION
CARRIER *TIGER CLAW*

ULYSSES CORRIDOR

MARCH 17, 2654
0630 HOURS
ZULU TIME

6.5 HOURS FROM
CHARYBDIS QUASAR
JUMP POINT

"Mr. Obutu? Prepare to power down the entire ship," Gerald said, sliding back into his command chair.

"Power down the ship. Aye-aye, sir." A layer of sweat dappled Obutu's face, but his voice did not waver.

Sansky, noting the renewed hope in his crew, rose to pace the bridge. He did not share their faith in the plan, despite having suggested it. Powerless and adrift, the *Tiger Claw* would become an object of curiosity to the Kilrathi. The dreadnought's captain might bring his ship in close enough for the *Claw* to launch a sudden, point-blank torpedo—providing that Mr. Rodriguez and the DCC got a tube back online.

Or, as Sansky more likely figured, the big cat would note the power-down, bare his fangs, and, without a second thought, blow the *Tiger Claw* into a memorial.

"Captain," Sasaki called excitedly. "I'm getting a friend or foe acknowledge from the new starfighters. They're ours, sir."

"It's Deveraux's strike force," Sansky said, guarding his emotions. The tide had still not turned.

But Gerald smiled back at the opportunity. "Mr. Obutu. Belay that power-down. And find out how that DCC is doing in Secondary Ordnance."

"Aye, sir."

Flying in wedge formation, Deveraux's fighters, still just pin-pricks of light, soared in behind the Kilrathi dreadnought and destroyer. For a moment, Sansky wished he were in one of those cockpits, responsible only for himself and his wingman, able to sit straight and tall, the crosses of command gone forever.

As a half-dozen targets presented themselves in Blair's HUD, instinct drove his gloved finger over the primary weapons trigger. He listened intently for the order to break and attack.

Deveraux hadn't said much since giving in to Taggart's pleas. They had returned to the *Claw* at full throttle, and when Forbes had sighted the destroyer and dreadnought, an odd mixture of relief, regret, and anticipation had filtered into the voices of Blair's comrades. Taggart had been right, but being right meant that the *Tiger Claw* had already faced a more powerful force sans some of her best fighter pilots. Although Blair and company would now join the party, the *Claw* hardly stood a chance.

"All right, ladies. All Rapiers except Maniac and Blair engage those Dralthi."

Blair bit back a curse. "Commander, I didn't come out here as an observer."

"Relax, Lieutenant. Drama equals danger plus desire, and it's about to become dramatic."

"See you later, nugget," Forbes told Maniac.

"Watch your ass, Rosie."

"Thought you had that covered," Blair said, unable to resist the barb yet wincing just the same.

The rest of the strike force peeled off in pairs to confront the Dralthi fighters streaking in at the wing's one o'clock low. Spiraling missiles and criss-crossing laser bolts produced a dense, expanding web that promised to snag any pilot who broke rhythm or got cocky. One look at the gauntlet instantly humbled Blair, and he grew fascinated by the sight of so many fighters dogging each other, grazing each other, navigating through a tangled mess of technology splayed across the otherwise simple, unassuming vacuum.

The furball had been born.

"Broadswords, follow me in," Deveraux said, her stony gaze infectious.

"Roger that," Taggart responded. "Beginning the bomb run."

"Maniac? Blair?" she called. "Cover us."

Wrenching her Rapier into a forty-five-degree turn, Deveraux raced under and ahead of the Broadswords. The bombers throttled up and swept in behind her. She rolled to level off, spearheading the quintet.

Blair had difficulty judging his distance. He yo-yoed to Taggart's seven o'clock after accidentally riding the crest of his wash. Recovered, he guided his targeting reticle over a distant fighter launching from the destroyer's forward flight deck. A beep told him he had the lock, and his thumb slammed down the secondary weapons button. Rays of simulated sunlight passed over his canopy as an Image Recognition missile let loose from his wing. Two more missiles joined his as Maniac fired upon another Dralthi rising from the dreadnought.

"And here comes the flak barrage," Deveraux said.

The capital ships' big turrets spat and coughed up triple-A fire that hung like handfuls of cotton balls tossed in zero G. And worse, the dreadnought's torpedo tubes opened to fire a salvo at the *Tiger Claw*, whose deck shields already cushioned rounds from dozens of strafing Dralthis.

Blair flipped his gaze to the image coming in from his missile. It finally reached, identified, and sliced the enemy fighter in two. Semicircular wings spun away to collide with the destroyer in a copper-colored shimmer.

Concurrently, Maniac's missiles kicked over a trio of Dralthis, two striking directly, a third falling prey to his wingman's fireball.

Maniac's face popped up on Blair's left VDU. "Three more kills for the Maniac, folks." Then he turned his head and sobered. "Hey, man. Look!"

A mere kilometer stood between the *Tiger Claw* and the four Kilrathi torpedoes.

From his position, Blair could do no more than watch.

Weakening phase shields, twenty-one centimeters of armor plating, and three meter-wide hull compartments stood between Engineer Davies and the void.

He never saw the torpedo coming.

It burrowed through the shields, impaled the twenty-one centimeters of armor, then exploded with a force that hammered through the hull compartments, bending durasteel like taffy.

Thrown a half-dozen meters across the engineering deck, Davies landed with a sharp thud and heard his arm crack. Broken. Then a whoosh filled his ears, rising into a wolf's howl as recycled air fled through a tremendous breach in the hull. A hand slapped his back, gripped his uniform. He craned his head to see big Oxendine, the engineer who could smell fear. He clutched a turbine ladder and began wresting Davies toward it. Davies looked at the man, wondering why he bothered.

But Oxendine's determination trivialized the animosity between them. In his gaze Davies saw no more than a man trying to save him. And for a second he felt good, really good about the company he had kept, about his faith in others, about his significance. Some people never knew that much.

A long tongue of fire licked across Oxendine's arm. His grip on the ladder faltered, fingers straining against searing heat until—

Davies thought he heard Oxendine shout, but he couldn't be sure. He tumbled several meters across the deck, then felt his arms and legs dangle in midair. A blunt object struck his back, another his leg. He tried to breathe. Tried. After a quick glance to the still and distant stars, he shut his eyes and waited for it to happen.

Sansky's command console tore apart, and a jagged section flew up at him before he could block it. His head snapped back as the bulky panel struck his forehead so hard that he swore it had torn a chunk out of his skull. His face, once sticky with sweat, now felt warm and slippery. He lay back on his chair, his neck growing numb, his breath ragged. He fought to lift a hand to his face, but the effort felt too great. He took in a bit of smoky air, coughed, then felt as though he were spinning through the chair.

Behind him, Obutu's voice penetrated the bass-drum booming of lower-deck explosions. "The hull has been breached at level three. Steering loss: eighty percent. Drone repair crew activated. Estimated recovery time: six minutes."

"Sir?" Gerald asked, standing somewhere nearby. "Sir? Medic! Medic to the bridge."

"Gerald," Sansky managed, gurgling blood. "What's Deveraux doing?"

"Blair? How's our six?" Deveraux asked.

"Clear for the moment," he replied, not that his report really mattered. The radar display—a living, breathing thing—could change in a heartbeat.

The proof lay in front of him as four Salthi light fighters broke from their box formation to intercept the bombers. Blair tracked their velocity at nearly one thousand KPS, their afterburners stoked. Forward-swept wings fixed to their broad, flat fuselages in an inverted V pattern gave the fighters a low profile while maintaining a respectable level of intimidation through design. One Salthi didn't pose a huge threat to a Rapier. But like killer bees, if you faced enough of them, they would drop you through attrition.

A Dumb-fire missile flared below Deveraux's starboard wing, then went from zero to 850 KPS in three seconds—enough time for the Salthi pilot she had targeted to curse her, beg for Sivar's forgiveness, then experience a more corporeal wrath.

As Deveraux's Salthi vanished in a short-lived conflagration, the fighter nearest it scissored across Blair's field of view. He dove after the Salthi, lined up on its six o'clock, then fixed his cross-hairs on the green circle leading the fighter. Target locked! He dished out a flurry of bolts from his rotating nose cannon. The first salvo struck the Salthi's shields, crooked fingers of energy scattering across a light blue hemisphere. Another volley stitched a pattern across the Salthi's cockpit, and the ship flipped into a barrel roll before bursting apart.

"Hey! Save some for me," Maniac said.

Pulling up from the Salthi's still-flashing rubble, Blair saw Maniac shoot off the third Salthi's wing. The cat inside fought for control but couldn't help spinning into the fourth Salthi flying toward it. A white-hot fireball enveloped both fighters.

Maniac howled with glee. "Buy one, get one free!"

Cannon fire from the cap ships scoured Blair's path as he strained to regroup with the bombers. He jammed the stick forward, plunging in a sixty-degree dive to evade.

But the autotracking systems aboard the cap ships refused to abandon their quarry. The thick, deadly bolts returned, raking space along his Rapier's portside.

"It's getting too hot," Deveraux said. "It's up to the bombers. Let's get back out there."

Blair pulled up, flying below the bombers, then banked hard on a new heading for Deveraux's six. He switched to his aft turret camera and watched the bombers zero in on the destroyer's starboard bow.

"Thanks for the escort," Taggart said, then addressed Knight, who had assumed point for the run. "Steady on course. Wait for them to drop shields and open tubes."

Triple-A and tachyon fire clogged the space around the bombers as their defense computers automatically released clouds of chaff and decoy missiles. Three of the destroyer's turreted cannons went after the countermeasures, but the others spat their venom at Taggart and Knight. The lightning of reflected rounds writhed across their shields. Blair couldn't believe that they held course. The wall of Triple-A began terrifying him, and he wasn't alone in that feeling.

"They're throwing up too much flak!" Knight screamed. His Broadsword's starboard wing grazed the expanding edge of a Triple-A cloud. Rivets popped as the wingtip tore off, violently rocking the bomber. "I'm hit!"

"Almost there," Taggart said, trying to calm the man. "Steady now. Steady."

Tachyon fire chewed into Knight's Broadsword, tearing open its belly to expose its synthetic bowels. Knight released a strangled cry as the bomber, now engulfed in flames, shattered across the destroyer's bow.

Taggart veered away from the flickering aftermath and vanished from Blair's screen.

In the meantime, Deveraux had engaged a pair of Krant fighters, who braked hard to get on her six. Blair guided his Rapier about 800 meters above the destroyer, then circled back to assist her. She wove left and right, dodging pairs of laser bolts, her tactics tight, efficient, practiced—but not enough against two Kilrathi pilots. The cats struck direct hits, and her shields glittered as bolts dissipated over them. A few more strikes and they would have her.

On full afterburners, Blair roared up behind the two Krants. Before he could lock a target, Deveraux pulled into a six-G loop parallel to his position. She leveled off and liberated a pair of IR missiles. One Krant swallowed a projectile, but the other blew chaff and pulled into a loop of his own. Deveraux's missile took the bait, detonating harmlessly.

Blair craned his neck to spot the Krant, now on Deveraux's tail, cutting loose a dense storm of fire. Her shields absorbed a half-dozen rounds before dying. Bolts passed over her canopy, each one tightening the gap as the cat adjusted its bead.

Narrowing his gaze, Blair locked on to the Krant, then lost the lock as Deveraux banked sharply. He considered firing but without a lock, friendly fire might do her in. Instead, he dove beneath them, his glance shifting between the radar display and the cap ship fire that seemed to lace up the space below. He yanked the stick back, thundering into a hard climb. Directly ahead stood the Krant, with Deveraux just off its starboard quarter. The targeting brackets in his HUD found the Krant, as did the smart targeting reticle.

Envisioning himself as a durasteel dragon, Blair incinerated the enemy fighter with a combination of laser and neutron fire. He spiraled up through the rubble to emerge just as Deveraux doubled back.

"What took you so long?" she asked.

"I took the scenic route," he said, glancing down at the dreadnought. "Where's Taggart?"

Maniac broke into the channel. "No visual contact. The son of a bitch booked."

"And that dreadnought's opening her tubes," Deveraux said.

Indeed, the huge vessel's tubes dilated open, and Blair beat a fist on his canopy. "Their shields are going down. We could've had them now."

The dreadnought's bow, shaped like two pairs of clamps forming a cross, raised as she passed over the first destroyer's wreckage. From one hundred meters below, the destroyer's tattered hull still glimmered, conduits jutting out like jagged teeth amid coils of lingering gas.

And from within that gas and those teeth, a ship appeared, a Broadsword, maneuvering thrusters firing to turn it up toward the dreadnought. "Baker leader. Get your fighters clear of the pulse wave," Taggart said.

"Roger that. Maniac? Blair? Break contact. Return to ship," Deveraux ordered.

Unsure of how Taggart would get himself clear of the pulse wave himself, Blair obeyed orders, lined his navigational crosshairs on the distant dot of the *Tiger Claw*, and started toward it, though only at half-speed. He focused his attention on Taggart, who flew bravely toward the dreadnought.

James "Paladin" Taggart lifted a shaky hand to fire the Broadsword's two piggyback torpedoes. Then he touched another button, releasing the other two bombs from their belly racks. HUD reports indicted that all four of the mighty rockets had targeted the unshielded dreadnought.

Holding his breath, he lit the afterburners and climbed away from the cap ship, Triple-A and cannon fire punching holes in his vaporous wake. His gaze locked on the scrolling numbers showing his distance relative to the target. He began to shake his head. Then a proximity alarm beeped. He looked up to spot the Jovian-like planet's third moon, its heavily cratered surface lowering into view.

The torpedoes struck the dreadnought.

A nanosecond later, the entire Area of Operations stood under a tarp of intense white light for one, two, three seconds . . .

The light dimmed to unveil a huge explosion tearing through the dreadnought, its hull breaking up as the widening rings of the blast wave stretched into space.

Caught unaware, the Kilrathi aboard the destroyer attempted to maneuver their vessel away from the wave, but the ship tacked only a few degrees before the inevitable force hit. The destroyer listed badly to port, then collided with the first destroyer's hull, producing fires amidships that began cooking off its ammunition. An internal blast erupted through its hull, breaking off the bow in a fountain of sparks and jetting gas.

Taggart's grin didn't last long as he tracked the wave encroaching on his airspace. It swallowed his exhaust, seemed to gain momentum, then struck his engines.

Displays crackled, fried, and went dead as the Broadsword groaned and took its beating. The bomber rolled onto its side, driving Taggart's head into the console. He felt the sting of a gash, and blood trickled into his eye. Blinking, he saw that the ship now barreled uncontrollably toward the moon. He seized the manual eject lever and jerked it down.

After a double click and a faint blast of air, the cockpit ejection pod shot free, slowly rotating away from the doomed bomber, ushered to the fringes of the weakening shock wave by sputtering retros.

The Broadsword impacted with the moon's surface in a cloud of ancient dust that would take days to settle.

Before Taggart could regain full control of the pod, he found himself caught in the third moon's gravitational pull. Rocking to and fro, he increased retros and tried to pull up from the cratered uplands. The retros teased him for a moment, then whooped and fell silent. He threw a toggle several times, trying to reactivate them. "Well, it was fun while it lasted."

As the gray-and-white surface hurtled toward him, he told himself that he had lived a glorious life, that while he had never been an Arthur or a Roland, he rested assured that he had inspired a young heart or two. And, he reasoned, by influencing just one soul, he had, in effect, changed the course of history. James Taggart had accomplished what he had set out to do. He had lived the warrior's life and would die the warrior's death.

Nothing could be more fitting.

He grinned, remembering a few lines from his schooldays: "My mind misgives some consequence, yet hanging in the stars, shall bitterly begin his fearful date with this night's revels . . ."

Thrown forward by a sudden, brutal jerk, Taggart grimaced, but that expression turned to surprise as he realized that the ejection pod no longer plunged toward the moon.

Or had he already struck the moon, died, and been sent to some purgatorial state wherein he would repeatedly relive his own death? Relive his own death. There was an oxymoron . . .

He touched his cheek. No, he felt real. The rest of his senses concurred. He spotted the faint illumination of a tractor beam hugging the pod's hull.

Then a Rapier descended beside the pod, and Taggart read the pilot's name along the cockpit's edge: Lt. Christopher Blair. The young man held his hand in a salute, which Taggart returned.

"You're bleeding, sir," Blair said.

Taggart touched the gash in his forehead. "And you had an order to retreat."

"Which I obeyed."

"Then why are you here?"

"Uh, I got lost, sir. Came looking for directions."

"Mr. Blair. Pilgrims never get lost."

⊠ ⊠ ⊠

Maniac's smile withered as the remaining Kilrathi fighters regrouped and began retreating behind the planet's moons. All but one of those pilots needed to die. The cat left alive would warn every clan of Maniac's fury. Maniac would become a legend among the Kilrathi, his picture posted in pilots' berths: Have you fought against this hairless ape? This foul-smelling being is the empire's most wanted pilot.

But none of that would happen unless Maniac went after the fleeing cats. "Hey, Rosie? You want some more?"

The VDU flickered, and she appeared, lifting her brow. "Like you have to ask?"

They gunned their Rapiers in a sudden U-turn, chasing after the Krant, Salthi, and Dralthi fighters still in the open.

"ETA to catville: five seconds," Maniac said through a returning grin.

"Baker One to all Baker pilots. Return to base. Repeat. Return to base."

Maniac fired a look of disgust at Lieutenant Commander Deveraux before her image went dark in his VDU. Luckily for him, his mask concealed the look. He eased on his throttle and held course.

"Maniac?" Forbes called in a warning tone.

"Hey. What about my needs?"

"Your needs? We just received—" She never finished.

Two Dralthi fighters that had been trailing the pack pulled up and away from their wing. Like mechanized manta rays, they swung around to target Maniac and Forbes.

"They'll try to ram," Forbes said, one Dralthi rushing straight for her. "Guess they don't wanna play nice." She opened up with everything she had, tearing the fighter into scraps of superheated plastisteel.

The second Dralthi aimed for Maniac, and the enemy pilot's disgusting mug suddenly spoiled Maniac's display. If that weren't enough, the computer translated its taunt. "You will bleed for Sivar, you ignorant descendant of monkeys!" The cat widened its urine-colored eyes.

Maniac let out a snort. "Tell Sivar he can kiss my ass." Then he switched to Forbes's channel. "Watch this, Rosie."

Putting the proverbial pedal to the metal, Maniac howled as the afterburners threw him back. He centered his targeting reticle over the Dralthi—but he had no intention of firing. A collision alarm blared.

Distance: 1,000 meters.

"Shoot him, Maniac!" Forbes hollered. "Open fire!"

700 meters.

"Warning. If you do not alter your present course—" Maniac switched off the computer warning.

500 meters.

He brought up the aft turret view and saw Forbes trailing at his five o'clock high.

"What are you waiting for, Maniac?"

"For him."

300 meters.

"Shoot him. Or I will!"

"It's all in the timing . . ."

100 meters.

Forbes fired over Maniac's shoulder, but the bolts fell wide.

50 meters.

"Pull out!"

"Not yet."

30 meters.

Realizing that the Kilrathi pilot had no intention of changing course and every intention of dying, Maniac rolled the Rapier to starboard. He express-delivered a volley of laser fire that stitched its way across the fighter's cockpit, mortally wounding the cat inside.

With only centimeters between them, the two fighters passed, the Dralthi now trailing nutrient gas and tumbling toward—

"Rosie!" Maniac cried. "Shit. Pull up!"

Her Rapier's nose lifted a few degrees.

Not enough.

The Dralthi's wings acted like the blades of a fan to tear

spark-lit gashes in her fighter's starboard side and belly. Forbes jerked the Rapier in an attempt to pull away, but the impact forced her into a roll that suddenly evolved into a flat spin. She throttled up to recover, flying straight but bobbing on invisible waves. One of her thrusters had been sheared away, and escaping fluids streaked her fuselage.

Maniac descended to form on her wing. "Rosie. Can you hold her?"

"I could fly this thing and cook you breakfast." Interference crept into her signal as her malfunctioning comm system promised to shut down. She had some control, but the Rapier wobbled and veered dangerously close to Maniac.

"Hey, quit showing off," he said, then widened the distance between them.

"Impressive, huh?"

"Eject. I'll tractor you in."

"You'd like that, wouldn't you? The ejection system is fried."

He took in a deep breath. "Just stay with me, Rosie. We'll do it together."

Ten minutes later, they neared the carrier's scorched flight deck.

"Oh, man," Maniac said, responding to the devastation.

"The ship looks worse than I do after a three-day shore pass," she said.

Maniac struggled to find just one section of the *Tiger Claw* that did not bear the wounds of combat. A gaping hole had been torn in her engineering deck. Her superstructure bore the jagged scars of hundreds of laser bolts and debris pitched off from explosions. Most of her dishes and antennae had been hacked away. Wrecked fighters from both sides floated near her upper decks, turning them into a labyrinth of graveyards. She limped through space, barely lit, her intimidating presence now tucked into her damaged recesses.

"Say, honey?" Maniac said. "Let's find another hotel. This place is a dive."

"Yeah, but she's the only dive in town."

He sighed. "Baker Three and Four to Flight Control. We're coming in for a side-by-sider. Clear away everything that ain't bolted down."

Boss Raznick, his beefy face hanging tiredly, replied, "Roger that, Baker Three and Four. Clear to land, SBS."

He and Forbes now flew level with the flight deck, bound for the translucent energy field and the flight hangar beyond. He tossed a look to Forbes. Bad idea. The sight of her bobbing Rapier turned his blood icy. He checked their speed and approach vector. "We're coming in too hot."

"Sorry, but my brakes are in the shop."

"Line it up," he said, unable to smile, his gaze riveted on her fighter. "That's it."

"Piece of cake. Just like before."

"Except that you're right-side up." Now he managed a fleeting grin.

"I knew something was wrong."

Through his HUD viewer, Maniac watched the deck rush toward them. "Almost there."

Her wingtip tapped a wall abutting the deck, but she wrestled the fighter straight as tiny groans escaped her lips.

"Okay. Easy. Just ease it in," he said. "Thirty meters."

"I . . . I love it when you . . . talk dirty." She could barely speak through her exertion. Her fighter lost power and fell behind his.

"Ten meters," he said as his own landing skids lowered and he glided over the flight deck, the energy curtain widening to fill his display. "Just five . . ." He trailed off as he realized her approach had gone awry. "Pull up! Pull up!"

But she didn't. She couldn't. Her port wing got caught on the flight deck's lip, and she started to flip over as the wing tore off and boomeranged away. The Rapier struck the deck with a gut-wrenching thunderclap, crushing her canopy. Shards of Plexi floated away as the fighter scraped along the runway, then spun out to a halt, snapping off the remaining engine, which rolled ahead of it.

Maniac frantically guided his Rapier through the energy field, then released his canopy before even landing. He could care less where he put down the fighter and wound up narrowly missing a wall of storage containers dead ahead because his hands weren't on the steering yoke; they were on his harness, throwing off buckles. He climbed onto the Rapier's wing, then leapt off, bolting toward the hangar entrance, toward Rosie.

Someone familiar shouted his name. Shouted again. Loud footsteps. Then someone collided with him, arms wrapping around his chest, forcing him to the deck. He fell forward, bracing his fall, not bothering to look up at his assailant, his gaze consumed by the wreckage just behind the force field.

"She's outside the airlock!" Blair screamed. "You go through the force field and you're Jell-O."

Maniac sprang to his feet. "Get me a suit! Get me a suit!" He started for the field as Blair seized his collar, holding him just a meter away. With the energy curtain so close that he could hear its hum, Maniac shivered as he realized that were it not for Blair, his panic would have driven him through it. He winced, staring at the twisted Rapier, then hollered, "Rosie! Rosie!" He could see her helmet, partially obscured by the shattered canopy. She did not move.

Sharp-angled shadows began wiping over the wreckage, cast by the half-dozen Rapiers circling overhead, waiting to land.

"Forbes? Rosie?" Deveraux called, her voice piped through the deckwide intercom. "Can you hear me? Rosie? Answer. Just key your mike, if you can. Come on, girl. Just one little click."

Maniac looked to the overhead speakers, waiting, waiting.

"I've got approximately ninety seconds of fuel left, Commander," Hunter said.

"Ditto for me," Polanski added.

"Rosie?" Deveraux's voice echoed hollowly through the hangar. Still no response. "Baker Leader to Flight Control. Clear that wreckage."

A sudden tightness gripped Maniac's throat, and he found it hard to breathe. "What?"

The roar of an engine startled him. He turned back to see a huge yellow deckdozer with a wide blade affixed to its nose come rumbling toward them. Its operator, seated behind a polarized windshield, blew a horn, and they dodged out of its way.

Maniac ran across the deck and looked up to the Flight Control windows. "Hey! What are you doing? Hey!" He spotted the grim-faced Raznick and began waving his arms. "Hey! You can't do this! You can't do this. Please! Stop! She's alive!"

The deckdozer neared the energy curtain and lowered its blade. Maniac abandoned his pleas and sprinted after the truck, determined to rip its driver from the cab. He came up hard on the driver's side, launched himself toward the cab door—

But Blair tackled him from behind, and they both rolled to the deck as the dozer disappeared with a ripple of energy.

Blair pinned Maniac and shouted, "There's nothing you can do."

"Get off of me, you Pilgrim son of a bitch!" Maniac struck a roundhouse to Blair's mouth. As Blair reached for the wound, he broke his grip, and Maniac squirmed away, heading back to the curtain.

"Are you going to kill yourself, too?" Blair asked, then dove for Maniac's legs, bringing him down.

Unable to break Blair's hold, Maniac lay there, panting and horrified as the deckdozer plowed Rosie's starfighter to the edge of the runway. The vehicle slowed, inching Rosie toward oblivion. Finally, the Rapier tipped over the side and tumbled slowly away, into space.

Maniac lowered his head, eyes tightly closed. His insides turned to vacuum.

"Baker Leader to Flight Control," Deveraux called solemnly. "Request permission to land."

Still in a haze of disbelief, Maniac sat on the deck, back to a bulkhead, legs pulled into his chest. He watched the Rapiers land, and with each touchdown, he thought he saw Rosie flashing him a thumbs-up.

He studied the others, hoping he would spot her just behind them. Polanski climbed out of his cockpit. Hunter tore off his helmet and brushed the sweat from his forehead. Taggart sat on the nose of his Broadsword's ejection pod, a medic attending to his forehead. Deveraux trudged down her cockpit ladder and turned back to face everyone.

"Come on," Blair said, kicking his boot. Maniac's friend had not left his side.

"What's there to debrief?" Maniac asked. "We went out, and two good pilots got killed. Not that these people know how to grieve." Then he tensed, stood, and joined Blair.

He would make them remember Rosie. Even if it killed him.

"Lieutenant Marshall," Deveraux began. And she could stop there. Maniac knew where this was going. "You disobeyed a direct order to return to base."

"I was—"

"Which, during wartime, is considered treason and punishable by death. Hunter? Give me your sidearm."

Hunter exchanged a worried glance with Polanski as he withdrew his pistol.

Blair took a step toward them. "Hunter, put the gun away."

"She's the CO, nugget."

After a nod, Blair lunged toward Hunter, but Polanski intervened, driving his shoulder into Blair's chest. Much larger than Blair, Polanski had little trouble sliding behind his opponent. He locked Blair's arms to his sides.

Deveraux accepted the gun and raised it to Maniac's head.

Part of Maniac wanted to shout "Do it!" but another part believed she would.

"What's with you?" Blair cried. "It was a stupid accident. He has to live with it."

"Or maybe I don't," Maniac said with a solid note of resignation. He stared into the cold wasteland of Deveraux's eyes. Rosie had been her friend, too. How could she remove herself so thoroughly from what had just happened? His gaze drifted to the gun's shaking muzzle.

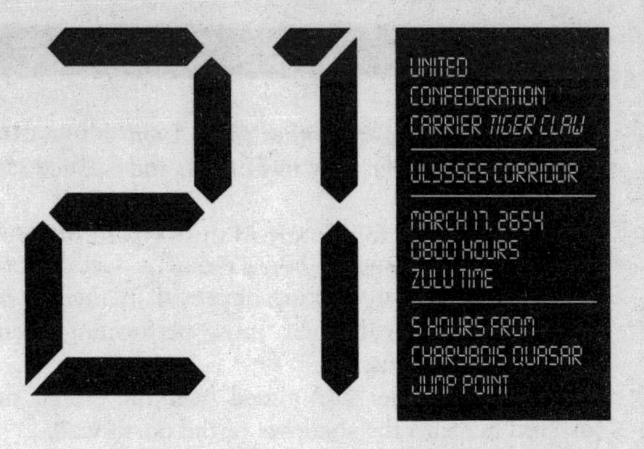

Captain Sansky had sustained a concussion from the blow to his head. And worse, on his way to sickbay, he had suffered an acute myocardial infarction that had rendered him unconscious. Commander Gerald now assumed command of the *Tiger Claw*. No stranger to the job, Gerald threw himself wholeheartedly into the challenge. Without Sansky's interference, he felt certain he could save the carrier from another onslaught, one that would surely finish her.

During the attack, Sansky had seemed strangely remote and indecisive. The Jay Sansky Gerald knew would have led them headfirst into the fray while barking orders and inspiring his officers to find an inner strength they never knew they possessed.

But the old man had shut down, and Gerald refused to believe that fear had caused that. In combat, fear could turn a man's mind to water that would pour out of his ears. No, something else troubled the captain, and the captain's preoccupation left Gerald uneasy.

As he focused on the images coming in from the *Claw's* tactical scanners that were being displayed on the helmsman's console, he cleared his mind of everything but the task at hand: finding cover from the Kilrathi battle group headed toward them.

Pictures from the Jovian-like planet's second moon revealed a string of deep craters, one of them large enough to conceal the carrier. "There," Gerald said, pointing at the screen. "Put her down there."

The helmsman touched a key, locked in the course, and the carrier lurched forward. For a moment, Gerald looked to Falk, Sasaki, and Obutu, seeking approval in their expressions. All were too busy with their jobs, performing them admirably despite their exhaustion.

Once the carrier had glided over the crater, the helmsman lowered her into the shadows of the north wall.

"I think it's time for that power-down, Mr. Obutu," Gerald said.

"No problem, sir. Most of our systems are down anyway."

Gerald spared a smile over that irony. "Is the decoy ready?"

"Yes, sir."

"Very well. Launch the decoy."

"Launch the decoy. Aye-aye, sir."

After a thump, the decoy blasted away from the carrier. Gerald tracked its progress on a monitor. Long antennae extended from its circular hull, while a pair of dishes began rotating. The drone slowed a moment to compute its bearings, then fired thrusters and aimed for the Jovian-like planet's ring system.

Gerald turned his head at the approach of Taggart and Deveraux. He noted a hint of surprise in their expressions as the bridge lights faded, then winked out.

"Decoy away, Commander," Obutu reported. "Systems nominal. She has a bigger electronic signature than the *Concordia*. I think she'll fool them, sir."

"I hope you're right. Secure all active scanners. Passive systems only." He dropped into the captain's chair and looked up to a bank of scanners above the forward viewport.

The first moon hung in the right corner of one display, and as Gerald studied it, he noticed tiny fluctuations in its glow. Then part of that glow seemed to burn off and materialize into brilliant dots. One after another the moon shed those dots, and they spread into a triangular formation.

"There," Obutu said. "The Kilrathi battle group."

Rapt by the image, Gerald felt his mouth falling open. Never had he been so close to so many Kilrathi ships. They stood at the eye of a sleeping giant.

"They've missed us," Mr. Falk said anxiously from his radar screen. He smiled broadly. "They're following the decoy."

The crew cheered. Even Gerald mouthed a "Yes!"

"Quiet!" Taggart shouted, startling everyone back into silence.

From that silence rose a steady beeping from one of Falk's passive radar detectors.

"I know that signature," Taggart said, charging toward the radar station. "It's a destroyer . . . hunting for us."

As if on cue, the beeping increased in pitch and rhythm. Falk's eyes bugged out. "They've spotted us!"

"No," Taggart said, his gaze shifting from the radar screen to the bank of scanners behind it. "We're still close enough to the radiation belt. Gamma rays are clouding their screens. If they don't see us, they won't find us."

Gerald found cold comfort in Taggart's assurance as the beeping grew more insistent. Out of habit, he swung his chair toward Mr. Falk, about to demand the destroyer's position.

However, with the scanners down they were blind. He swung the chair back, then the deck lifted sharply.

"Did you feel that?" Deveraux asked, shifting to his side.

His chair shook as another vibration passed under the ship. He gritted his teeth and puffed air. "Shit. They're nuking every crater. Methodical bastards."

As though they had heard the insult, the Kilrathi released another bomb, whose shock wave rumbled through the carrier like a thousand ancient cavalrymen.

"The next one will hit us," Deveraux said.

"Or it won't," he countered. "We're not moving."

Taggart placed his hand on Deveraux's shoulder and gently eased her back. "Mr. Gerald is right, Commander. We're not moving."

"They've launched again," Falk shouted. "Here it comes."

Although Boss Raznick's voice continued to blare over the intercom, Specialist Justin Jones ignored him. He knew his job, had assessed the situation, and didn't need the old man breathing down his neck. The Kilrathi were launching nukes nearby and everything in the flight hangar needed to be secure. Simple math. Rocket science not required.

Jones knew that Olivia felt the same and would back him up, so long as he didn't vanish on one of his treks to the latrine. But Jones could make no promises.

He double-checked the moorings on a Rapier with heavily damaged landing skids, got the signal from Olivia to move on—

Then felt the deck drop away from his boots. He fell onto his side as a deafening screech resounded from the bulkheads. The dozens of bombers and fighters surrounding him convulsed as the tremor worked its way farther into the ship. A few taut cables securing fighters to the deck popped free and whipped over fuselages. The wire Jones had just checked snapped, as did the one near Olivia, who shouted something, but a creaking noise drowned him out.

Jones looked over his shoulder and saw the Rapier coming down on him. Astonished, he thought, *I'm not gonna make it.* He raised his hands in reflex, in a vain effort to stop the fighter, and in surrender to his fate.

Rodriguez clung to the bulkhead as the temblor paid an unwelcome visit to his Secondary Ordnance room. It seemed odd that alarms did not accompany the quake, but nearly all of his systems had been shut down. Were they online, he would have noticed that tube integrity had been compromised in station number four. The only notice he received came in the form of a sudden rush of air that dragged Spaceman Taesha Douglas across the room, up the bulkhead, and into the tube. She died without time to scream.

Ashley Galaway rushed toward the hatchway, and Rodriguez pounded his fist on the emergency hatch control, sealing himself inside the ordnance room. He could see Ashley's pleading eyes through the hatch's window. She pounded on the durasteel, pointed at the control, screamed for him to open the door.

But Rodriguez could no longer hear her. The lack of oxygen made him grow faint, and his fingers slipped free of the conduit he had been gripping. He felt his legs being forced into the tube. His vision grew dark around the edges.

Miguel Rodriguez knew he was going to die, and that was okay. He had saved the ship from a major breech. But he wished he could bargain for one more hour to spend with Ashley. He could already hear the melodies of salsa, carried on the wind.

After Maniac had fled the hangar, Blair had tried to smooth things over with Hunter and Polanski. But after being cursed at by a jock who called himself "Maniac," a jock who had disobeyed orders, and a jock who they deemed responsible for the death of their unofficial leader, the two had simply walked away. And Blair had known better than to press the issue. He had left them to go after Maniac and had returned to the hangar, where he had, ironically, found Maniac seated in his Rapier. Then the Kilrathi had begun nuking the moon, and more death had fallen upon the *Tiger Claw*.

Now, as Blair picked himself off the deck, a whistling sound had him eyeing the bulkhead, the overhead, and the fighters that had collapsed or collided with each other. He shot a look to Maniac, who had left his fighter to squat near the lift doors and stare blankly at the chaos. Even the sight of two men being crushed by a Rapier had not drawn a reaction from him. Blair turned his attention to Deckmaster Peterson, who came sprinting by. "What's that sound?"

Peterson froze, and his head slowly tilted back as he took in the massive hangar bay doors. "Oh my God," he mumbled. Then the electricity of the moment struck him. He whirled around and shouted to his crew. "The door seal is failing! Boss? Activate the energy curtain!"

"Can't do that," Raznick said over the intercom. "The cats are just outside. They'll pick up the surge."

"Damn it." Peterson looked very much alone, despite the three techs who now surrounded him. "All right, all right! Grab anything that will seal it. Now!"

As the techs scattered, Blair quickly scanned the deck and spotted a Rapier's detached wing laying amid several toppled tool carts. He bolted across the deck, rounded one of the hangar's columns, then kicked power tools off of the wing. Seizing one end, he tried to lift it. "Hey! Over here! Someone help me."

Peterson answered the call and grabbed the wing's opposite end as the whistling grew louder and lower in pitch. Styrofoam cups, paper, pens, and anything else lighter than a kilo or so flew toward the widening breech in the doors. Peterson lost his grip on the wing, and it dropped to his hip. He began shaking his head, ready to give up.

"Come on!" Blair urged him. "We can do it!"

With a guttural hiss, Peterson took up the wing once more. They hauled it closer to the doors, and Blair realized that the only thing keeping them anchored to the floor now was the wing's weight.

Out of nowhere, something struck his skull, knocking him off the wing. He fell onto his back and got caught in the gale of escaping atmosphere, dragged feet-first toward the buckling, yawning doors. He spread his arms and palmed the deck in a futile effort to slow himself.

Techs shouted, their voices whisked away by the tornado-like roar.

More debris struck the doors with the *rat-tat-tat* of an automatic weapon.

Blair's hands stung from the building heat, and rubber burned off his heels as he dug them in for support.

He came up on a mooring rung that jutted from the deck. He reached for it. Missed. Another passed before he had time to react. A third rushed up and he reached for it, extending his arm until the pain brought tears and fingers touched, slid over, and clutched the metal. Jerked hard by the sudden stop and feeling as though his arm would rip from the socket, Blair rolled onto his stomach and gripped the rung with both hands. His cheeks rippled as the wind lifted him from the deck, and he began flapping like a flag in a hurricane.

He could see the others now, far ahead, watching in stunned fascination. Maniac stood. Hunter lingered behind. Peterson kept his grip on the wing as two techs joined him.

Then Maniac did something surprising. He turned to the others and shouted, "You sons of bitches just going to watch him die?" He raced to the bomber behind him, retrieved a broken piece of mooring cable, then fastened it around his waist. He jabbed the other end in Hunter's hand, saying, "Secure this."

And if Maniac were afraid, no evidence reached his face. He seemed angry, enraged even, as he started forward. The doors abruptly parted a quarter-meter, and the increased suction yanked him off his feet. He flew headlong at Blair, his crimson flight suit ruffling like fanned flames.

Then he jerked to a halt, dangling just a meter away, the cable cinching so tightly around his waist that Blair swore it would cut him in two. He swallowed a scream, turned back and seized the cable with one hand, then waved to the others for more slack. He rappelled down the deck like a rock climber until the cable stopped coming. He waved for more. Hunter shook his head. Maniac turned back, released the cable, then, hanging only by his waist, thrust out his hands. "Grab on!"

Blair took one hand off the rung and screamed as he tried to reach his friend. Maniac jerked himself a little closer, crying out as the cable dug deeper into his waist. He seized Blair's wrist with both hands, then looked back to Hunter and the others bracing the line. "Come on!"

Something wet spattered in Blair's eye as the cable jerked and he felt himself moving away from the doors. Another droplet struck his cheek. Then another. He spotted a dark stain forming around Maniac's waist. He called his friend's name to no response. He called again. And again.

Meanwhile, Peterson and the other techs hoisted the wing upright, and, anchoring themselves to the deck, eased it toward the doors. Blair caught sight of the wing suddenly flying through the air to slap across the gap with a terrific thud. The timpani roll of rushing air fell off into the soft simmer of a tea kettle.

And while that comforted him, he and Maniac suddenly found themselves gunned down and dropping to the deck. Blair belly-flopped and lost his breath. Maniac struck his shoulder and gave a half-strangled cry. As Blair sat up, a service vehicle trundled by, a tech standing in its turret behind a sealant gun with a barrel nearly two meters long. The truck stopped short at the doors, and the tech sprayed his viscous containment foam over the wing and the gaps above and below it. The foam quickly hardened into a solid mass, sealing off the leak.

Blair gazed over at Maniac, who lay inert on his back. He crawled over and untied the cable from Maniac's waist, exposing torn fabric and bloody flesh.

Grabbing Blair's arm, Maniac lifted himself up, then rose shakily to his feet. "What are you going to do when I'm not around to watch your ass?"

"Save your energy."

Maniac's eyes rolled back for a second, and he dropped to his knees. Blair rushed behind him, and Maniac fell into his lap. Blair's gaze swept over the hangar. "Medic!"

Then Maniac stirred. "It's my fault. She would've come back in, Blair."

"She knew what she was doing."

"I should have protected her."

"Forbes was a fighter pilot in a war zone," he said in a tone so cold that it shocked him. "She didn't need any protection from anybody. She's dead. And that's that."

"How can you be so—" Maniac's eyelids fluttered, and his head fell slack.

"Medic! Medic!"

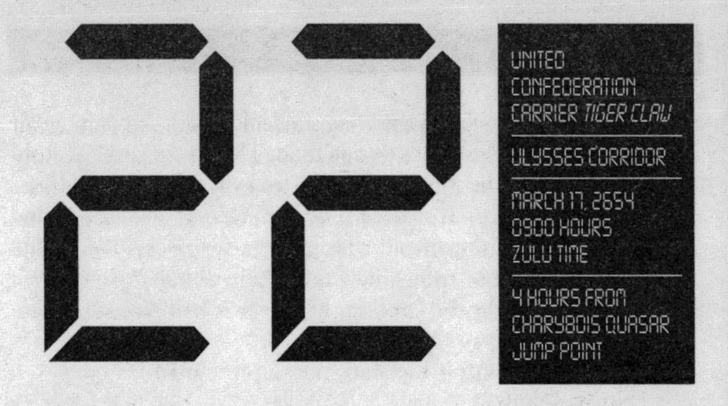

"The destroyer has moved on, sir," Falk said, observing its progress on his radar screen.

Gerald released an inaudible sigh, then rubbed his tired eyes. "Mr. Obutu? Give me the numbers."

"Reports are still incomplete. Thirty-five confirmed dead. One hundred and twenty-three wounded. We're still venting atmosphere on decks eleven and twenty-one. The breeches in Engineering and Secondary Ordnance have been contained. The flight boss reports hangar doors inoperative. No estimate yet on repair time. And he's still tallying up the damage to our fighters and bombers. It doesn't look good, sir."

"No, it doesn't. You have the con." Gerald pushed himself up and headed off the bridge.

As he turned into the corridor, Obutu's report rang in his ears. *How the hell did it come to this?*

And his answer kept falling upon the arrival of three individuals.

He found his way to the lift and took it down to the living quarters. Someone accosted him, but he marched by, not looking up, the rest of his journey a blur until he reached Sansky's hatch.

Inside, he found the captain propped up in bed and connected to a half-dozen tubes and wires that snaked into a small rolling tower of sensors. The doctors had successfully cleared the blockage of his coronary artery, yet they could not understand why his condition had not improved. "He says he wants to live," one doctor had said. "But somehow I don't believe him."

Gerald stood over the captain, whose eyes had trouble focusing. "How are you, sir?"

"They say the man is the ship, the ship the man."

"That bad, huh?"

Sansky managed a wan grin. "Tell me."

After giving the captain a capsule summary of the *Claw*'s present condition, Gerald folded his arms over his chest and waited for a reaction. And, to his astonishment, Sansky looked relieved. "Mr. Gerald, we could have sustained even greater losses were it not for your leadership. Thank you. I'm resuming command."

"Aye-aye, sir. But if I may speak frankly, we wouldn't have sustained any losses if—"

"I know where you're going, Paul. Stow that argument."

"Sir, they know our every move before we make it. And all since Commodore Taggart or Paladin or whoever the hell he is came aboard with that half-breed and his reckless buddy. Then there's the question of the ULF signals. We didn't send them, yet Blair detected them. He's trying to throw us off his trail. In any event, it is my firm belief that there is a traitor aboard the *Tiger Claw*."

Sansky opened his mouth, but a ring came from the hatch bell. "Enter."

Taggart straightened and ran his finger along the sliding door. "This hatch is wearing a little thin, Mr. Gerald. Sound tends to carry right through it. So make your point."

"The boy's a Pilgrim. Could my point be any more clear?"

Grinning crookedly, Taggart crossed to the bed. "So he's a Pilgrim. In your eyes, that makes him guilty of treason?"

"Yes, sir. It does."

"Barring the lieutenant's blood, do you have any other evidence that suggests he's a traitor?"

"We don't need any more evidence, sir. He arrives on this ship and things go to hell. That's not a coincidence. It's a fact."

But Taggart wasn't buying the facts. "Lieutenant Blair risked his life to save mine today. He's as good as they get. And I've fought with the best. He can fly my wing any mission, any time. Now I urge you to get over that damned war, Commander. We have another to fight."

"Commodore," Gerald spat. "With all due respect to your apparent rank, you're a Naval Intelligence officer. You don't know a damned thing about space combat, strategy, or war."

"I knew enough not to send Deveraux's wing on a wild-goose chase while the *Tiger Claw* was attacked."

"And if we had been destroyed, you would've been safely out of harm's way. Tell me, sir, was it just intuition that you knew about the Kilrathi diversion? Or are you withholding information?"

"Commander, I can stand here for hours trying to justify my loyalty to you. I could tell you that I flew off this ship during Custer's Carnival, remind you that I carry Admiral Tolwyn's ring, but what difference would that make? You've made up your mind."

"Gentlemen," Sansky interjected. "None of this matters now. What matters is our survival and our mission."

"Both of which are threatened by this man's presence," Gerald said.

Sansky glared back. "Enough!" He proffered his hand to Taggart. "Welcome aboard, Commodore. Do you have any orders for me?"

Tensing, Gerald could not watch his captain shake hands with the half-breed's champion, a handshake that might seal their fate.

"Sir, this is your ship," Taggart said. "I offer you every assistance in the current crisis."

Gerald nodded. "Assist us by leaving."

"As matters stand, we need all the help we can get," Sansky

said, lifting his voice, then lapsing into a cough. "This ship has suffered massive damage, and we have almost no operational fighters left. If you have any suggestions—any at all—I'd be glad to entertain them."

Taggart paced before the bed, eyes narrowed in thought. "The Kilrathi will be at the jump point in just under four hours, and we still don't know their capabilities or plan of attack." His hand brushed along the bulkhead. "I think this old lady's got a little fight left. All she needs is a little coaxing."

The man's naïveté astounded Gerald. "Engineering took a direct hit. Our fuel cells are nearly gone. We don't have enough power to keep up with the air recyclers, let alone get under-way. Barring a miracle, we've failed."

"Failure is not an option, Commander," Taggart said. "And if it's a miracle we need, I suggest we find a way to make one. Understood?"

"Yes, sir."

"You're dismissed, Commander."

Wanting to throttle the man instead of saluting him, Gerald went through the motions, spun on his heel, and got the hell out of there.

It was high time that he had a talk with the command staff. High time, indeed.

Commander Ke'Soick looked toward the lift doors at the back of the bridge. Thiraka took the suggestion and moved cautiously away from his captain's station, eyes trained on Admiral Bokoth. The kalralahr stood at the forward viewport, contemplating the swirls and hues of the quasar. No one dared interrupt him.

"Kal Shintahr," Ke'Soick whispered, standing near the doors and well out of Bokoth's earshot. "I want to kill him. Permit me the honor."

"No."

Ke'Soick's lips curled back. "Then his trust in the Pilgrim will kill us all."

"Easy, my friend. It won't come to that."

"You've let it come this far, haven't you? He's of your clan. You have much more to lose. I understand, Thiraka. So permit me the honor."

"I won't sacrifice you."

"There's no other way. We must be aggressive, decisive, and above all, ruthless. *You* should lead this battle group."

"But I won't lead it without you."

"Kal Shintahr?"

Thiraka glanced across the bridge. The admiral had turned from the viewport, his one eye panning the room. "Here, Kalralahr," Thiraka said. He hastened away from Ke'Soick and tensed as he arrived at the admiral's side.

"The whispering of young warriors troubles me," Bokoth said, resuming his study of the quasar. "As we grow older, our power shifts from muscle to mind. Does that shift weaken us? Hardly. But you don't believe that. You'd like to be rid of this old one who has taken over your ship and your battle group. Am I correct?"

Thiraka hesitated. "If I answer yes, I admit to treason. If I answer no, I call you a liar."

"And if you don't answer honestly, you will die where you stand."

Retreating a step, Thiraka said, "Your presence here undermines my authority. It reminds my crew that my own father doesn't trust me. And the loss of two destroyers and a dreadnought does little to—"

"I alone accept responsibility for those losses."

"You should have sent more ships," came a tinny voice from the shadows. The Pilgrim neared them, his face pale, his small lips quivering. "The *Tiger Claw* is alive and still a threat."

Bokoth flared at the traitor. "Go to the ConCom. Prepare the jump coordinates and transmit them to the fleet."

The human held his scowl a moment, the stormed off.

"What about the *Tiger Claw*?" Thiraka asked.

"We'll place the ConCom within range to find her." The admiral glanced at Thiraka. "You don't agree?"

"You serve the Emperor, Kalralahr. And I serve you." Thiraka bowed before his superior.

"That is no answer."

"For the moment, it is the only one I have."

The doctors in sickbay had done an excellent job of sealing Maniac's wounds, and they had instructed him to stay off his feet for forty-eight hours. Blair had guessed that Maniac would not last more than forty-eight minutes lying in bed. But once he had helped his friend back to their quarters, Maniac had fallen into a deep sleep, his body jerking as though the day's painful events were replaying in his subconscious.

Blair could have used some sleep himself, but too much had to be done. He returned to the flight deck, where he found pilots heading up their own maintenance teams. Three techs had already cleared the rubble from his Rapier, and while one sat in the cockpit, running diagnostics, the other two waved x-ray scanners over the fuselage, checking hull integrity. Although Blair's Rapier had not sustained major damage, many of the other fighters and bombers, nearly one hundred in all, had fared far worse. Wings had been crushed, cockpits shattered, landing gear snapped off. Blair stared across the great sea of mangled metal and still had difficulty believing what had happened.

To his right, a dozen techs led by Deckmaster Peterson hung from four rolling cranes near the hangar doors. Bulkhead panels running parallel with the doors had been removed, exposing a complex network of hydraulic lines and electronic pumps. Peterson barked commands, demanded reports, and challenged his people with time limits.

After catching the attention of his crew chief, Blair started toward the woman. Then he shifted course as he spied Deveraux. She squatted near her fighter's portside landing skid and stared up into the runner's compartment.

"Angel?"

She emerged from under her fighter, eyes swollen, hair disheveled. "What is it, Lieutenant?"

"Can we stop the bullshit, please?" He had her attention. "I'm sorry about Forbes."

"Who?"

"Don't." He shook his head. "It's a shitty game, Angel. I tried to play it with Maniac, and you know what? It hurt. It's supposed to."

"You're the authority?"

"You don't forget the people you loved. They deserve more than that."

She closed her eyes. "What do you want?"

"Maybe I can help. Maybe we can help each other."

"I'm all out." She turned away.

"He was crazy about her."

"He was crazy about her?" She spun to face him, all woman, all fire. "She was my best friend. I loved her."

"You weren't alone. You know he blames himself for what happened."

"And so he should."

"His confidence is shot. He's questioning every move he made. He can't go back up in that condition. And right now, we need every pilot we have."

"That's right. But you expect me to put him back on the duty roster?"

"Just do the right thing."

"I'll think about it."

"Maybe you can talk to the others. Maniac's a good guy. And he's sorry, really sorry. There's no reason for anyone to hate him."

She drew in a long breath and seemed to consider that. With nothing left to say, Blair started for his fighter.

"Blair?"

He glanced back. "Yeah?"

"Thanks."

Commander Gerald sat in one of the carrier's conference rooms with Lieutenant Commander Obutu and Lieutenants Falk and Sasaki. Lieutenant Commander Deveraux blew into the room, the sleeves of her flight suit rolled up, her forearms stained. "Sorry I'm late, sir," she told Gerald, then plopped into a chair.

Gerald stood. "I'll get right to the point. Captain Sansky, despite being incapacitated, has resumed command of this ship. Confederation naval regulations permit him to do so as long as he remains conscious and rational. The captain is conscious, but he continues to trust Mr. Taggart."

"What the hell are you saying?" Deveraux asked.

"I specifically asked you to be here, Commander, so that I'd have a witness. This isn't a conspiracy to commit mutiny. All I'm asking is that you keep your eyes open. We didn't get our asses whacked because we're stupid. Someone's been feeding the Kilrathi our location. Maybe it's Taggart and the half-breed and maybe it isn't. I just need to know that when the shit goes down, you'll be there."

Falk and Sasaki nodded their compliance.

"Sir, I can alert Security," Obutu said. "They'll work quietly."

"Very well. Monitor all communications. And we have a detail outside the ship doing hull repairs. I'd like surveillance there and at all other major repair sites."

Obutu tapped a command into the computer slate in front of him. "Done."

"Commander, if you think there's a saboteur on board and you'd like to react to that suspicion, then I'm all for a quiet little shakedown," Deveraux said. "But don't point fingers at Taggart, Blair, or Marshall. For God's sake, Paladin single-handedly took out that dreadnought. And Blair pulled him out of there. I'm not worried about Marshall. I'll bring him around myself."

"Yes, they're all great officers—or they're simply keeping their enemies close." A tone came from the messenger clipped onto Gerald's waist. He checked the note. "Well, our friends are back. Thank you for coming. Dismissed. And Deveraux? Your friend Mr. Taggart would like to see you on the bridge."

She made a face and hurried out.

They took the lift together. Neither spoke. The lift hummed. Finally, Gerald broke down. "So how are you doing, Commander?"

"Sir?"

"How are you?"

She gave him an odd look. "I'm fine. And you?"

"Never mind."

Thankfully, the ride did not last long, and they stepped onto the bridge to find Taggart at the radar station, staring into nothingness as the telltale beep of an incoming ship grew louder.

Deveraux headed for the transparent wall of the radar screen. "What's out there? Another destroyer?"

"It doesn't matter," Gerald called after her. "We can't take another round of bombardment."

Her expression grew hard, meant for him and Taggart. "I have four Rapiers ready to go. We'll go down kicking and screaming."

"We'll do better than that, Angel," Taggart said. "That ship up there is going to save our assess."

Maniac had tried to sleep, but Rosie's death played itself out in his dreams like a holo trapped in a loop. His chest felt heavy, and the thought of food made him sick. He had risen from bed and had accessed the ship's datanet to lose himself in video recorded during the attack. But he found it difficult to concentrate and twice thought he sensed Rosie staring over his shoulder.

In short, living hurt.

Now he rolled onto his stomach, his bandages tugging painfully on his waist. His pillow smelled like her perfume, and he took a deep breath, his eyes rimmed by tears.

Then he suddenly felt angry for what had happened. *It wasn't my fault! Do you think I wanted to get her killed?*

He wasn't sure who he had asked. God, maybe. The lack of a reply drove him farther inward, where he found his guilt waiting for him. He had not known Rosie Forbes for very long, but war affected time as efficiently as a gravity well. Two days or twenty years . . . it didn't matter. Life grew more intense when you lived on the border of death. You met someone, and in your minds you got married, had kids, retired, and died—all in the span of a one- or two-day stand-down. So Maniac had shared a lifetime with Rosie during their two days. Then he had thrown it all away by believing that he had ultimate power and control over his life. The safe world, the just world, had died with her. He no longer trusted anyone or anything. And he believed in nothing.

An alert call echoed from the intercom, but it seemed distant and unreal. He buried his head deeper in the pillow and stared across a black void until he saw two Dralthi detach themselves from their wing and fly toward him. He fired all guns and launched all missiles, but every round missed. To starboard, Rosie's bright eyes flashed a second before both Dralthi slammed into her fighter. He jerked up from the pillow, his body rocked by chills.

"Lieutenant? C'mon. Open the goddamned door. Lieutenant?"

Someone had been calling him. "Come," he said, and the hatch slid aside.

Deveraux wore a new flight suit and had a computer slate tucked under her arm. "I just came from a conversation with your doctor. He wants you off your feet. I think you can handle that—seated in a cockpit. Let's go. Time to suit up."

He pulled the blanket over his boxers. "Ma'am?"

"I need my best pilots out there."

"I don't know if I'm one of your best pilots."

Her face drew up in mild disgust. "Does everyone here think I go around making *suggestions*?"

"No, ma'am."

"Then I guess I gave you an order. Be on the flight deck in five minutes." She turned to the hatch. "And do it for Rosie."

Deveraux left him floored. She had returned him to the duty roster, but more importantly, she had acknowledged the existence of a dead pilot. And that made Maniac suddenly want to live. To fight. He sprang from his bed, grimacing as the needles of pain dug in. He snatched up his flight suit and fumbled with the zipper. Now it seemed okay to smile through his tears.

From a position just inside the *Diligent*'s loading hatch, Blair watched Commander Paul Gerald lead a squad of Marines up the ramp. Dressed in gray-and-red armored space suits and packing toy chests of anti-cat weaponry, the cocky jarheads appeared to have just blasted their way out of Hell's prison. Scarred faces and hardened expressions testified that they had made the escape more than once.

The commander also wore armor, and his presence had Blair frowning. During the briefing, there had been no mention of his accompaniment. "What the hell is *he* doing here?"

"Let's find out," Taggart said.

As he reached the hatchway, Gerald eyed them contemptuously.

Mirroring the look, Taggart said, "I think you're on the wrong ship, Commander."

Gerald lifted a gloved index finger and aimed it at Taggart's nose. "I still have a responsibility to this crew, Commodore. And, excuse my bluntness, but if you think I'm going to let *my* men be flown into combat by a rogue and a half-breed, you're sadly mistaken." He pushed past them.

Taggart winked at Blair. "He's really a great guy once you get to know him."

Blair smiled tightly, then started toward the ramp. "I'll be right back."

"Two minutes, Lieutenant."

He jogged across the hangar, where he found Maniac in a Rapier, going over the loadout with his crew chief. "Hey."

"Hey, Blair."

"I wanted to talk to you after the briefing."

"Yeah, I had to get down here."

"How's the . . ." Blair rubbed his own waist.

"Better."

"Good." He stared at his friend, and Maniac suddenly looked away.

"I'm all right, Chris. Really."

"I know you are."

"Then get out of here."

Blair smiled. "I'm gone." He dashed back toward the *Diligent*, circling around a fast-moving ordnance cart headed in Maniac's direction.

Inside the merchantman's hold, Blair found the Marines seated on both sides of the bulkhead, their rifles standing upright at their sides.

"Hey, Lieutenant?" a grunt seated near the back called. "Tell the commodore to hurry up. We're so wired we're gonna start shooting each other."

Blair cocked a brow. "I'll let him know."

He made it to the bridge and saluted Deveraux as she noticed him. He took a position behind Taggart, who manned the helm. Gerald sat beside the commodore in the co-pilot's chair, looking as thrilled as ever.

"That's a little big on you, Lieutenant," Deveraux said, studying his atmospheric suit. "Or you're a little too small for it." Though she still sounded glum, her teasing was a good sign.

"If you'd like, I can take it off, ma'am." Blair wanted to pull back the words; his suggestion drew Taggart's stare, followed up quickly by Gerald's.

"*Diligent*? You're cleared to launch," Boss Raznick said through the comm.

Taggart looked back to his console. "Roger, control. External moorings and power detached. Internals powering."

Blair made a mental note to thank Raznick for his timing. He edged away from Deveraux to stand beside Taggart. The commodore took the merchantman past the now-open and repaired hangar doors. The ship rocked a little as it parted the energy curtain and skimmed over the dark runway. The crater's deep shadows fell off as they neared a trio of colossal asteroids. Taggart rotated ninety degrees to port so the *Diligent*'s lines now formed with one asteroid's ragged ridgeline. The two Rapiers that ran escort hovered just below. Only a careful-eyed Kilrathi could spot them now.

"Passive radar engaged," Gerald said, his announcement punctuated by a faint beeping.

Taggart looked up, eyes distant as he interpreted the sound. "We have the target."

"There she is," Blair said, pointing to the forward viewports. A large ship glided overhead, her thrusters filling the bridge with a bright orange glow. As the glare abated, Blair thought he recognized her configuration. Two Dralthis flew at her sides.

"That's no destroyer," Deveraux said.

Blair went to the window for a closer look. "It's the ConCom ship we came up against."

"They'll spot our heat corona soon," Gerald said.

"They won't have the chance," Taggart corrected. "Blair. Man the Ion gun." He opened a channel to the Rapiers. "Marshall? Polanski? Hit it."

As Blair hurried off the bridge, he heard Gerald moaning about the *Diligent* not being a bomber, that they should not have come out flying only what was available. The techs had promised Gerald a Broadsword but had failed to deliver. For once, Blair agreed with the commander; however, the *Diligent* did boast a formidable weapons package, if not quad torpedoes. He climbed up into the gunner's domed nest, then buckled into his seat. The system automatically powered up, and he booted a pedal, swiveling 360 degrees in one fluid rotation. He took hold of the firing grips and got a feel for the ion cannon's range of motion, its barrel protruding about three meters from the transparent hemisphere. The asteroids and stars began wheeling around as the merchantman broke cover.

The ConCom ship veered away as the Rapiers chased after on full afterburners. Blair had flown enough missions with Maniac to recognize his friend's, well, maniacal flying style. Maniac performed a corkscrewing dive through a sleetstorm of fire, juked right, then hit one of the Dralthis with a rapid succession of expertly directed bolts that drummed shields to zero and quartered the fighter into sizzling sections.

"Yeah," Maniac shouted.

Polanski's Rapier overshot the second Dralthi, and his swearing crackled over the comm. The Dralthi tore after him, and Polanski led the enemy pilot on a torturous, laser-lit course through the rubble.

With reflexes hotwired to the battle, Maniac pulled into an eighty-degree climb, aiming for the Dralthi on Polanski's tail.

A radar screen superimposed on the Plexi bubble caught Blair's eye. He whirled to discover a pair of Dralthis rising from behind the moon. "Two more bogies at six o'clock." He squinted and opened up on one of the fighters. Charged atomic particles magnetically accelerated at high speeds pulsed from the gun. The Dralthi swerved out of Blair's glowing bead and answered with a volley that thundered across the *Diligent*'s shields. Blair cursed his unfamiliarity with the weapon. He should have had that bastard.

The ship jolted suddenly as Taggart increased throttle, bringing them up toward the larger ConCom ship. "Marines, to your stations," he ordered.

From below, Blair heard the Marines putting on their helmets, locking and loading their rifles, and gathering around the bay door. A sergeant's voice carried above the racket. "All right, sweethearts. If this dispersion doesn't go by the numbers, each of you will sacrifice a limb. Got it?"

"We got it, sir!"

"Hey, Sarge. Montauk says he'll sacrifice his—"

"Shuddup!"

"As soon as you get in, go straight for the bridge," Taggart said. "We have to get control of that ship before they scuttle her."

Another Dralthi zoomed across Blair's sights. He pivoted to track the fighter and, grating his teeth, unloosed a barrage. The agile little ship darted to port, but Blair found it once more, this time locking on. An intense multicolored flash ended the cat's mission. "Yes!"

Now alongside the ConCom, the *Diligent's* docking umbilical began to extend. Blair watched it for a second, then swung around, wary of more contacts.

On the *Diligent*'s bridge, Deveraux repressed a chill as the ship inched closer to the ConCom's wide upper deck.

"Their missiles are hot," Gerald said, reading his screen.

The news did not move her. "They can't use 'em now. We're too close."

"They're Kilrathi, Commander. They can do whatever the hell they want."

Before she could retort, a fighter dove into view, headed straight for the bridge.

"He's going to ram," Gerald cried.

From a twelve o'clock bird's-eye view, Maniac looked down on the Dralthi making a kamikaze run for the *Diligent*. A long-range image from his forward camera showed the pilot wearing an opaque helmet, the ship's bow reflected across its face. *Too bad*, Maniac thought. He wanted to glimpse the terror in the cat's eyes as he parted the starry heavens like Sivar incarnate. "Heads up, asshole."

Turbines wailed as Maniac bore down on the Dralthi in his own kamikaze run. He saw the pilot's head snap back and did the only natural thing: He flipped him the bird. Then the big barrel of his Rapier's nose sheared off the enemy fighter's cockpit as Maniac pulled four Gs to recover from the dive. He shot a look over his shoulder as the Dralthi did a pilotless jig cut short by the ConCom's stern.

Damage reports flashed in Maniac's VDUs. The Rapier handled sluggishly, but Maniac didn't care. "That's for you, Rosie."

He arced back toward the *Diligent*, whose umbilical now latched onto the ConCom. A few seconds later, the Kilrathi ship's hull turned pink as the umbilical's lasers began to cut through.

"Hey, Maniac? Form on my wing," Polanski ordered.

"On it."

"And thanks for the assist."

"You're buying when we get back."

"You kidding? I already owe Shotglass a week's pay. I've run out of credit with him."

"Let me do the talking. I'm sure we can work out a mutually beneficial deal."

"I don't like the sound of that."

"You're a wise man, Polanski."

They drew close to the two ships and circled overhead. Maniac fixed his gaze on his radar display.

He did not trust the calm.

Deveraux knew that Sergeant Cogan did not appreciate her leading his Marines into the ConCom ship. His jowly face screwed up into a knot when he first heard about the plan, and his expression had not changed. Deveraux was not a Confed Marine Corps lieutenant, nor did she have any special training in tactical boarding operations. For all intents and purposes, she should not be commanding the Marines.

However, she possessed one piece of knowledge that had convinced Commander Gerald to assign her the task. As part of her academy training she had spent two months flying a captured Dorkir-class freighter similar to the ConCom. She knew the layout of those vessels better than any grunt in Cogan's squad. Sure, Marines received intense training in enemy ship design, but no solider could memorize thousands of deck plans. Without her, the squad would rely on field slates and constantly have to pause to check their coordinates via computer. She could get them to the bridge far more swiftly—not that Cogan appreciated the advantage. Deveraux was not a Marine. Period.

And while she stood at the front of the squad, immersed in the sparks and shimmer of the superheated hull, Cogan reminded her of that fact. "When the door blows, hold back, Commander. Let my people do their jobs." His face shield barely hid his contempt.

"I'm leading this group, Sergeant. I recommend that you take that literally. Are we clear?"

"Yeah, we are. At least your corpse won't weigh very much in zero G." He marched back and began shouting at his troops.

"Five seconds," a Marine reported, waving a small scanner near the cutting line.

Deveraux began a mental countdown, but the copper-colored section of plastisteel thudded to the deck before she reached one. She felt the umbilical's air tug on her shoulders as it fled into the Kilrathi ship. As suspected, the cats had turned off the artificial gravity in this section in order to slow the Marines' progress. In a surreal zero-G dance, she glided forward and turned into a triangular corridor clogged with a thick green gas and festooned with conduits. A silhouette stirred ahead, and she strained to see through the fog, her rifle stock already jammed into her shoulder.

A yellow bolt tore a jagged hole in the bulkhead just a half-meter away. She returned fire but couldn't pick out a target. She touched a button on her helmet, engaging her thermal scanner. Data bars beamed at the corners of her faceplate. Forms grew more defined, details less so. The torn-up bulkhead throbbed red.

The Marines charged in around her, cutting loose an incredible wave of suppressing fire that stirred the alien gas into hundreds of tiny whirlpools.

"Hold your fire," Cogan ordered.

She studied the corridor via the thermal scope. No movement or heat sources. "Tito! Marx! Take point. Second team. Watch our backs. Let's move."

Blair kept Polanski and Maniac in his sights as the two engaged another pair of Dralthis that had sprung from behind the asteroids.

"They're coming up behind. Let's kickstop 'em," Polanski told Maniac.

"Affirmative."

"On my mark. Hold . . . hold . . . hold . . . mark!"

Maniac and Polanski broke into hard ninety-degree turns, holding their new courses for a moment. The Dralthis overshot them, and the Rapiers spun back 180 degrees to lock targets. Missiles flew, and the cats paid with interest for their mistake.

"Lieutenant, can I have a word with you?" Merlin asked, his voice coming abruptly from the intercom.

"Little busy right now."

The hologram flashed into view with his usual flourish and sat cross-legged on the Ion cannon's console. He thrust out his lower lip and blew a stray lock of hair from his eyes. "I'm picking up some strange electromagnetic emissions from the Kilrathi ship."

"So?"

He leaped onto the crossbar joining the firing grips and obscured Blair's view. "They're Pilgrim. The ULF frequency I picked up earlier. Do I have your attention?"

"Yeah. Can you pinpoint the signal?"

"Of course. I wouldn't have brought it up if I couldn't."

Blair gaped at the little man. "Well?"

"Deck two, aft section. The bridge."

Decision time. He glanced at the radar display: all clear. Maniac and Polanski could handle themselves for at least a little while, barring an onslaught. *Man, that's weak justification, but it makes me feel a little less guilty.* He lifted out his cross, kissed it, then climbed down from the gunner's dome. Moving gingerly away from the ladder, he stole a glance at the bridge. Taggart and Gerald sat at their consoles, their backs to him. Good. He unlatched a rifle from its bulkhead mount, checked the charge, then fetched his helmet from the rack.

He winced as the airlock doors parted, and tossed another look back at the bridge. Taggart and Gerald had heard nothing. He double-checked his helmet's binding, then ventured into the umbilical, feeling his weight decrease before the suit's gravity boots automatically kicked in.

Dense fog unfurled toward him, and once he reached the opening to the ConCom ship, visibility had been reduced to a meter. He turned into a corridor

And something brushed his shoulder. He recoiled with a cry, lifting the rifle, finger tensing over the trigger.

An abomination floated next to him, a uniformed beast so hideous that nature had not yet forgiven herself for its creation. The thing's pale, elongated head had been torn open by laser fire, and its huge paws were locked in a death clutch. The corpse rolled over, and the yellow eyes stared at Blair, convex irises now inert, lids twitching involuntarily.

Taggart had been right. The Kilrathi would not be entering beauty pageants anytime soon. And Blair felt fortunate that his first close encounter was with a dead one.

"Nice," Merlin said through the comm. "I believe there's another way. To the right."

His gravity boots peeled off the deck and made traveling furtively more than a little difficult, though the haze did help. He reached a door at the corridor's end and frowned at the control panel labeled in Kilrathi.

"Translating," Merlin said. "Hit the big button."

"Of course."

Green fumes poured through the doors as they slid apart. He touched a control on his helmet, bringing the thermal scanner online. Two pipes affixed to the bulkhead glowed red, otherwise the corridor appeared cool. With his rifle at the ready, he moved inside.

"Aw, hell," Deveraux moaned as a half-dozen Kilrathi troopers stamped up the corridor. The Marines traded a dozen bolts with the aliens, then fell back into an intersecting passage.

"That the only way?" Cogan asked, popping out an energy magazine and popping in another.

"It is now," she answered grimly. "They've reported our position. They're already sealing us off back there."

"Grenade!" someone cried.

Deveraux looked down as the cylindrical concussion grenade

rolled across the deck, just two meters away. Cogan seized her shoulders, driving her back as the bomb exploded. A bluish-red fireball swelled overhead. They collapsed, and Deveraux fought to recover her breath. Somehow, she managed to sit up.

Three Marines lay dead in the intersection, their arms and legs gone or twisted at unnatural angles, their space suits whistling as O_2 units mindlessly pumped air.

A sweaty and scared-looking grunt rounded the corner, ducking from incoming fire. He took one look at his dismembered comrades, gagged, then forced himself toward Deveraux. "Ma'am? Got another squad moving in behind us. We are pinned down."

"Lieutenant Polanski? Report," Gerald ordered.

The young man's masked face shown on the comm screen. "No contacts, sir."

"I concur," Marshall added. "We're jamming local transmissions, but that doesn't mean our buddies didn't get off a signal. Better set the table anyway."

"Understood," Gerald said. "How are we doing back there, Blair?"

No response.

"Lieutenant Blair? Answer your station." Gerald tapped on the ship's security cameras. He flipped through the images until he found the empty gunner's dome. "Look at this," he shouted at Taggart. "You should've never brought that half-breed on this mission. His orders were to remain on this ship." Gerald bolted up. "Stay here. I'll find him."

Picturing himself with a gun shoved into Blair's forehead, Gerald slapped on his helmet and tore a rifle from the rack. He glanced to Taggart. *That's right, Commodore. You should look worried. Now your boy is going down.*

"Which way, Merlin?"

Blair had reached the end of the corridor, where a more narrow passage ran through it at a seventy-five-degree angle.

“Go left. Then down.”

His elbow scraped along the wall of the tube, which quickly widened into a standard-size corridor with increasing gravity. Blair’s stomach suddenly greeted his knees.

“There’s a floor panel on the deck. Pull it up,” Merlin instructed.

He found the handle and slowly lifted the panel while balancing his weapon. He peered into the hallway below, hoped to God that it would remain clear, then dropped to the deck.

“See that hatch up ahead?” Merlin asked. “That’s the bridge. ULF signals are peaking the meter now.”

After a second glance at the hatch, Blair dodged to the bulkhead. Large, cross-shaped windows built into the doors revealed two Kilrathi officers, their heads lowered to their consoles, their bodies outlined in the faint red of his thermal scanner. He cocked his rifle. Full charge. Keeping to the shadows and thicker fog near the wall, Blair advanced. He threw a look back, and when he faced forward, light flickered across his display.

Two towering Kilrathi skulked out of the gloom near the bridge door, and one of them took massive strides toward him, its booted feet rumbling the deck, its mouth opening to expose diseased gums and a grotesque set of gnarled, razor-sharp teeth. Blair stood immobilized in the image as the warrior launched itself toward him with improbable speed.

His finger found the trigger, and he blew open the alien’s abdomen at point-blank range. The thing gurgled and bled over its legs, took a step back, and dropped.

In a blur, the second Kilrathi appeared behind the first.

Blair lifted the rifle. The cat came at him, bulbous eyes widening, arms lifting, claws springing from its paw. A victory grin split open its horrid face.

Blair fired!

Pain rocked visibly through the alien, robbing its smile and narrowing its gaze. It released a spinetingling shriek and stumbled onto its back.

As Blair stepped around the cat, he exchanged a look with a

Kilrathi officer behind the bridge's door, then stole his way to the windows.

On the other side, one alien stood fixated on a monitor while another, presumably the captain, turned to kneel before a copper-colored statue of Sivar. The captain's mouth moved.

"This is not good," Merlin said. "That Kilrathi in there just spoke a ritual phrase. He says that he's honored to die for the glory of Kilrah, the Emperor, and the Empire."

The captain rose and turned back to a center console, where Blair spotted a red button that needed no translation.

He fell back from the door, dropped an explosive round into his rifle's grenade launcher, aimed, and—

With a faint *thump* the bomb left his weapon, struck the door, and blew it off its tracks in a column of flames edged in black smoke. Exploiting the lingering cloud, Blair rushed toward the hatch, then crouched to pick a target.

Reaching for the red button, the Kilrathi captain jerked as Blair's first round tore a ragged hunk out of its shoulder. Two more bolts punched the now-howling captain to the deck.

Blair flinched as the remaining two bridge officers returned fire from the cover of consoles. He dodged through showers of sparks and flying debris, then dropped to his stomach behind a long row of stations. He inched forward, careful not to move the colossal swivel chairs beside him. From between the widely spaced console legs he saw armored feet closing in on him from flanking positions. In a half-dozen heartbeats, the cats would be standing over him.

He waited for four of those beats, then rolled under the stations and popped up behind a warrior, jabbed his rifle into the thing's long head, and squeezed off a bolt. The warrior dropped, most of its brain on the wall behind it.

But where was the other officer?

Pivoting frantically, Blair couldn't find him. Then, out of nowhere, the thing abandoned its rifle and sprang. An armored fist sent Blair's weapon tumbling, and an even faster paw across his face hurled him to the deck.

This Kilrathi did not smile as the earlier one had. The pure thought of killing narrowed its eyes to slits, kept its lip crimped in a sneer, and fueled a long, steady growl. It reached for Blair's chest, grabbing him by the fabric of his space suit. With little effort, the thing hoisted him high into the air as it extended the talons of its free paw. Then it lowered him a little, wanting to stare him down before the unceremonious gutting.

In a second of movement so well choreographed that it made Blair feel he had stepped outside himself, he jabbed his thumbs into the cat's large, yellow eyes. The paw gripping him relaxed, and he fell, palming a console for balance as the alien wailed in agony.

Blair bounded for his rifle, came up with it, and finished off the Kilrathi with a pair of bolts to the head. Flesh sizzled.

"Nicely done," Merlin said, seated on the forward edge of a nearby monitor.

"Thanks for the help."

"I'm just running my program. And by the way, don't touch the red button."

He looked at the self-destruct switch and sighed. Then his gaze wandered the rest of the bridge, and he noticed a black box partially hidden behind a piece of the exploded hatch, the letters N-A-V visible on one side. The box sat on the station he had hidden behind, and a score of cables emanated from it, some leading to a monitor that scrolled numbers and letters, some into a bank of consoles he guessed were part of the ConCom's communication system. "What the hell?"

After crossing to the device, he set down his rifle and lifted away the piece of plastisteel. His mind raced as he read the words PEGASUS NAVCOM AI. "They have the Charybdis jump coordinates, Merlin."

"They have more than that. I'm picking up strong electromagnetic emissions from the panel to your right. It's a ULF signal. I finished translating the code. They're relaying a ship's coordinates."

"What ship?"

"The *Tiger Claw.*"

"Damn it. What's the source?"

"The original signal comes from the *Tiger Claw* herself."

Blair's jaw dropped. "A traitor on the *Claw*?"

"It gets worse. It's encrypted with an executive-level code, one I recognized immediately."

"Who has access to those codes?"

"Only Captain Sansky and Commander Gerald."

The monitor flashed, and the code numbers and letters scrolled by at an increasing rate.

"What's happening?" Blair huddled over the screen.

"The signal just went from ULF to Ultra High Frequency. The *Tiger Claw* just became a beacon."

"Every Kilrathi ship in the sector will be able to find her," Blair said, nearly losing his voice.

"Lieutenant, someone is—"

Reacting to the sound of footfalls, Blair whirled to lock gazes with Commander Gerald, who, with inflamed eyes and teeth flashing obscenely, raised his rifle and started onto the bridge. "You'd like my ship to fall, wouldn't you, you treacherous piece of shit." He gestured with his weapon toward one of the dead Kilrathi. "I should feed you to these things."

"Looks like you'll get your chance," Blair said, then patted the NAVCOM. "They owe you a few favors, don't they, Mr. Gerald?"

Gerald crossed the ConCom's bridge in several long, deliberate strides. "Mr. Blair," he began, then suddenly smashed Blair's helmet with the butt of his rifle. "I believe you just called me a traitor."

Blair rolled across a console, then fell to his knees.

After flipping the weapon around, Gerald aimed it at Blair's head. He pulled the slide back, then nodded at the NAVCOM. "Turn it off."

Three simple words . . . yet they shocked Blair. If Gerald wasn't the traitor, then—

A hollow laugh resounded from the rear corner of the bridge. "To think we came from you."

Wearing a space suit and clutching a large Kilrathi pistol, a man stepped from the shadows, a man whose gaunt face seemed familiar, but Blair couldn't summon a name.

"Wilson?" Gerald said, his tone so full of astonishment that the word had barely escaped his lips. "But the Pegasus—"

The admiral took a step forward, and Blair had never seen a man more consumed by hatred; it clung to his face like a parasite. "Twenty years of service. Ironic, isn't it?" He extended his arm, the pistol directed at Gerald.

"Wait," Blair cried. He lifted his pilgrim cross with a trembling hand.

Wilson drew back, gazing suspiciously at the cross, then at Blair. "Where did you get that?"

"It was my mother's. She was killed at Peron." Extending a palm in truce, Blair slowly got to his feet, holding the cross like a shield in front of him.

For a second, Wilson's eyes glazed over, as though he had taken himself across the light-years and back to the massacre. "When you remember Peron, what do you feel?"

Before answering, Blair turned his glower on Commander Gerald. "I feel hate."

"So you think you're a Pilgrim? Do you have any idea what it's like to wait a lifetime for justice?" He waved the pistol at Gerald. "My people gave them the stars . . . our greatest folly."

"Your people murdered millions," Gerald said. "Your regrets should lie there, you bastard."

Wilson seemed unaffected by the remark. He favored Blair, his expression brightening. "So, boy, if you're a Pilgrim, prove it." He raised his chin to Gerald. "Kill him."

Blair's nod came easily, and he turned back for his rifle, his thoughts colliding as he fully comprehended the moment. He had enough bitterness stored inside to fight Gerald, but could he kill the man? The answer was obvious.

"No rifles," Wilson said. "Use the blade."

Shifting back, Blair pulled the cross from its chain and touched the center symbol. The cutting edge flashed out.

Gerald withdrew a long, ugly-looking fighting knife from his vest. Not standard-issue to be sure, the blade seemed to bear a charge of winking silver. Gerald assumed a fighting stance, grinning ominously. "I was right all along. Come on, Pilgrim. Pass your test." The commander lunged at him.

Skirting behind a console, Blair saw that he had reached a dead end at the bulkhead. He climbed atop one of the stations and leaped into an open area, behind the helm controls. Gerald followed. Now they circled each other, feinting with their blades.

Time slowed for Blair, his arm moving in a hypnotic pattern as the feeling of hopelessness grew. Gerald seemed part of some bad dream, while Wilson, looking on, had emerged from a nightmare. *Mother? Father? Is this what we are?*

I can't be in this place. I can't do this.

Sparks skittered along his blade as Gerald's big knife made contact. Blair fought against the other man's weight, then flipped his wrist, breaking pressure while spinning behind Gerald.

But the commander whirled around, boot raised, and kicked Blair in the ribs. As Blair fought to remain standing, he saw Gerald lift his blade—

A horrible tearing sound came from the sleeve of Blair's space suit. He reached for the tear, reeling back farther from the commander. Automatic voice alarms warned him that Gerald's blade had penetrated the suit's first layer.

He tensed once more as Gerald, now wild-eyed, searched for an opening. The man's blade shot at him once, twice, a third time, and Blair parried each assault. He remained defensive, caught his breath, and watched as the commander's face grew more flushed.

"Is that all you have, Mr. Gerald?" Wilson taunted.

Swearing at the admiral, Gerald feinted right, lowered his head, and came in with a thrust toward Blair's abdomen.

Instead of parrying, Blair grabbed Gerald's wrist with his free hand, then threw himself beneath the commander, sweeping out the man's legs in a classic jujitsu move he remembered from boot camp. Gerald landed hard on his back as Blair followed through with the maneuver, exploiting his momentum to roll and hover over the commander, blade centered over the man's heart.

"Finish him!" Wilson cried.

He looked at Gerald, whose face paled in the half-light. The commander mouthed a curse, and Blair suddenly felt as though he had been dipped in ice water as he imagined Gerald writhing in agony. He lifted the blade a few inches, preparing to drive it home—

Then turned, flicking his wrist.

The blade warbled, threw off dazzles of gold and silver, then . . .

Thump!

The admiral flinched, looked down at the cross stuck in his chest, then raised his head, wearing a new mask of horror as his space suit began hissing loudly. He stumbled, reaching blindly for support, then slumped against a column.

Gerald sat up, and Blair proffered his hand. "Take it, sir."

After a moment's consideration, Gerald accepted. He went to the admiral, whose face looked contorted and skeletal. "Wilson!"

Despite his agony, the man remained conscious.

"Why warn Tolwyn?" Gerald demanded. "Your Kilrathi friends could've destroyed Pegasus, taken the NAVCOM, and jumped to Earth with no interference."

He smiled weakly. "I used to think the stars were not my destiny. I used to think I was human. But I'm a Pilgrim. And the stars were the Pilgrims' destiny. Not Earth's. Not Kilrah's."

A faint click drew Blair's gaze to the admiral's hand, which slowly opened. A concussion grenade sat in his palm, its firing button triggered.

"Shit!" Blair cried, already turning to retreat. He crashed into a pair of big chairs as he and Gerald darted toward the hatch.

At the first hint of the explosion, they dove toward the corridor. An intense wave of heat wiped over Blair's legs as he hit the rattling deck. His comm unit crackled as the boom overloaded his mike. He crawled toward the corridor, but a second explosion had him cowering again. Black smoke poured over them, and the snapping of flames grew louder. He forced himself to stand and took a deep breath to ward off the dizziness. Gerald was already on his feet.

"Now do you want to know who your traitor is?" Blair asked.

The hatch at the corridor's end opened, drawing Gerald's attention. A Marine crouched near the edge, directing the business end of his rifle at the commander. "Halt!" he shouted as two other Marines joined him.

"Cogan? Deveraux?" Gerald called back.

Deveraux jogged from behind the Marines and through the hatch. "Sir? What are you doing here?"

"Never mind. Secure the fuel cells. Blair and I have some business to take care of." He marched past her.

She looked after him, then turned her troubled expression to Blair.

"It's okay," he said.

"What business do you—"

"Gotta go." He sprinted to catch up with Gerald.

Once on board the *Diligent*, Blair gave Taggart the bad news while Gerald prepared an escape pod for an express ride back to the *Tiger Claw*.

"You're in the intelligence business, sir. Did we ever suspect Captain Sansky of espionage?"

"No," Taggart said, still overwhelmed by the news. "He's had a long and distinguished career."

"Is he a Pilgrim?"

"Who knows?"

Gerald stood in the hatchway. "Let's go, Lieutenant."

The pod came in for a rough landing, and Gerald ignored the flight boss's complaints as he hustled toward the lift. Blair struggled to keep up with him and tried to ignore the stares of the deck crew. Two officers rushing off with drawn pistols would invariably raise an eyebrow or two.

At Sansky's hatch, Gerald overrode the lock. The door slid aside, and they rushed in like military police.

The captain sat up in bed, his sallow face registering only mild surprise. "Gentlemen, I don't pose a threat." He checked his watch. "In fact, I'll be dead in a few minutes." Noting Blair's frown, Sansky waved a finger at a syringe lying on his nightstand. "In the old days they used cyanide. The plecadome, I'm told, makes for a more peaceful retreat."

"Jesus Christ, Jay. You were the best CO I had." Gerald lowered his pistol and huffed his disappointment. "Why?"

"Because, Paul, sometimes the role you play isn't the one you were born for."

"You've failed at both," Gerald growled.

"Have I?" he asked, his voice heavy with irony. "A bad spy and a bad captain." His eyelids grew heavy as the poison took effect. He battled against it, lifting his hand toward Blair. "Here. Give this back to Tolwyn. Please."

Blair took the ring as the admiral's hand fell limp. He held the ring tightly, needing something to believe in for the moment, something tangible, something that wasn't a lie.

"Look," Gerald said, raising a holopic from the nightstand. He thumbed through the images of Sansky's graduating class at the academy. Admiral Wilson stood close by in every hologram. There was even one of him at the podium, accepting his Confederation commission.

"They're my age," Blair said. "I was just there."

"Here's the past," Gerald said, shaking the holopic. He pointed at Sansky. "There's the future—if you let your Pilgrim roots get in the way."

"I just want to know who I am, sir. That's all."

"I think you already know."

"Commander?" Obutu said over the intercom.

"Talk to me, Mr. Obutu."

"Engineering reports that the Kilrathi fuel cells have arrived. They'll have them adapted in a few minutes. They estimate that we'll have sixty percent power."

"Very well. Prepare to get under way." Gerald, realizing he still held the holopic, threw it violently across the room. "If we live," he began, trying to contain his fury, "it's going to take me a long time to get over this."

Blair nodded somberly. "At least one of us will."

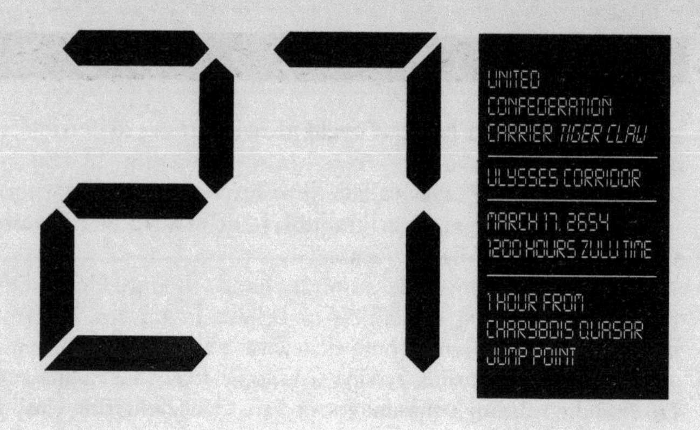

"Hey, Blair. What happened to you out there? One minute you're manning the Ion cannon, the next you're gone. Not that Polanski and I needed your help, but it's nice to know your ass'll be covered in a clutch."

Blair sat on his bunk, rubbing his eyes with the heels of his hands.

"I didn't mean to make you cry . . ."

He made a face at Maniac, who lay bare-chested on his bunk, scratching at his bandages.

"C'mon, Chris. What's up?"

"In a couple of minutes, Gerald's going to announce that Captain Sansky is dead. He might even mention how Sansky betrayed the Confederation. Hell, he betrayed humanity."

"You're shitting."

"Wish I were. I think Sansky was a Pilgrim. At the least, a Pilgrim sympathizer."

"So that's why you're bummed. Well, you've been wanting to find out more about the Pilgrims. Satisfied?"

Blair shot to his feet and unzipped his flight suit. Leaving a trail of clothes, he headed into the shower. As the hot spray warmed and loosened his aching muscles, he closed his eyes and wondered if his mother had engaged in anything as terrible as Sansky and Wilson.

"Hey, Chris?" Maniac called. "I'm sorry, man. Really."

Without answering, Blair grabbed a bar of soap and a washcloth.

He needed to get clean.

By the time Blair finished his shower, Maniac had already changed and left. He had probably headed down to the rec to get that drink Polanski owed him. Thankful for the solitude, Blair stood in his towel and reached instinctively for his cross, feeling only the chain. He panicked for a moment, then slumped in resignation as he remembered where he had left it.

Was its loss another omen that he should not explore his roots? Maybe. But he knew he would never abandon that goal no matter how much pain it caused. Not knowing hurt more.

He padded to where he had dropped his clothes and dug out Admiral Tolwyn's ring from a pocket. He needed to give it to Taggart, who could return it to the admiral.

After donning a new flight suit, he made sure to place the ring in his breast pocket. He wished now he could keep it, a new symbol of who he might become.

But the ring had to go back.

Blair felt a distinct jolt as he stepped onto the bridge. The *Tiger Claw* ascended, and the shadows folded back to expose the pockmarked and grooved surface of the crater's wall.

Lieutenant Commander Obutu lay on his back, assisting a tech with repairs on the portside observation station. The other officers stared determinedly at their screens, uttering reports into headsets.

"I heard about your business," Deveraux said, meeting him at the rail. "Gerald's not going to inform the crew until we're dead or out of this. He's breaking regs, but he's right. We have to keep morale high, speaking of which, how's yours?"

"I'm all right."

"Wow. Very convincing."

"I'll be all right. Soon. Maybe."

"At least now you're honest."

He gestured toward Taggart, who stood behind Gerald's command chair. "I need to speak with him." Deveraux released him with a nod, and he crossed to stand at attention beside Taggart. "Sir, I have something for you." He fished out Tolwyn's ring.

Taggart grinned at the sight, then shook his head as Blair offered it to him. "Keep it for now. We get out of this, you can return it yourself."

"Thank you, sir."

"Have you ever met the admiral?"

"No, I haven't."

"I'm sure you'll find the experience . . . memorable."

"Yes, sir."

"We're clear of the crater," the helmsman abruptly reported.

"Very well," Gerald said. "Mr. Obutu. Prepare a drone. Input the Kilrathi jump coordinates. Send it through the Charybdis Quasar to Admiral Tolwyn."

"Aye-aye, sir." Obutu slid out from beneath the observation station.

Gerald glanced back to Taggart. "They should be able to target the exact location of the Kilrathi jump entry. It'll be over before they can get their weapons online."

"If Tolwyn's there, Mr. Gerald. If he's there."

Out of the corner of his eye, Blair saw Mr. Obutu smite his fist on a touchpad. The radar and comm officers gathered around him, and all three murmured excitedly.

Finally, Obutu spun to face Gerald. "Sir, we have a problem. All communications and decoy drones are off-line. Executive override."

"Sansky," Gerald said as though swearing. "Without those coordinates, Tolwyn doesn't have a chance—and we're too big to slip past the Kilrathi and warn the fleet."

Taggart gave Blair an appraising glance, then said, "We'll have to send a fighter through."

"Impossible," Gerald argued. "There are over a thousand singularities in that quasar. To jump it would be suicide without NAVCOM coordinates."

"We don't need a NAVCOM, Mr. Gerald." Taggart placed a hand on Blair's shoulder. "Lieutenant, you will navigate the quasar. Lieutenant Commander Deveraux will follow your lead."

Stunned by the order, Blair's voice cracked. "It's statistically impossible, sir."

The commodore tightened his grip. "We don't have another option." His voice lowered to a near whisper. "You have the gift."

Blair slid out of Taggart's hold and looked to the deck, reaching for his phantom cross. "I don't have the faith."

"It's not faith," Taggart said, coming up behind him. "It's genetics. It's the capacity to feel magnetic fields. But if you believe you need faith—" He circled in front, reached into his tunic, and withdrew a Pilgrim cross. "Here. Take mine."

Awestruck, Blair took the cross, then gazed curiously at its owner. "Why didn't you tell me?"

Taggart cocked a brow. "You didn't ask."

The reverence in Taggart's eyes when he had examined Blair's cross and the pain he suffered when speaking of the Pilgrims were now clear. But how had he come to fight for the Confederation? Blair hoped he lived long enough to find out. He attached the cross to his own chain, then thought better of tucking it under his flight suit. People should see it. People needed to see it.

"Long-range scanners are picking up Kilrathi ships, sir," Obutu told Gerald. "Looks like a destroyer and a cruiser."

"Mr. Blair. Can you do it?" Gerald asked.

"I think so, sir."

"Not good enough, Lieutenant!"

"Sir, I can do it, sir!"

"Very well. I'll have the Kilrathi jump coordinates transferred to your Rapier and copied to Deveraux's. We'll create the diversion. Just get those coordinates to Tolwyn."

"Aye-aye, sir." Blair quickly exited the bridge, and Deveraux joined him in the lift.

"I guess we're in for a wild ride," she said.

"You don't have to come. I can get Maniac to fly my wing. He's brave *and* stupid enough."

"And I'm not?

"You're smart, Angel. Very smart. That's why everyone respects you."

"I'd like to believe that."

"You should."

"Well, in any event, I'm coming along. Commodore's orders. And you can't change my mind."

"Then I'm honored to fly with you, ma'am." He eyed her sternly. "Just don't get me killed."

Men sacrificed themselves over a smile like hers. Blair would be no exception.

As Deveraux hurried off toward her fighter, Blair continued along the flight line. The order had come down from the bridge to prep two Rapiers, followed by a second order for battle stations. Flight crews jogged to Rapiers and Broadswords, finished hasty repairs, and criss-crossed the hangar in ordnance carts. The energy created by them struck and excited Blair. He saw Polanski, Hunter, and Maniac in the throes of preflighting their fighters. He thought of saying good-bye to Maniac, but his friend seemed too busy for the interruption. Ahead, his own flight crew swarmed his Rapier, and he quickened his pace, wanting to lend them a hand.

"Pilgrim," a familiar man called out.

Blair craned his head as Hunter came toward him. *I don't need this now*, he thought. *Why can't this bastard just let it go?* Blair held his ground, muscles growing tighter with Hunter's every step.

"I heard what you did on that Kilrathi ship," the big Aussie said. "We all heard. I was wrong." He extended a hand.

Trying to hide his feeling of relief, Blair took the hand and give the pilot his firmest shake.

"Good luck." Hunter ambled back to his Rapier.

As Blair turned, he found Maniac standing in his path. "You trying to sneak out and die without me knowing?"

"I—"

"Unh-uh, don't say anything. I want to remember your pretty face just like this. See you on the other side, bro." He banged fists with Blair, then winked and dashed off.

The bellow of firing turbines seized the flight deck as he reached his fighter. She had waited faithfully for him, and Blair ran fingers along her fuselage. *One last hurrah, old lady. That's all I ask.* With the crew already finished, he settled into the cockpit as the commotion outside came to a crescendo.

"Somebody said you're going to navigate the quasar, sir," his crew chief shouted, her short blond hair tossed by thruster wash. "Is that true?"

"How did you hear?"

"I just did. Is it true?"

He nodded. "Wanna come?"

"Sure. But I got nothing to wear." She slipped under the Rapier and emerged on the starboard side to lift a thumbs-up. "That's a nice loadout." Then she stared wistfully at him, as though he were already dead.

Blair returned a tight smile and a thumbs-up, then tapped a switch, lowering the canopy. He broke external moorings and routinely performed the rest of his preparations, despite the growing lump in his throat.

Within sixty seconds the deckmaster waved him into position for launch. He saluted, got clearance from Raznick, and for the first time in his military career felt uneasy about punching his thrusters. The Rapier accelerated through the energy curtain and over the runway. He flipped on his VDU and watched the *Tiger Claw* shrink into the vast tableau. Deveraux formed on his wing and sent him the order to maintain radio silence as they entered the asteroid belt.

He glanced down at Taggart's cross, which had turned onto its back. He noticed an inscription and lifted the cross to read it:

> **TO JAMES**
> **REMEMBER LOVE ACROSS THE DISTANCE**
> **REMEMBER ME**
> **AMITY**

He turned over the cross and whispered, "Well, Amity, I think he does."

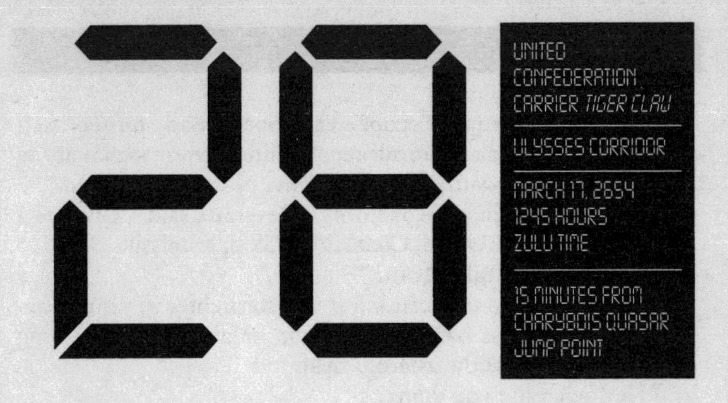

"Report," Gerald yelled as a klaxon reverberated through the bridge.

"I have a bogie, vector one-nine-seven mark three," Mr. Obutu said, "approaching at a velocity of . . . now it's gone. Attempting to reestablish contact, sir."

Taggart studied Obutu's display, played back a recording of the contact, then breathed a curse. He moved to Mr. Falk's primary radar screen and squinted at the glowing numbers.

"You have something, Commodore?" Gerald asked.

"It's a Skipper missile. Must be a prototype. We only pick it up when it decloaks to take a radar fix."

"That technology is years away from the Kilrathi—or at least Intelligence said so." Gerald fixed the commodore with a sharp look. "That's your department, Mr. Taggart. Do you have any intelligence on how to stop it?"

The commodore appeared at a loss, then quickly snapped toward Falk. "Estimated time until impact?"

Falk plugged the coordinates into his terminal, then waited for the results on his big screen. "Nine minutes, sir."

Blair peered at his radar scope. The contact had spirited itself away. Time to break radio silence. "I had a strong signal at ten o'clock, headed toward the *Tiger Claw*. Now it's vanished."

"Accessing intelligence database," Deveraux said. "Give me a sec. All right. Here we go. Contact is a Skipper missile. Shit."

"Can the *Claw* take it out?"

"The only thing that can kill it is a starfighter in visual contact." With that she banked hard right, breaking from his wing and climbing above the asteroid field.

"Hey, what are you doing?"

"Stay on course. Get through that jump point."

"What about our orders?"

"You mean the one I just gave you?"

"But you're flying *my* wing."

"I was."

"Angel? Angel? Don't do this."

On the *Tiger Claw*'s bridge, Gerald felt his pulse surge as he faced Mr. Falk. "ETA on missile?"

"Six minutes, five seconds, four, three, two, one, mark. It should decloak in a minute or so."

Mr. Obutu spoke quietly into his headset, his expression holding little promise. "Sir, our shields are too weak to take a direct hit. DCCs are doing everything they can, but they can't restore full shield power without being spacedocked."

"Countermeasures?"

"Decoys remain down, but the standard array is back on line. Won't matter much. That missile has a smart recognition system against anything we throw at it."

Gerald nodded, then found Taggart's vacant gaze. "Commodore, isn't there anything we can do?"

The man slumped in his chair. "It's in Blair's and Deveraux's hands now."

Blair jolted as the blip reappeared on his display. "It's back, Angel. Check your scope."

"I got jack," she said. "Come on . . . wait . . . got it!"

Deveraux's fighter, now a blue blip on his screen, chased after the red blip. "It's off to your starboard, bearing two-two-four by one-three-one."

She followed his coordinates, winding toward the contact.

"I'm coming back to assist."

"Negative."

He lit the burners and slammed the steering yoke right, riding the tube of an invisible breaker. Her thrusters gleamed ahead, and she fired lasers at the missile even as it cloaked. She continued to lead the Skipper, directing her bolts along its trajectory, shrinking the gap.

"Angel. You're too close," Blair said. "Back off."

A sudden and harrowing inferno erupted ahead of her Rapier. The Skipper materialized and corkscrewed through space, shedding jagged hunks of red-hot plastisteel.

"Target destroyed," she reported tersely, then scaled a trail of vapor to evade.

But her report had been premature. The Skipper exploded with a burst like an antique flashbulb. The light gave way to a visible shock wave, concentric circles of force ripping through space and sweeping up Deveraux's Rapier as though it were a paper airplane in a typhoon.

Her scream shocked Blair. "Angel! Angel!"

The Rapier's wings tore off as it barrel-rolled through the wave. A faint burst of light came from her canopy as she ejected. Tumbling like the Rapier, the escape pod rode the crest of the wave, then suddenly broke free as retros slowed its progress.

Blair held fast to the stick as the remnants of the explosion buffeted his fighter. He turned ninety degrees and flew parallel to the wave, nearing the pod and the meandering line of wreckage floating beside it. The pod's retros fired again, rolling it inverted relative to him. He flew under Deveraux, then slid up so that his cockpit stood within a meter of hers. "You okay?"

"Nothing broken," she said, staring down at him through the Plexi.

He glanced back to the Skipper missile's widespread debris and the speck beyond: the *Tiger Claw*. "You got it."

She shook her head. "It got me."

Blair regarded a panel at his elbow. He touched a button, bringing the system online. "Hang on. I'm going to tractor you back to the ship."

"No. Go on. We can't both disobey orders."

"I'm not leaving you here, Commander. You'll be out of air in an hour."

"An hour and four minutes."

"You're going back to the ship."

She raised a gloved finger. "You disobey my direct order, and I'll have you court-martialed."

"Like I care."

"Then care about the billions who will die if the fleet doesn't get those Kilrathi jump coordinates. You've been around long enough to know that in this war, some of us get a shitty deal. That's the way it is."

"It doesn't have to be."

"Fight *in* the war Blair—not against it. Go now. You have to. You know that."

Yes, he did. And choked by the thought, he punched the canopy. "You're all right, Angel."

She unclipped her mask and smiled ruefully, then pulled off her glove and placed her hand on the Plexi. "You too, Chris."

He could barely look at her as he touched his thruster control, sliding away from the pod, his wash gently rocking it.

That soft face. That hand pressed on the glass. Like Taggart, he would remember across the distance.

Gerald swiveled his command chair toward the radar station. "Repeat?"

Falk gazed at his screen in wonder. "I said there's no sign of the Skipper missile, sir. One of the Rapiers must've shot it down."

"Where are they now?" Taggart asked, staring pensively through the viewport.

"One continuing on course, and one . . . picking up an auto beacon from an ejection pod." Falk jerked his head toward another quadrant on his display. "Got two Kilrathi ships at extreme range."

"Yes, that's about right," Taggart thought aloud. "Knowing our condition they would only send two, keeping the rest for an ambush at the jump point."

Rising, Gerald joined the commodore at the viewport. "So what now? We have just a half-dozen operational fighters and can barely maneuver."

The commodore faced him with a renewed zeal in his eyes. "What now, Mr. Gerald? Now we make the Kilrathi on those ships sorry they were ever born." He regarded the bridge crew and roared, "Battle stations!"

Obutu punched a bank of controls. Alarms echoed along with automated warnings.

Gerald scrambled to his chair. "All right, ladies and gentleman," he barked over the shipwide comm. "Prepare to kick some ass!"

"Hello," Blair said, staring off to starboard. A Kilrathi cruiser and destroyer glided away from him as he held his position inside the shadowy crevice of an asteroid. He checked their course, saw they were headed for the *Tiger Claw*, and could do little more than hope that the ship's scanners had already detected them. Hearing the mental tick of the clock, he sped off, threading his way through the rocks, occasionally glimpsing the quasar's spectral arms.

Maniac sat in his Rapier with his eyes closed, listening to the drone of his breath. He hoped the launch order would come before he turned gray, lost his sex drive, and had to wear a truss.

Hunter had already fallen asleep and had accidentally left his comm open. The sound of his snoring seemed amusing at first, but the humor was short-lived. Polanski had shouted for the pilot to wake up, but old Hunter sat in mid-dream, tooting his horn at the sights and sounds of his subconscious. Even the flight boss could not wake him.

Finally, the penetrating buzz of the launch alarm jolted Maniac out of his doze. "Man, another two minutes and I would've been out."

"Hear that," Polanski said. "Hey, Hunter? You with us?"

"In spirit," he groaned.

"Don't worry about him," Polanski assured Maniac. "Now that he's pissed over losing his beauty sleep, he'll whack a couple extra cats for us."

"I'm not sure there'll be any left for you guys by the time I'm done."

"Listen to this guy."

"Mister, you fly straight and true. You do what I tell you," Hunter warned.

"Yes, sir," Maniac said. "When we get back, stogies on me."

Hunter snickered. "You'll have to go Cuban if you want to impress us, Mr. Marshall."

"Cuban? All right. I'm there."

"Good. You're up."

Following the deckmaster's signals, Maniac positioned his Rapier for launch. He saluted, yawned into his mask, then the thundering turbines rocked him fully awake.

"All fighters away," Gerald told the commodore. The thought of going head-to-head with two Kilrathi cap ships brought on the gooseflesh and the cotton mouth, but Gerald wouldn't call them reactions to fear; they were simply reactions to respect for the enemy—an enemy who was about to die.

"Kilrathi cruiser and destroyer are in missile range," Falk said anxiously. "They're launching."

Taggart's eyes widened. "Open fire, Mr. Gerald."

"Aye-aye, sir." He switched on the shipwide comm. "All batteries, fire as she bears."

"Mr. Obutu?" Taggart said. "Report charge status."

"Batteries operating at forty percent and falling fast, sir. Those Kilrathi fuel cells don't hold a charge as well as ours."

"But our gunners know that. They'll make every shot count."

"That they will, sir."

Gerald suppressed his reaction as dozens of Kilrathi missiles flared and locked on.

Deveraux had powered down all but the most vital systems in the ejection pod—especially its auto beacon that would betray her location. She shivered as the pod grew colder than a Belgian winter. Out to port, missiles streaked across the blackness, creating rainbows of vapor. She strained for a better look, but her breath condensed on the Plexi. She wiped it away and took a tiny, rationed breath.

The end, she figured, wouldn't be all that painful. The cold would turn her numb, and perhaps she would experience that warm feeling she had heard about. She would eventually pass out from the lack of oxygen, but even then there would be no genuine suffering.

No, it wouldn't hurt much . . . *physically*. But the contemplation of dying tore up her soul. A thousand desires, a thousand regrets—and no power to act on them.

She took herself back to the fragmented memories of her parents, saw the images of her holo, then put herself back into the moment as a first-person participant, her senses fully alive. Her father, very tall, eyes very dark, lifted her into the air. Her head fit perfectly on his shoulder, and he smelled like the North Sea. Her mother came to them, stroked her hair, and sang to her about the cool green Ardennes, about picnicking under oak and beech trees, about the eternity of her love.

Blair reached the periphery of the asteroid field, then flipped over his HUD viewer. *All right, all right*, he thought, trying to calm himself as he took in Charybdis's kaleidoscopic fury. Her reds seemed like blood, her blues like veins. He maxed out the throttle and leaned over to power up the jump drive computer. A pair of screens showed multiple glide paths through the quasar, all of them wrong. Or at least they felt so. "Merlin? Check my coordinates."

The hologram directed his voice into the Rapier's comm. "Coordinates a-okay, boss. Three minutes to jump."

"Firing jump drive." He touched the switch—

And an enormous six-G jolt struck the Rapier as the drive drop-kicked him forward. His lips flapped, and his cheeks flirted with his ears.

The quasar smeared into a striped tunnel, and thousands of ghostly claws tugged on the fighter. An atonal chorus of moaning fuselage and wings resounded over the beeping of instrumentation. The stick felt as though it were melting in his glove.

He no longer flew the Rapier; it flew him.

The Kilrathi cruiser lumbered into visual range, and Gerald shook his head at her menacing form as she came head-on. "What tack, sir?"

"Steady on, Mr. Gerald," Taggart said. "Make them the first to blink."

"Aye, sir. Steady on."

"Report from our fighters?"

"Hunter's wing has already engaged, sir," Obutu told Taggart. "But they're outnumbered about ten to one."

Blair's Rapier shimmied, and the jump drive made a noise akin to a mortally wounded animal. His breath came in rapid bursts as the thousands of singularities continued vying for the ship.

"Ninety seconds to jump point," Merlin said. "But you're drifting off course."

"The quasar's gravity is affecting you."

"Running diagnostic. All systems nominal. Christopher, you must change course. Patching new coordinates into the nav computer."

"Negative. Shut up, or I'll shut you off."

"So you've finally decided to kill yourself?"

"Merlin . . ."

The little man wisely fell silent. Blair skimmed the jump drive screens, then shut his eyes.

Mother, you don't want me to come here. But this time I have to. I hope you'll understand. I hope you won't try to stop me.

"Warning. Jump drive system reaching point five light speed, PNR velocity for this system," the ship's computer said. "Do you wish to continue?"

"Affirmative."

"PNR velocity achieved. System lock activated. Pilot, you are committed to the jump."

Admiral Bokoth's plans, based on an unholy pact between himself and a now-dead Pilgrim, were falling apart before him. But Captain Thiraka would not wave his prior reservations in the admiral's face. He delivered his report meekly, comfortable with the knowledge that the admiral's next error would be his last. Commander Ke'Soick's fingers itched with the desire to murder Bokoth, and Thiraka would permit his shintahr that honor now. Thiraka would sacrifice the life of a dear friend for the preservation of the Empire. As agonizing as it was to lose Ke'Soick—who would be executed for the admiral's murder—Thiraka had come to see the truth and the honor in disposing of Bokoth. He bowed before the old one. "Kalralahr. A manned Confederation fighter is approaching the quasar with its jump drive engaged. We're not in position to intercept."

"A fighter?" Bokoth asked, turning in the command chair. "Using what coordinates?"

"Apparently the right ones, sir. The ship is on course."

Bokoth's good eye bulged. "He's going to warn the Confed fleet of our jump coordinates. Follow him. Instruct all ships to mark our course but follow original coordinates through. Sixty-second intervals."

"As you wish. But I should remind you that our enemy is capable of jumping gravity wells, pulsars, and now a quasar. They must have Pilgrims among them. If the *Tiger Claw* is not destroyed, I believe she will jump behind our fleet."

"If she does, then I'll have three destroyers from the fleet waiting for her. Satisfied?"

"Only with victory, Kalralahr. Only with victory." Thiraka nodded and stepped away. He gave the new orders to the helm, then stood beside Ke'Soick.

"Now?" the commander asked.

"I agree with his orders," Thiraka said. "We'll wait until after the jump. But don't worry, my friend. You'll have your chance."

Gerald did a double-take as he watched the Kilrathi cruiser turn hard to port, away from the *Tiger Claw*. "Mr. Falk?"

"She's changing course, sir."

"Why?"

"Frankly, sir, I'm not sure."

"Mr. Gerald," Taggart said. "Prepare to lower our shield. Starboard missile battery prepare to fire."

After setting the shield to perform a flash shutdown, Gerald discovered an error in Taggart's order. "Sir, missile guidance systems won't activate at this range."

"They won't need to. Arm warheads."

In the Secondary Ordnance room, Spaceman Ashley Galaway rushed down her line of torpedoes, typing in arming codes on each missile's control panel.

When she finished, she looked across the room at a cocky, good-looking ghost who smiled back.

Boss Raznick slammed down his computer slate and opened up the deckwide intercom. "Peterson? Why has my flight deck not been policed? Why am I looking at tools all over my runway? Why is my flight deck not one hundred percent battle-ready?"

"I don't know, sir. But I'm on it, sir. Flight crews? Get your unprofessional butts over here. Now!"

So many concussions rumbled through Blair's Rapier that he swore he now plunged into an atmosphere, a degree shy of burning up. To call the vibration infernal was to appreciate it only as a spectator.

"Merlin?" he shouted, warping the computer's name. "Velocity?"

"Light speed mach-point-eight-two," the little man responded, his voice as shaky as Blair's. "Twenty seconds to jump. Can you do it?"

"Only one way to find out."

When Blair had plotted the course through Scylla, he had closed his eyes, fingered the touchpad, and played a song of coordinates written at the subatomic level. He had obeyed the feeling and felt the need to surrender to it now. "Computer. Switch to voice recognition and prepare to plot course."

"Acknowledged. System ready."

He reached out with his mind, with his body, into the quasar, feeling his way through a transparent maze of gravity and magnetic fields. Then he pictured the correct trajectory, a star-rich vortex yawning open. "Coordinates: one-seven-two-nine-four mark three-three-four-eight. Vector: four-four-two-seven-one. Angle of attack: six-three-nine-five-six-one by three-two-four-nine."

"First set of coordinates plotted. Warning. Deviation in jump course found. Do you wish to adjust course?"

"Ignore deviation. Maintain speed and heading."

The *Tiger Claw* convulsed as the Kilrathi cruiser came abreast, its cannons spewing thousands of bolts that struck and irresistibly weakened her shields. The two great ships would soon pass each other, headed in opposite directions.

Gerald buckled into his seat, seeking assurance in his torpedo status display. "Commodore. Four tubes loaded and online.

Warheads armed. Range of target: four hundred and six meters and closing."

Taggart sat in the command chair, his expression of quiet intensity reminiscent of Captain Sansky during battle. He clutched his armrests and leaned toward the Kilrathi cruiser, as though he would leap at it himself. "Lower shields. Give 'em a broadside, Mr. Gerald."

"Fire all batteries!" Gerald cried.

"Aye-aye. Fire all batteries," came the reply from the starboard ordnance room.

Kilrathi cannon fire hammered the unshielded cruiser in rumbling waves, but Gerald ignored it, focusing on the four torpedoes. Three lanced through the cruiser's shield to impact on its hull, ravaging portside batteries and a launch bay in an impressive conflagration. The fourth torpedo found the ship's bridge and severed the entire superstructure from the hull in a cascade of detonations.

As the cruiser yawed, a dozen of the *Claw*'s guided missiles burrowed into her hull, stopped short somewhere inside the ship, then exploded. Fiery light filtered through the ruptures.

"Commodore," Falk said. "Two fighters have broken through our wing. One has targeted ion engine control. If he scores a direct hit, we'll lose all propulsion."

"Where are our fighters?" Taggart demanded.

Falk grimaced. "They're being swarmed."

"Hey, Maniac? Where the hell are you going? Don't leave my wing!" Polanski shouted.

Maniac continued in his eighty-degree dive to escape the raging furball over the cap ships. "Two Krants broke loose. They're after the *Claw*. Now don't leave *my* wing!"

"I'm with you, buddy."

The blue blip that was Polanski's Rapier slid onto Maniac's radar display. "Take the one going for the bridge. I'll get the other."

"Dammit, he's really moving," Polanski said.

"Get him, man! Get him!"

Jamming the stick back, Maniac pulled out of his dive and streaked toward the carrier's stern. He targeted the Krant swooping down on the *Claw*, and his VDU showed that the bastard had missile lock. Maniac hollered his war cry and issued last rites to the cat with Neutron guns. Once a fighter, the Krant blew into a flaming trail that cut through Maniac's path. "Whoa, whoa, whoa," he muttered, going inverted. Showers of burning fuel doused the Rapier's belly. He angled away, and the last of the fuel burned off.

From his new vantage point, Maniac saw that the *Tiger Claw* glided alongside the cruiser at point-blank range. "And they say I'm crazy."

A flash at his port quarter gained his attention. Polanski's Rapier cut a jagged line across the heavens. "That's six kills today, Maniac. You won't top me."

"Oh, no?" Maniac pinned the throttle and went ballistic. The horde of fighters rushed toward him.

"Hey, don't do anything reckless," Polanski warned. "Not without me."

Obutu actually grinned as he looked up from his console. "Commander. The cruiser has lost guidance and propulsion. Life support failing. We got her, sir."

As the bridge crew whooped and cheered, Gerald unbuckled and went to the viewport. The cruiser's stern floated ahead, fires still flashing behind breaches and portholes. Were she a seafaring vessel, she would be capsized and ringed in foam. As it was, she plunged into the void, expelling gas and fluids and sloughing off scorched and twisted plates of plastisteel.

"Clearing the cruiser," Obutu said. "The destroyer has moved out of range."

Taggart left his command chair. "Not bad for a rogue, eh?" he asked, coming toward Gerald.

"Sir, you have to understand that I was putting the safety of this ship and her crew—"

"Relax," Taggart said, backhanding sweat from his brow. "You don't surrender your trust to just anyone. Know what? Neither do I."

The jump drive shrieked, and the rattle had become an indistinct noise that made it nearly impossible to concentrate. "Second set of coordinates at four-seven-five-five-three-nine-nine," Blair shouted.

"Warning. Course deviation. Do you wish to—"

"Hell, no. Stay on course."

"Five seconds," Merlin reported. "Four, three, two—"

The striped vortex winked out of existence.

"Mother?"

"You shouldn't do this to yourself, Christopher. You weren't meant to see me. This is not your continuum."

"It is mine. I chose it."

"You don't have the right to choose. Only one does."

"What do you mean? There aren't any rules. I feel this. I can do what I feel."

"Then you'll fall. Like the others."

"You're not my mother, are you?"

"I'm everything your mother was, is, and will be. I'm in every part of the universe at once, as you are now, as you shouldn't be."

"Why?"

"I wish you could understand. I wish that more than anything. But I've seen your path. And there's nothing I can do to change it."

"Wait. We've had this conversation before. This has already happened."

"No, it hasn't. But it will."

"I don't understand."

"You don't need to."

"Where are you going? We have to talk! I need to know—"

Thunder overpowered his words, and the harness dug into his shoulders. His head fell forward, then ripped back. Star lines whirled, grew shorter, coalesced into points as the jump drive disengaged with a whine. The faint stench of heated metal permeated his O_2 flow. He shook his head to clear the mental gossamers of the gravity field, then squinted at the stars and knew, knew with his eyes and with his blood, that he was on the perimeter of the Sol system. "We did it," he muttered. "We did it!" He patted the canopy. "I love this baby. She held together."

"I'm not sure I did," Merlin moaned.

Blair quickly dialed up a secure Confederation channel on his comm system. "This is Lieutenant Christopher Blair of the TCS *Tiger Claw* calling any Confed ship. A Kilrathi battle group has the Charybdis jump coordinates. They'll breech at one-six-seven mark eight-eight-nine, Sol system. Do you read?"

Only static replied.

"Merlin. Check your frequencies for signs of the fleet."

"Nothing . . . Wait a minute. Check behind us."

"Behind us?"

The still and silent void exploded in a terrific white orb spanned by phosphorescent webs of energy. Out of the orb surfaced a colossal vessel whose copper-colored hull and sharp angles betrayed it as a—

"Kilrathi capital ship," Merlin said gravely. "Snakeir-class."

Blair pounded the instrument panel. "Shit! We're too late."

Admiral Geoffrey Tolwyn had pushed his battle group to one hundred and twenty percent, having lost a total of five ships en route to Sol. But he had reduced the Kilrathi's two-hour lead down to a mere three minutes, much to the dismay of his engineering crew and the crews aboard his escorts. No battle group in the history of the Confederation had made better time. Commodore Bellegarde had said they would have to break every jump record to reach Sol within forty-two hours. Tolwyn had embraced the challenge.

The *Concordia* would soon reach Pluto, then bound toward the bluish, ringed dot of Neptune.

"Are you all right, sir?"

Tolwyn did not look back at Bellegarde. The man's concern, while sincere, had become vexing. "Have you come again to suggest I sleep, Commodore? Because—"

"No, sir. Comm reports a faint message from Lieutenant Christopher Blair. He's in the system and broadcasting the Kilrathi jump coordinates."

That sent Tolwyn spinning around. "Blair?" Was it a coincidence? Hardly. "Like father, like son."

"Should we respond, sir?"

"Identifying Confed Rapier," Radar Officer Abrams called

out. "He's heading toward Earth at LSM point nine."

"What is it, Mr. Abrams?" Tolwyn asked, reacting to the man's troubled voice.

"He's being followed by something massive, Admiral. I've analyzed its signature. Looks like a Snakeir."

Bellegarde tensed. "Permission to intercept it, Admiral?"

"No," Tolwyn said, stroking his two-day-old beard in thought. "We wait."

"But the Snakeir will overtake Blair's fighter."

Tolwyn only nodded.

"Sir, if we don't intercept, that ship will reach Earth orbit before us. The casualties could be significant."

"I'm bloody well aware of that, Richard." Tolwyn bolted from his chair and spoke through gritted teeth. "All ships are to hold their positions and target those jump coordinates."

"But . . ." Bellegarde trailed off. He thought a moment, then his mouth opened in realization. "Ah, if we jump him, we'd be out of position when the Kilrathi fleet comes through."

"We're after bigger game than that Snakeir. We need a resounding victory—or this war is over." Tolwyn faced the stars, their age-old light seeming to shine on his own past. "For that victory, I have to risk the lives of innocent civilians and one very brave young lieutenant."

Blair ran the diagnostic twice, and twice he cursed the damage to his engines. Yes, the Rapier had survived the jump, but now he could only pry eighty-seven percent thrust from the machine.

And the massive blip on his radar screen inched closer.

"Blair to Confed fleet," he said shakily. "Do you read me? Kilrathi capital ship has penetrated the quasar jump point and is in Earth space. Copy?"

Static upon static.

"Confed fleet, do you copy?" He threw back his head. "If they're here, they're out of range. Earth will never see the Kilrathi coming."

"Ironic that we made it this far," Merlin said. "Of course,

irony is an essential ingredient in every tragedy."

"Shuddup. Or at least help us out."

"I knew this was all going to end horribly. Did I mention that we'll be in range of the Snakeir's guns in ten minutes?"

"At least they can't launch torpedoes at this speed."

"I'm sorry, Christopher. But they won't have to."

A radar alarm beeped rhythmically, and Blair stared through his HUD viewer. "There! Got a contact dead ahead. It's the fleet signaling. They've heard us!" He opened the channel. "Blair to Confed fleet. Kilrathi capital ship on my course, aft of my position. Confed fleet, do you read me?"

The alarm drummed louder. Blair checked his scope and saw the blip. "Only one ship. But it's huge."

"It isn't a ship," Merlin said in a dire tone. "Check your scanners."

Blair engaged his telescopic scanner, its readout now rippling across his HUD. Space shimmered for a moment, then unveiled a lonely beacon signaling in the night. He glimpsed a data bar for identification.

And wished he hadn't.

Beacon 147.

"All we need," Merlin grumbled. "Scylla. Bane to sailors and monster of myth."

"We're hove to for repair inspection, sir," Lieutenant Commander Obutu said.

Taggart smiled wistfully. In the days of ancient sailing, *hove to* meant that a ship would turn its bow into the wind and drift, in order to meet a storm. Thankfully, Taggart's storm had already passed. "Report on Lieutenant Blair?"

"We're not sure, sir, but we think one of the Rapiers jumped."

He looked past Obutu at Falk, ever standing behind his large radar screen. "What about the locator beacon from that Rapier pod?"

"Nothing, sir. Lost contact during the battle."

Taggart shook his head at the news. "We've sacrificed too

many good pilots already. Have the *Diligent* prepared for launch. I'm going after that pod."

"Aye-aye, sir."

Taggart double-timed off the bridge, growing more anxious as he imagined Deveraux or Blair slowly suffocating in that cramped durasteel box.

"Christopher? Why haven't you changed course?"

He sweated over the controls and had trouble listening to Merlin over the incessant proximity alarm. He would shut it down, and a moment later it would return. "Merlin, can you turn this damned thing off?"

"I will, but in case the alarm hasn't cued you, you'll be past Scylla's Point of No Return in ninety seconds. Its gravitational pull will tear us to pieces. More precisely, to minute, highly dense particles."

"Solutions, Merlin! No more problems." Blair glimpsed the stars as they contorted into the gravity well's whirlpool of space-time.

Solutions. The word rang in his head and ironically sparked something. Blair had a Snakeir behind him, a gravity well ahead. Solution? In his mind's eye he saw one, but he balked at the notion. Still, it was the only one he had. "How much does a Snakeir weigh?"

"Accessing specs. About two hundred thousand tons, give or take a few thousand."

A smile passed over his lips. One throw of a switch, and the afterburners slammed him into his seat. Space seemed to open up around him as he bulleted toward Scylla, the well fringed by silvery ribbons of stars. Warning lights now dotted Blair's HUD, but at least Merlin had successfully turned off the proximity alarm.

"What are you doing?" the little man cried. "The afterburners will use all our fuel."

"I know, but I need more thrust. Eighty-seven percent won't cut it." Excitement tingled along his spine.

Merlin's voice quavered. "But we're still headed for that thing . . ."

⌂ ⌂ ⌂

Captain Thiraka took in a long breath of nutrient gas, then went to Bokoth, who reposed in the command chair and looked for all the Empire like the vandalized statue of a war hero. "Kalralahr, planetary torpedoes online. We are almost in range. There is no response to the Rapier's transmissions. Sivar smiles on us. The surprise is total."

Bokoth's lips flared. "Yes," he said slowly, "it is."

Something punched into Thiraka's back, found a seam in his armor, and penetrated flesh. The sudden agony felt so severe that he shamed himself by screaming. Rigid in shock, he turned.

Commander Ke'Soick held a bloody *vorshooka* blade, the ritual instrument for cub-bearing and murder. "Forgive me, Kal Shintahr."

"He's a skilled warrior," Bokoth rasped through a sinister grin. "You won't die quickly, Thiraka. I wanted you to see our victory and know, really know . . . regret. How dare you plot my murder. Did you really believe that Ke'Soick's loyalty could not be turned?"

"My father will have your life," Thiraka said, collapsing to his knees.

"I kill you *with* your father's consent. The Kiranka clan will soon be clean."

Thiraka's shoulders grew numb, and he realized he could no longer lift his arms. His thoughts were swept into a gale of panic. He thought of calling for help, but who would listen? Who would dare defy Bokoth?

Second Fang Norsh'kal suddenly rang the ancient tocsin to alert the bridge crew.

"What is it?" Bokoth demanded.

Hissing nervously, Norsh'kal delivered his report. "The Rapier is homing in on a beacon signal. It could be a Confederation guidance buoy."

"Or a capital ship," Bokoth amended, then winced as he forced his wizened frame toward the infrared monitor in front of him. "Identify and report. Full battle stations."

On the admiral's screen, Thiraka saw a red speck heading toward the beacon.

And he suddenly realized where they were and what that beacon marked. He opened his mouth to warn Bokoth, then smiled wanly. The Rapier pilot had become an ally in revenge.

Deveraux had thought she could die peacefully. She had thought she might experience a warm state of bliss before the cold draped her in an eternal sleep.

She had been idealistic about death.

Now reality had stolen most of her air. Reality had iced up her canopy so that even the pleasure she took from the stars was gone. *I did all right*, she thought. *It wasn't such a bad life. I helped some people. I wasn't as selfish as I could've been, I guess. If only I could take this cold. But I can't. I'm a fighter, but I can't take this. Call me weak. I don't care anymore.*

She reached for the pod's main panel, her hand shaking so badly that she could barely bring her finger down on the correct button. The panel lit.

"Self-destruct system armed. T minus thirty seconds until self-destruct," the computer said. "System will lock out override at T minus five seconds."

A song came to Deveraux, a song from her youth. "And as the moon rose high and high, and the twilight fled the sky, we saw the night was really here, and listened for the owl's cheer. Soon the stars began to shine, and we heard music in our minds, we heard music in our minds . . ."

Blair gazed at his HUD, never more determined. A half-dozen warnings kept lighting his screens, as though the ship's systems now conspired against him. A thousand meters to starboard, an asteroid plummeted toward the raging well. He blinked sweat out of his eyes and checked the VDU. "They're still back there," he told Merlin. "Good."

"If you say so. Kilrathi radar locked on. Ten seconds to the Point of No Return . . . and you're almost out of fuel. You won't be able to turn."

"Give me a count."

"Four . . . three—"

"Holy shit!"

"—two . . . "

He jerked the stick hard to starboard, but the engines coughed before responding. Numbers clicked backward on his velocity gauge. Five and a half Gs pinned him to the seat. "We're not going to break free," he cried, eyeing another gauge. "We don't have enough fuel."

"You've got ten more seconds of thrust."

"Not enough!"

"Then find a weakness in the gravity field. Feel it."

Every rivet, plate, wire, and switch seemed to cry in protest as the Rapier grappled with Scylla. Blair projected himself into her swelling arms and felt for a way out.

He pulled the stick back, climbed a moment—

Then abruptly dove while slaloming away.

"Five seconds of thrust."

"Sorry, old girl," he whispered, feeling a fluctuation in her pull.

"Two seconds!"

With a last jerk, the Rapier tore from Scylla's clutches, rocketing away at a ninety-degree angle.

"We're free," Blair said, only half-believing it.

Thiraka had lost the use of his legs. He poured all of his energy into breathing. He could no longer smile as he watched Bokoth foolishly chase after the Rapier.

Second Fang Norsh'kal's voice spilt open the tense silence that had fallen upon the bridge. "Kalralahr, the Rapier has veered away. Confederation ship, dead ahead."

Bokoth nodded and took a second glance at his screen. The horror that befell his face thrilled Thiraka. "That isn't a ship! Hard to port! Reverse all thrusters!"

Blair's engines whined a decrescendo and died. The Rapier glided via inertia through space, and the cockpit's eerie silence unnerved him.

"We're out of fuel," Merlin said. "And battery power's nearly exhausted."

But Merlin's report seemed distant, blighted by a beautiful sight that took form in the distance. The huge Kilrathi cap ship sailed straight for Scylla's undulating throat, its retros and reverse thrusters firing futilely against the laws of physics. "The Kilrathi's too heavy," Blair confirmed. "Scylla's got her."

Thiraka battled to lift his chin as the gravity well bloomed across the starboard viewport. Its glistening, inescapable maw turned the bridge crew into babbling cowards, including Bokoth.

"All engines full!" the admiral shrieked, his face draining of color.

The deck under Thiraka quaked as the gravity well leapt on its prey.

Norsh'kal jolted from his sparking console. "Engines overheating!"

Bokoth shrank to his chair. "But Sivar chose us." He looked down at Thiraka—

Who mustered his remaining strength to scowl at the admiral.

Behind them, a bulkhead burst open. Nutrient gas rushed toward the gaping seam and jetted into space.

Ke'Soick and Norsh'kal screeched and pounded past Thiraka, their bodies stretching unnaturally toward the viewport and the singularity beyond.

The chaos darkened into silhouette, and the cries diminished.

Thiraka wondered if he had died, then, through the numbness, he sensed himself being pulled apart.

"Record this, Merlin," Blair said, marveling at the Snakeir as it turned sharply to port in a final effort to dodge Scylla.

The well flung the ship around and drew it in, stern-first. Fissures opened across the Snakeir's hull, met other cracks, then released colossal sections that formed a parade of flotsam stretching toward the vortex.

Blair could not see Scylla's mythical six heads as they

devoured the ship, but their effect humbled him. In less than ten seconds the last pieces of the Snakeir's bow spun into the well, leaving a fleeting band of distortion in their wake.

"Can I stop recording?" Merlin asked.

"Yeah."

"What's wrong? We got them."

"I know. I just can't imagine dying that way."

"Then how does freezing to death sound? You've got four minutes of battery power."

"Send an automatic distress, along with the jump coordinates."

"I already have. No ships in range."

"Then I guess you'll have your tragedy."

"Christopher, if you die, I cease to function. Your father made me that way."

Blair unclipped his mask and palmed sweat from his face. "I'm sorry."

"When people know they're going to die, they confess things to each other, say things they—"

"What is it?"

"You don't know much about how I was designed. Your father wanted it that way. But I don't believe he wanted you to die without knowing. My chips were manufactured with protein from your father. It was his way of never saying good-bye."

"But he left."

"In the physical sense, yes. He knew he would. He loved you, Christopher. More than anything. And he wanted me to show you how much. I hope I didn't let you down."

"First sarcasm and now melodrama," Blair said with a half-grin. "How could you ever let me down?"

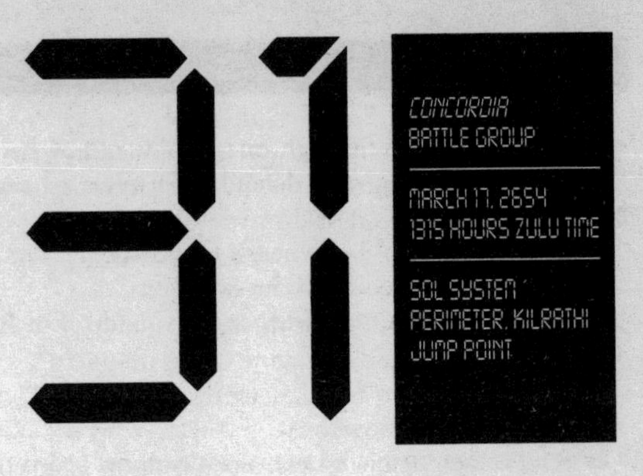

Admiral Tolwyn held his breath as the *Concordia* decreased thrust and the battle group dispersed into attack formation.

"What do you think, sir?" Bellegarde asked as they stared ahead. "Are we too early or too late for the party?"

Tolwyn squinted at a flickering gleam in the distance, a gleam that quickly burst into a ringlet of light. "We're right on time." He favored the radar officer. "Identify that ship."

"She's a Fralthi-class cruiser," Abrams said.

"Fire all batteries."

Laser bolts and guided missile exhausts sewed a hundred translucent trails into the gap between the Fralthi and the battle group. Tight-lipped, Tolwyn observed the bombardment and noted another ship flashing through the jump point.

Even as he faced Abrams, the young man shouted, "Ralari-class destroyer in our sights, sir."

"Take her out."

Pummeled by a surprise attack, the Fralthi got off only a half-dozen salvos of return fire, then emitted a spectacular light show as it broke apart. The destroyer plowed into the Fralthi's wreckage, then took a score of torpedo strikes to her stern.

"They're coming through one ship at time," Bellegarde said. "They have no chance to defend themselves or warn the ships behind."

Tolwyn nodded. "But where's that Snakeir?"

"She's disappeared from our scanners."

"Launch two Rapier wings and a squadron of Broadswords. We have to find her."

"Aye-aye, sir."

The status light on Blair's life support panel faded. He probably had a couple, maybe three more minutes of oxygen left if the cold didn't kill him first. The shivering had come, grown worse, and now he sat with chattering teeth, rocking himself toward death.

His Rapier had glided well past Pluto. Far beyond the gas giants and beyond Mars lay that precious planet, homeworld of humans, the only home, some said. He wanted to go there and see the legendary beauty that everyone fought so fiercely to preserve. Too late now.

"Hey, Merlin. You there?"

With the fighter's systems down, the little man took holographic form, his image flickering on Blair's knee. "Here, Christopher."

"You were right all along."

"I was?"

"We're doomed."

Merlin folded his arms over his chest and glared like a drill sergeant. "Don't say that. You're a fighter. So fight. We're going to make it."

"Cold got to you, Merlin? You sound downright optimistic."

"Let's just call it intuition—"

Blair fell forward as the Rapier lurched.

"—or a working array of scanners."

"What the hell . . ." A powerful spotlight shone on the cockpit. The light panned away, and behind it floated a Broadsword bomber that literally brought tears to Blair's eyes. The pilot snapped off a salute, and Blair managed a shaky reply.

A tube extended from the bomber's belly and locked onto the

Rapier's primary external coupling. Blair threw back a row of toggles, and systems blinked on. One screen showed his Rapier firmly locked in the Broadsword's tractor beam.

"Good afternoon," the pilot said, his masked face now on Blair's VDU. "I'm Lieutenant C. W. McCubbin of the TCS *Concordia*. Who's Saranya Carr?"

"She's the star of *Luna Jones, Jumpscout.*"

"That's good. But even the cats know that."

"C'mon, buddy. Do I look like a Kilrathi to you?"

"Well, Lieutenant, you're pretty damned ugly." The pilot chuckled, then fired thrusters, towing Blair off.

"TCS *Tiger Claw* entering low Earth orbit," Abrams said.

"Jesus," Tolwyn muttered as he surveyed the old carrier's shattered and blackened hull. When Gerald had made his report, he had obviously understated the ship's condition. As expected, the commander had spent more time discussing his disappointment and disbelief over Captain Sansky's actions. Tolwyn had taken the news with only mild astonishment. Sansky wasn't the first or last traitor to wear a Confederation uniform.

The lift doors opened, and a familiar young man hurried onto the bridge, looking about as tattered and battle-weary as the admiral himself. Lieutenant Blair brightened as he met gazes with Tolwyn, then steered himself to the viewport.

Tolwyn returned the boy's salute, then proffered his hand. "Your father would've been proud."

"Thank you, sir. And it's an honor to finally meet you." He stood starry-eyed a moment, then jolted. "Oh, I almost forgot. I have something for you." He removed a ring from his breast pocket. "Captain Sansky asked me to return it."

Tolwyn took the ring, eyed it with a deep affection, then slipped it on. He tried to mask his sorrow over Sansky's betrayal, but Blair's reaction said he had failed. "The wounds of civil war run deep. He was a good captain, despite everything."

"Yes, sir. And sir? Did anyone locate Lieutenant Commander Deveraux?"

"Paladin went after her. No word yet."

Bellegarde, who had been sitting at an observation station, went to the comm console. He conferred a moment with the officer there, then slipped on a headset. "We're monitoring the *Tiger Claw*'s transmissions. She's been in contact with the *Diligent*. Commodore Taggart's requesting clearance to land."

The young lieutenant hastened toward Bellegarde. "Is she with him?"

"Lieutenant Commander Deveraux is on board," Bellegarde said, concentrating on the signals.

"I knew she'd make it," Blair said with a hearty nod.

"Taggart is requesting an emergency medical team to meet him on the flight deck immediately."

Blair froze. "What's wrong?"

"I'm sorry." Bellegarde pursed his lips and removed his headset. "The rest of the transmission got cut off as they entered the *Tiger Claw*'s airlock."

The lieutenant's expression harbored more than simple worry over a comrade. Tolwyn smiled inwardly. "Mr. Blair? I think you're on the wrong ship."

"Sir, if I can borrow—"

"Get down to the flight deck. I'll have a fighter waiting for you."

He raced toward the exit, remembered his salute, then knifed through the lift doors before they had fully opened.

"Well," Tolwyn said, hearing the melancholy in his voice, "there we go, just yesterday, his age."

Bellegarde's face reflected his own yearning. Then his gaze settled upon Earth, and he studied the planet with an odd intent. "Sir? I've a leave coming up. Maybe it's time I go to Scotland. Have a look around, as it were. With your permission—"

"Granted, Richard," Tolwyn blurted out in surprise. "I think you'll find a lot more there than you've expected."

"I hope so, sir."

Blair switched off the comm in his borrowed Rapier, silencing Boss Raznick's tirade. The boss would have to forgive Blair's reckless approach. He plowed through the energy curtain and blew the canopy as the Rapier came to a wailing hover and abruptly descended. Landing skids slapped hard on the deck.

Standing in his cockpit, Blair spotted the *Diligent* across the hangar. A crowd had gathered near her loading ramp. He jumped from the fighter, then sprinted toward the commotion.

Taggart, Gerald, and Maniac stared over the shoulders of two medics as they struggled to revive Deveraux. She lay on a lowered gurney, and her back arched as one medic waved a pen-shaped defibrillator over her heart.

Maniac broke away from the group. "Son of a bitch, you made it."

Blair's gaze returned to Deveraux. "What about her?"

"Pure luck that I found her at all," Taggart said. "She must've turned off her beacon so as not to tip off the Kilrathi. She had eight seconds left on her self-destruct when I nudged the pod, woke her up, and got her to deactivate. She passed out before I got her moored. Brave girl."

He slipped past Taggart and dropped to his knees beside Deveraux. Her ashen face made him tremble. "Come on, Angel. Come back. Don't you die on me." He took her cold, limp hand in his own. "Come on, Angel."

Maniac hunkered down and placed a comforting hand on his shoulder.

The grim-faced medics continued waving their instruments over Deveraux. One placed a small disc on the base of her neck and studied readings on a palmtop scanner. "Hold on now. Wait. Yeah, there it is. I got a pulse."

"That's right, Angel," Blair said, squeezing her hand. "Don't you die on me."

Her eyelids fluttered and finally opened. She coughed a little, then turned her head and smiled through her grogginess. "What did you say?"

"I said don't you die on me."

She licked her parched lips. "Is that a suggestion or an order?"

"That's a definite order," he said with a stifled laugh.

Their gazes locked, and she did not look away. Her lips welcomed him. He learned toward her, going in for the kiss

"We have to get her down to sickbay," one of the medics said, blocking Deveraux's face with his arm. He winked. "Don't worry. She'll be fine."

Blair stood as the medics raised the gurney and wheeled Deveraux toward the lift doors. He kept his eyes on her until she rounded a cargo container, out of sight.

"So, Mr. Blair," Gerald began. "I heard you single-handedly took out a Snakeir. Lured the ship into that gravity well at One-four-seven."

"That's correct, sir."

"Well, despite that, despite everything, I still don't like you." The commander flicked an ugly stare at Taggart's cross. "However, you've earned a little of my trust. In all likelihood, I'll be assuming command of the *Tiger Claw*, and I want only the best wing commanders I can find."

Taggart rolled his eyes. "The commander's trying to promote you, Lieutenant. I understand he's got a short list of command-approved wing commanders. You want the job or what?"

Blair grinned at the joke. "Wing commander? Me?"

"I can use you, Lieutenant," Gerald said. "We stopped the Kilrathi—"

"They'll be back," Taggart cut in. "The only question is when."

"We'll be ready for them this time," Blair said. "No more surprises."

"He'll take the job," Taggart told Gerald with a wink.

"I don't know," Maniac said, having been remarkably silent until now. "Maybe it's just me, but I didn't think they were all that tough."

Gerald and Taggart looked at Maniac as though he had finally lost his mind. Even Blair could not repress his frown.

"What?" Maniac asked, feeling the heat. "I mean it."

That drew hoots and guffaws from everyone, then Polanski

pulled Maniac away while the deckmaster flagged down Gerald.

Taggart gestured toward the lift. “C’mon. I owe you a drink.”

“And I owe you this.” Blair tugged the cross from his chain.

After withdrawing his own chain from beneath his vest, Taggart clipped on the cross. “I assume the admiral has his ring?”

“He does. Can I ask you something, sir?”

Taggart smiled. “You’d like to know about Amity.”

“How did you know?”

“The way you just looked at the cross.”

“I’m sorry if I—”

“No, it’s okay,” Taggart said. “Let’s get that drink. I’ll need it to tell that story.”

EPILOGUE

PLANET MYLON III,
DOWNING QUADRANT

VEGA SECTOR

NORTH HILLS COUNTY

SANTYANA FARM

MARCH 18, 2654
1900 HOURS
LOCAL TIME

At thirty-three, few things delighted William Santyana more than spending a Sunday afternoon with his wife and three-year-old daughter. He stood on the back patio of his farmhouse, breathing in the wonderful aroma from the hot dogs and burgers cooking on his grill. He wondered just how many fathers out there were doing the same thing on a thousand other worlds, in a billion other backyards. Santyana let his gaze wander past the patio to a green carpet of corn that unfurled to the twilit horizon. Tiny flashes of light appeared in the violet haze that banded the sky, and he stared curiously at them a moment, then lifted the cover on his grill.

"Will!" his wife cried from inside the house.

"Just another minute, Pris. We don't want to eat 'em raw."

"Get in here. Now!" Her horrified tone sent him racing toward the open patio door.

Inside, he found her seated on the sofa, balancing little Lacey on her knee. The holoplayer was tuned to the news channel, and a life-sized holographic anchorman stood on their rug, pointing back to a computer-animated globe that showed dozens of red dots encircling it.

"We're under attack," Pris said, visibly trembling. "Listen."

". . . And the planetary defense net has been shut down. MyGov officials have yet to respond. We do know that the ship is a Confederation-class carrier, now in low orbit, but any other insignia have been removed from her hull. She's already dispatched hundreds of fighters, bombers, and troopships. We go now to George Okoee, who's standing by at Blue Mountain Spaceport. Can you hear me, George?"

The holovid switched to a wavering image of the young, teary-eyed reporter, hunkered down near a row of seats in a vast terminal. "Got you, Rick. Ladies and gentlemen, just outside this terminal, a wing of Confederation Broadswords is descending upon this, Mylon's largest spaceport. The people here are in a state of shock. We'd expect this from the Kilrathi. But from our own forces? Still, there's no confirmation yet on who's piloting those ships. A major evacuation is in progress, but estimates put the bombers at just a few minutes away. We've received word that two dozen more Broadswords are headed toward the Confed Strike Base in North Hills County. Wait. I think I can hear them . . ."

"George, get out of there!" The anchorman's image returned. He placed a hand to the tiny receiver in his ear. "George? George!" He looked off-camera. "What's that?"

Distant booming piped in through the farmhouse's open windows. Santyana looked beyond the patio door and saw a dozen pillars of black smoke fencing off the western sky. A humming noise came from the south, and he frowned even as it grew into a sudden, excruciating roar. Gale-force winds keened through the house. Pris and Lacey screamed as with burning eyes he fought his way to the door.

A long shadow bled across the patio. He looked up as the menacing-looking troopship passed just three meters above his house. Shaped like an arrowhead, the craft pivoted and ignited retros, blasting up clumps of grass as it set down.

He bolted back into house, already picturing himself and his family climbing into their beat-up hover and fleeing. "Pris! C'mon! C'mon! C'mon! We gotta go!"

"Ohmygod," she said as he sprinted past her. "What's happening?"

"Daddy?" Lacey called. "Daddy?"

In the kitchen, he scooped up his driving card and turned to go—

When an amplified voice struck him motionless. "Mr. William Santyana. Please come out."

"Will?" Pris cried. "They know you."

He returned to the living room, and out of the corner of his eye he saw dark-clad figures lurking outside the windows. He stroked his wife's cheek, kissed his daughter, and muttered, "Stay here." With buckling knees, he moved toward the patio.

Outside, two people dressed in fancy Confederation Space Force uniforms came forward, flanked by a half-dozen rifle-toting soldiers. Santyana figured the duo for officers. One of them, a trim woman about his age with moss-green eyes and a confident gait, raised a thick eyebrow and evaluated him with her glance. "Mr. Santyana?" she asked.

"What the hell is this?"

Her shoulder-length black hair whipped like smoke in the lingering thruster wash. "Are your wife and daughter still inside?"

"What do you want?"

The woman nodded to her troops, who jogged toward the house.

"Pris! Run! Run!"

"No, William," the woman said. "We're here to save you."

"Are you people from the strike base? Wait a minute, even if you were, you wouldn't know my name."

"Will!"

He glanced back. Pris carried Lacey as two soldiers led them outside.

"You're from that carrier, aren't you," Santyana said. "Why are you attacking us?"

"Not you, William. Or your family. We're only killing the humans who live here."

"Humans? Than what are you?"

She reached under her uniform and withdrew a Pilgrim cross. "Do you know what this is?"

He did. His parents had carried them, and they had died because of what those crosses represented. "You people . . . you're fanatics. What have you done?"

"It's what we're *going to do*, William. We're taking back the stars. And you're going to help."

"You mean I don't have a choice."

"You couldn't choose your blood, no. And you'll never change who you are."

The other officer, an old man whose hazel eyes seemed forever distant, spoke in the alluring lilt of some Border Worlds tribesman. "William. You're a fine man, a wonderful father. Amity here asked me to come out because I fought with your parents. We're bringing everybody home now. You need to come."

"Home?" he asked incredulously. "This is my home."

"Just leave us alone," Pris shouted. "We don't want any part of you Pilgrims."

Amity tightened her lips and nodded. "I understand. But in a few hours, every living thing on this planet will be dead. Maybe you'd like to be a part of us—at least for now."

Santyana looked to his wife, searching for an answer, but she seemed lost in a blur of fear. He faced Amity and sighed. "We'll come. But you'll never take the stars."

She lifted a condescending grin. "We've been waiting nearly twenty years for this moment, William. We lost that war. We won't lose this one."

PETER TELEP earned his B.A. and M.A. from the University of Central Florida, where he now teaches English. Mr. Telep is a recipient of the prestigious John Steinbeck Award for fiction and has written a number of science fiction and fantasy novels, including *Descent* (based on the popular computer game), the Squire Trilogy, and the *Space: Above and Beyond* books. Contact him at PTelep@aol.com or care of HarperEntertainment. Visit his website at www.ptelep.com for news on upcoming books.